THE WEST'S AWAKE

THE QUEENSTOWN SERIES - BOOK 2

JEAN GRAINGER

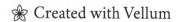

Dedicated to my mother, my most powerful ally and dearest friend.

CHAPTER 1

ueenstown, County Cork. July 1916

'IS THAT ALL, MISS DEVEREAUX?' Cissy Devlin asked, wrapping the ham she'd just cut from the large joint in greaseproof paper. Almost everyone in Queenstown called Harp 'Miss Devereaux' now, ever since Henry had named her as his daughter in his will.

Harp smiled and checked her list. 'Em…a tin of mustard powder and some Epsom salts too please.' If she arrived back to Cliff House without all the items she'd been sent for, her mother would not be happy.

It was mid-July and they were full every night in the guest house, which meant she was constantly having to run out for one essential or another. The Devlins' shop was the best grocer in the town; it was immaculately clean, the produce arranged neatly and held mostly behind the counter. The more discerning housewives preferred it to the cheaper huckster shops, where rats and mice were hard to keep out and everything always smelled a bit off.

'And what about you, Mr Quinn?' Cissy smiled over Harp's shoulder. 'What can we delight you with today?'

Harp turned in pleased surprise to find Brian Quinn behind her. *He must be home from Dublin for the holidays*, she thought. The undertaker's son was universally liked and instantly recognisable, tall and thin with freckles peppered across his pale skin and a shock of red curls that he tried to tame with hair oil with limited success.

'Nothing, Miss Devlin, thanks. I'm a penniless student. I just popped in to say hello.'

Brian smiled warmly at Harp, and she suspected he had spotted her on her way into the shop and was there to see her as well.

Cissy arched an eyebrow at them both. 'I suppose the two of ye have gone too big and sophisticated altogether for a few pear drops?'

'Never.' Brian chuckled as she poured a few of the boiled sweets into two paper cones and handed them to him and Harp. 'I might look grown up, but you know my weakness, Miss Devlin.'

'I do well. Didn't I serve you enough of them over the years? Now tell me, how are the studies above in Dublin going? I'd say medicine is very hard all the same.'

Cissy was a great one for talk, whereas Liz, who was quietly stacking tins on the shelves behind her sister, was much more reserved. Neither woman had ever married, but they seemed very contented living together. They looked alike, both small and wiry with dark hair set in respectable waves. They wore housecoats, one pink, one blue, and only took them off for Mass. Liz had thick glasses and Cissy was the friendlier of the two, but when they weren't wearing the different coloured housecoats, people often confused one for the other.

'Medical college is fine and hard, I can tell you, Miss Devlin. I don't know if I'll make it at all some days,' Brian said ruefully. "Tis Harp here should be doing the complicated books of anatomy and physiology – she's the brains of the town.'

Harp glanced at him with a shy smile. She'd always thought he'd make a good doctor; he had the sort of open face and gentle manner that people trusted.

'We'll be losing Miss Devereaux to the halls of the university soon enough, I'd say. You'll be the first girl from here I ever heard of to do it, fair play to you. I suppose 'tis to Cork you'll go, is it? What will you be studying?' Cissy asked as Harp popped a pear drop into her mouth.

At sixteen she probably shouldn't be accepting free sweets like a child, but the Devlin sisters had been so nice and kind to her all her life, from when she was a tiny little scrap of an oddball. 'Well, I have to matriculate next year, but I think it will be all right if I work hard enough. And then I'm still not sure – it will depend on lots of things, I suppose.' She reddened as she spoke but was still pleased at how confident she sounded. What a difference four short years had made to her. Having the whole town know her as the daughter of Mr Devereaux had changed her. She looked even more like him now as she grew older, her strawberry-blond hair the exact shade of his. She loved it when people remarked upon it.

Cissy nodded. 'Well, you've all the time in the world – sure you're only a child still. Are ye busy above? The place is teeming with people all the week.'

'We are busy,' agreed Harp. 'There are two ships going this week, one to Boston, the other to Canada.'

After Henry had left her the Cliff House in his will, she and her mother had converted it into a successful guest house. They catered mostly to the second-class passengers, as the first-class passengers stayed at the Queen's Hotel and the third class were consigned to Mrs O'Flaherty's boarding house in the part of Queenstown known as the Holy Ground, an area best avoided if possible.

The guest house had gained quite the reputation as a lovely place to stay, without the hefty price tag of the hotel, so the Cliff House was becoming increasingly popular with well-to-do Irish who could afford a holiday by the sea, or British officers and their wives and families enjoying some leave. It meant they were no longer dependent on sea passengers alone, which was just as well, because with the war raging in Europe, passenger travel wasn't what it was. The deliberate sinking of the *Lusitania* last May had really rattled people. The Germans had given an undertaking to allow civilian traffic across the ocean, but people were still nervous. The sinking of *Titanic* in 1912 had shaken Queenstown to its foundations, and though the *Lusitania* was sunk off Kinsale, on the other side of the harbour, the rescue mission was launched from Queenstown.

Harp remembered the pathetic sight of the notice board up in the hotel, people seeking information about family and friends who were aboard. She and her mother had watched in horror as the ship went down, nine miles off the Old Head of Kinsale. They had a view from the top window of the Cliff House. It sank in eleven minutes, with the loss of 1198 lives. The British said it wasn't carrying munitions, but it would be hard to imagine how it would have sunk so fast if it weren't.

'And another one next week,' added Cissy. 'Though just to England. There seems to be an awful exodus altogether on.'

'I suppose the carry on above in Dublin at Easter means there's plenty need to get out of sight of the authorities,' said Brian darkly. 'Idiots. You should see the state of the city in Dublin after

them and their shenanigans. Hotheads and romantic fools is all they were, and what have we to
show for it? A needless waste of lives and a city in
ruins.'

'It wasn't a "needless waste of lives",' Harp
protested indignantly. 'It was an armed insurrection demanding independence from our oppressors. And you shouldn't speak about the rebels so
disrespectfully, when their leaders were slaughtered so coldly and callously.' She had liked Brian
ever since he stuck up for her as a tiny terrified
child in the schoolyard, but he was a person who
saw the world very differently to her and she
wondered if they would ever agree on anything.
Clearly, he considered the Easter Rising a reck-
less adventure, but Harp had felt a thrill of excitement and patriotism. She'd followed the progress
of the rebels carefully and felt the pain of the
Cork men and women who were not given the
opportunity to participate due to a series of mis-
informed messages that said the Rising was off.

'Populist claptrap.' Brian dismissed her objec-
tions. 'If the rebels were so wonderful, how come
they allowed women to fight? Big brave men they
were for sure, sending girls no older than yourself out to die.'

'Why shouldn't women fight? I think they

were marvellous. Why should we not have a voice? We are part of this country too, and we suffer at the hands of the British even more than the men sometimes. If you listened – and I mean actually listened – rather than scoffed at what Countess Markievicz had to say about women's suffrage and the links between the equality of the sexes and the ideas of sovereignty, you might learn something.'

The Devlin sisters shot each other a look, and Harp blushed once more. She knew she shouldn't argue in public, but honestly, Brian Quinn was infuriating sometimes.

The undertaker's son smiled at the sisters. 'I'm sorry, Misses Devlin, for our outbursts. Harp and I have a lot of debates. She's a young lady who knows her own mind, I'm afraid.' He nudged Harp affectionately, but she didn't respond. He was typical of so many men and boys, thinking women were there to have babies and keep houses.

'What are you afraid of, Brian?' Cissy asked, her blue eyes innocent.

'Oh, I'm not afraid of anything, Miss Devlin. I just don't want my young impressionable friend here falling under the spell of glory-hunting hotheads.'

Liz stopped putting tins on the shelves and turned to face him. 'Oh, I don't think Miss Devereaux is in any danger of being impressionable. She's clever enough to know her own mind.'

'Thank you, Misses Devlin.' Harp was pleasantly surprised, first at Cissy's question and then at Liz's intervention. Smiling, she placed the groceries in her basket and turned to leave.

'Good day to you both,' called Cissy as Brian followed Harp out and another customer entered. 'And, Harp, please make sure to come again soon.'

CHAPTER 2

'Ah, Harp, you were ages!' Rose Delaney exclaimed as Harp entered the Cliff House by the back door. 'I thought I'd have to send out a search party.'

'Sorry, Mammy. I met Brian. He insisted on carrying my shopping, and we argued all the way here about the Rising.' Harp placed the basket on the large table in the centre of the kitchen, then glanced up at her mother, who looked beautiful in a pale-green dress. Harp envied her mother's beauty. Her dark hair and eyes, her alabaster skin and her slim figure made people stop and admire her wherever she went. *Unlike me,* thought Harp. *I still have the scrawny figure of a child.*

Rose looked concerned. 'Matt and Brian are coming to supper tonight – is that all right?'

'Of course. Why wouldn't it be?'

'I just thought if you and Brian had fallen out...' Rose turned back to the pot on the range, and Harp wondered what had got into her mother; she was normally never flustered by little things.

'Oh, that. Don't worry about that. I like Brian, but it's just he's so infuriating when he's losing. He makes it personal, trying to make me feel like a silly little girl when he's such a worldly man according to himself. Just because he's studying medicine up in Dublin. Cicero was right – he said that when you have no basis for an argument, abuse the plaintiff.'

'Harp...' Her mother stopped stirring and gave Harp her full attention. 'I think Brian Quinn might have an eye for you, and maybe that's why he teases you. You really are a lovely looking girl, so no wonder he does, but it doesn't do to lead boys on, thinking there might be something going to happen if there isn't. Do you know what I mean?'

Harp was astonished. It was the first time her mother had made such a suggestion. If anything, she treated Harp like she was younger than her sixteen years, and so her raising the possibility of Harp having a boyfriend or anything like it was astounding. 'Brian Quinn has no more interest in me than the man in the moon, Mammy, I can assure you. He thinks I'm an annoying little twerp with ideas above my station, so you need have no worries about that.'

'I'm not so sure.' Rose clearly wasn't convinced. 'He rushes to see you the moment he's back from college, and Matt says he talks about you a lot. He says you're fascinating, which of course you are, but I just want you to be on your guard, you know?'

'He doesn't find me fascinating – that's just Matt being nice. I'd say it's more like giving out about me, no doubt.' Harp was sure her mother was worrying unnecessarily.

'All right, but just be careful. You are growing into a very pretty woman, Harp. Men will notice you, and you need to be careful, for lots of reasons, not just having them think something that isn't there, but...well...other things too. Even walking alone with him might set tongues wagging.'

'Don't worry, Mammy. I'm no Fanny Hill.' Harp chuckled.

'Harp! How do you even know about that book? It's banned, isn't it?'

Rose was extremely proper. She had been only seventeen when Henry's brother, Ralph, had seduced her with false promises; later, Henry had told the world in his will that Harp was his child and a Devereaux. As a result of being known as an unmarried mother, Rose was very anxious never to give anyone the impression she was a woman of loose morals. Since becoming lady of the house, she had started to wear brighter clothes, but she kept her slim figure covered up completely.

'Don't tell me Henry had a copy in the library.' Rose rolled her eyes and sighed. 'That man.'

'He did. He didn't believe in banning books. But he made me promise to wait until I was sixteen to read it, so I did.'

'Harp, that's not suitable reading for a girl of any age. It's…well, it's…' Rose flushed, struggling to explain what was so objectionable. Everyone knew the book *Fanny Hill: Memoirs of a Woman of Pleasure*, but nobody admitted to reading it.

'Mammy, this is all part of the problem, making women feel less important than men. Why shouldn't a woman appreciate her body? Why shouldn't she get pleasure from it? What's so wrong with that? Men's pleasure is all that seems to matter, with women just helpless objects to be used. Either the men are gentlemen and want to marry a nice chaste girl, or they are cads seeking wanton seduction. It's all so demeaning to us. We're expected to take their names, have their children, run their houses and bend to their wills. I'll tell you what I think – I won't ever do that. I mean it, Mammy. I'll never marry. Who on earth would sign up for that life of drudgery, at a man's beck and call?'

Rose laughed despite herself. 'Henry said you were unique, Harp, and he was right – you really are. And I suppose you've got a point. I'm hardly in a position to judge anyway, but maybe you'll fall in love, and what will you do then?' Rose placed the apple pie in the oven and washed her hands.

'I won't, simple as that.' Harp was certain. 'I know my own mind. Socrates said to know yourself, for once you know yourself, then you can begin to care for yourself. I'm paraphrasing, mind you.'

'Yes, well, Socrates had no opinion on peeling potatoes, I take it?' Rose replied, nodding at the pile of dirty potatoes in the sink.

'Not that I know of.' Harp grinned and began peeling.

Still fired up by the argument with Brian, her young mind was not on love but on the Rising. The treatment of the Irish by the British was never good, but it was getting worse. The police were taking on a much more military stance nowadays, swaggering about like they were cock of the walk and sending officers over from England all the time, who treated the local people with disdain. She glanced at her mother. 'You know Liam O'Halloran?'

'The Liam in your class at school?'

'Yes, that one. Well, Lieutenant Groves and about ten RIC men barged into his family's house one evening last week when the little ones were in bed and started shouting and demanding that Mrs O'Halloran tell them where Liam's father was. They suspect him of being involved with the Volunteers. They got very rough with Mrs O'Halloran, so Liam stepped in to defend his mother, and when he arrived to school, he had a big bruise on his chin and a split lip. Groves himself hit him, and Liam is not big, as you know.'

Rose stirred the gravy to go with the lamb, a shadow of concern on her face. 'Harp, it's best if we stay out of things. Since the Rising, everyone is jumpy, and it's best to keep a low profile. I know you feel strongly about it, and I don't blame you, but we are a single woman and a girl and we don't need to be drawing the likes of Groves on us, do you hear me? So please keep your opinions on that matter inside these four walls, do you promise me?'

Harp gave a derisory snort, and Rose shot her a warning glance. Her mother preferred her as a docile little girl, but Harp had been awakened by the plays performed in the newly founded Abbey Theatre and by the performances and writings of Maud Gonne and Yeats and Countess Markiewicz. She'd only been able to read the plays, of course, but one day she would go to Dublin and see them on stage for herself. She'd read all she could get her hands on, especially about the women of the freedom movement, and she rejected the claims made by many that the Irish women's movement was subservient to the male revolutionaries. She knew her heroines didn't see it that way, and neither did she.

She thought of how Henry Devereaux would have understood her growing interest in the equality of the sexes. He'd pointed her in the direction of Karl Marx, Millicent Fawcett and Emmeline Pankhurst. She felt a pang of loneliness;

she missed him still, his gentle presence, his love for her. He had written her a letter to be given to her after his death, explaining how he cared for her and how proud he was of her. The truth was, he was not her biological father despite him claiming her as such in order to make her his heir. But she saw him as her father in every way that mattered.

'Has everyone checked in?' she asked her mother, changing the subject away from the thorny matter of politics.

'Yes. There's a couple in the blue room that seem a bit strange – I don't know why. They are older than the usual couple that emigrate, easily in their fifties, and I don't know, they seem kind of furtive or something.' Rose was chopping the carrots and parsnips. 'And there are the three brothers – they're joining Sean O'Sullivan on his ranch in Kentucky, would you believe? They are cousins of his mother's.'

'Sean O'Sullivan! Imagine! He left here with Gwen, having no idea what the future held. They wouldn't even have been going together if Molly O'Brien didn't give Gwen her ticket. And now look at him. In his last letter, he told me he owns his own ranch in America, breeding winning racehorses. Life is so strange, isn't it?' Harp put

17

the peeled potatoes into the large saucepan to boil.

'I'm so glad things worked out for him,' Rose agreed. 'That's another one for your book, isn't it?'

Since the guest house opened, Harp had been keeping a record of all their guests and their adventures.

'And talking of letters,' Rose added, 'there are three for you on the hallstand, and one is from JohnJoe, judging by the clever little drawing on the envelope.'

'Oh, really?' Harp was delighted. 'I haven't heard from him for weeks and weeks. I hope he's all right.'

Rose shot her a curious glance. 'Why wouldn't he be all right?'

'Oh, no reason. I just like to hear from him, that's all.' Harp reddened; she was a terrible liar and her mother could see right through her.

'Hmm.' Rose's gaze locked with Harp's. 'Would I be correct in thinking that your feelings for JohnJoe might extend beyond a childhood friendship?'

'No! Of course not! We're just friends –'

A deep, smooth voice interrupted her. 'Fall in

18

love or not, my charming niece, one day soon you'll have to be married...'

In mutual shock, Harp and her mother turned towards the garden doorway. There stood Ralph Devereaux, Henry's younger brother, clearly back from India for the second time that year. Tall and muscular, he had suspiciously dark wavy hair for a man his age, and his skin was tanned from years under the Indian sun. He always dressed fashionably and smelled of a woody cologne; he was said to be attractive to women, and he could be charming at times. Yet whenever she looked at him, Harp was reminded of the words of Cicero: *'Ut imago est animi voltus'* – the face is a picture of the mind. That was true in the case of most people, but not her uncle. She never knew what was going on behind those eyes. It felt like a malevolent force.

Of course, to be fair, there were things that Ralph Devereaux didn't know about Harp either, for instance that he wasn't her uncle – he was her biological father. And therefore that his brother, Henry, had not the right to leave the crumbling family home to Harp when he'd named her as his own daughter in his will.

Rose tried to put a good face on the sudden

appearance of her one-time seducer. 'Ralph! When did you arrive?'

He lounged in the doorway, preening. 'Got here on the one o'clock train. Might stay for a month or even more this time. The house looks well. You've done a lot more work on it. I assume I can have my usual room?'

'Of course.'

Harp's mother always gave the best bedroom to Ralph. Harp knew that part of Rose felt guilty; Cliff House was, after all, his ancestral home. Six generations of Devereauxes had lived there, and to have his inheritance snatched from under his nose by the former maid and her daughter must have been hard to take. So whenever he arrived, she treated him as an honoured guest, with room service, meals and drink – and never once did he put his hand in his pocket to pay for any of it.

'Then I'll go on up. No need for dinner. I'll be going out later. That excellent fellow Groves is staying at the Queen's Hotel, and he wants to stand me a drink. You should join us, Rose.'

Rose kept her head down. 'I have other dinners to cook...'

'What a shame. You shouldn't work so hard. Yet even with all the skivvying, you're as beautiful as ever. And, Harp, you're looking very grown up. Very pretty as well, in your own little way.'

Harp emptied the potato peels into the bucket for the hens without answering. She hated the way Ralph's eyes rolled over her and her mother as he spoke, as if they were cows at the mart. And it disgusted her that her biological father would drink with Lieutenant Groves, or any British officer.

When he had left for his room, she blurted, 'Urgh. What's he doing back here so soon? He's only been gone a few months. And he says he might stay for more than a month! That's not acceptable. Honestly, who does he think he is? I can't bear him, Mammy, I really can't.'

'I know, Harp, but what choice have we?' Rose said gently. 'He's here, and I can hardly ask him to go. Look, we'll just endure it, try to stay out of his way, and hopefully it won't be for as long as he says.'

CHAPTER 3

*H*arp finished in the kitchen and headed up to her bedroom with her three letters from the hallstand, including the one from America. As she rounded the corner of the stairs, she was so engrossed in JohnJoe's sketch of two pigeons on his envelope that she bumped into a British officer in full uniform, her face colliding with his broad chest.

'Oh, I'm sorry!' She dropped JohnJoe's letter and went to retrieve it, but before she could, the officer swept it up and held it above her head, a gleam in his eye.

She straightened. 'Can I have my letter?' she asked politely but coldly.

'You'll have to ask me nicely,' he said in clipped English tones, smirking.

Stifling the urge to stamp on his foot, she made an effort to compose herself. She resented having any British officers staying in the guest house as it was – let alone a horrible smarmy fellow like this one, with his oiled-back hair and thin moustache. She hated how he flirted with her each morning as she served him breakfast, in between droning on to the other guests, showing off about his service in France and name-dropping field marshal this and governor general that. Only that morning he'd grabbed her hand as she put his toast down, ostensibly to ask for marmalade.

'May I please have my letter, Captain Pennington?'

'Call me Robert,' he said quietly in her ear.

Harp shuddered. He was in his thirties at least, and his breath smelled of fish. As she opened her mouth to say something less than polite, her mother appeared at the bottom of the stairs.

'Oh, Captain Pennington, I didn't realise you were back. You had a nice walk, I trust?' If Rose knew she'd arrived in the nick of time, she gave no indication of it.

The officer stepped hastily back from Harp. 'Ah, yes, Mrs Delaney, very pleasant, thank you. The views across the harbour really are spectacular. I enjoyed lunch at the hotel, and I just came back for my tennis whites.' He showed her the bag he was carrying in his other hand, and his voice was nothing but polite and friendly. 'I'm playing doubles with Mr Bridges and Colonel Jennings at Hazelmere House this evening, and Harp's uncle has just told me he'll be glad to make a fourth. What a pleasant fellow he is! I'm delighted to have met him. And Mrs Bridges is kindly providing dinner for us afterwards.'

'Well, you'll have a lovely evening for it. Enjoy yourself. Harp, could you help me with the potatoes, please?' asked Rose, despite the fact that Harp had only just finished peeling them.

'Of course.'

Pennington handed her JohnJoe's letter with a slight bow and a smarmy smile, and she turned to run back downstairs.

'Are you all right?' her mother asked as Harp shut the door of the kitchen behind her. 'I heard that man's voice and thought I should come and check on you.'

'I'm fine. He took my letter from JohnJoe and was holding it above his head, and when I asked him politely for it back, he asked me to call him

Robert.' She shuddered. 'He's awful, though. No doubt he and Ralph will become best friends. It's a shame to waste two houses between them.'

Rose looked worried. 'Be careful of that one, Harp, and try not to be alone with him. I don't trust him.'

'I'll wait until he's gone before I go back upstairs. I really wish we could refuse the British, Mammy – I hate having them here. Even the ones who are not lecherous seem to exude superiority and look at all of us like we were something they brought in on their shoe.'

Rose sighed. 'I know, Harp, but to refuse them would be to draw adverse attention to us. Just last week, that Colonel Froggatt – remember him, the one with the large, demanding wife? – dropped in and said he and his wife wanted the large front room for four nights, and I said we were full. We weren't, not really, and I could have moved some guests around. He just bellowed, "Nonsense, Mrs Delaney! You shall have to make room. We'll be here at four." And then marched out as if he owned the place.'

Harp did remember him; she remembered them all. And she hated every single one of them.

They looked out the window. Pennington emerged a few moments later, his tennis bag slung over his shoulder, and strolled across the garden towards the Smuggler's Stairs. Queenstown was crisscrossed with flights of medieval steps that allowed pedestrian access all over the port town; the Cliff House garden had a side gate to one of those sets of steps, and its main driveway was rarely used by those on foot.

Catching them watching out the kitchen window, Pennington waved cheekily. Rose nodded but didn't smile. It didn't pay to be too rude or too friendly to the British officers; either way could get an Irish woman into trouble.

'The coast is clear,' Harp said with relief. She picked up her letters and left for her room again, this time without running into any other guests. She knew the three boys who were going to work for Sean in Kentucky were down the town, having a drink before dinner, their last in Ireland. Her uncle's door was open, but he wasn't anywhere to be seen. She guessed the few other guests must also be out and about. But as she passed the upstairs sitting room, she spotted through the open door a middle-aged couple sitting close together, speaking quietly; she thought they must be the odd pair her mother had mentioned.

She skipped up the last flight of stairs. She and

her mother had moved up into the attic, expertly converted by a local builder to create two bedrooms and a bathroom so they could have their own space. In Harp's room, her small iron bedstead had been replaced by a lovely black cast-iron bed with a russet-coloured bedspread. The floorboards were varnished, and a silk rug of oranges and yellows went almost to the walls; even the matching chest of drawers and wardrobe looked welcoming. What she loved best, though, was the dormer window that gave a panoramic view of Cork Harbour. Despite her mother offering to make her curtains, she preferred the inky sky at night with its twinkling stars and the bright morning sunshine to waken her. She would sit for hours by the window, in the frayed royal-blue Queen Anne chair that she had liberated from Henry's former office; it had been his favourite and was the one he had died in. She would watch the comings and goings of the port below, as she'd done all her life. And she would read and read, for hours.

She had already decided what and where she wanted to study – classics at Trinity College in Dublin. The university had been in existence since 1592, its charter granted by an unmarried woman, Queen Elizabeth I. Yet women had only recently been admitted to that seat of learning. The previous provost had said a female would enter the college over his dead body; he had died in 1904, and now Harp could apply. She wouldn't enjoy the same privileges as her male counterparts, but at least she could study. She could have chosen medicine or law, but she loved the Ancient Greeks and Romans and decided she would get a degree in the languages, literature and history of those cultures first. Her plan was to become a teacher, possibly at a third-level institution, ideally one that taught women. That way she could travel during the school holidays.

Her mother had assumed Harp would be happy to go to Queen's College in Cork, so Harp had decided to say nothing and apply to Trinity once she'd matriculated and see what happened. The college might refuse her, and then the worry she would inevitably cause her mother would have been for nothing. She had, however, confided her plans to JohnJoe and was dying to hear what he had to say.

The teenage boy had been illiterate when he'd stayed at the Cliff House on his way to America, but Harp had taught him his letters and they'd had an unending stream of correspondence over the past four years. They told each other everything; nothing was off limits. He wrote about how his Uncle Pat was a character, and a great friend and financial supporter of John Devoy, the Irish rebel in exile in America. He told her how he had become his Aunt Kathy's son in a way he could never have imagined and how they loved each other. He'd mentioned his first girlfriend, a redhead called Erin O'Malley from Dorchester Street who'd never set foot in Ireland but was, he joked, more Irish than either him or Harp. That relationship didn't last long. JohnJoe thought she was being pushed on him in order to form a closer bond between her father, Ernie O'Malley, and Uncle Pat. Anyway, she wasn't his type, he explained.

She wondered what his type was. She tried to picture him now. When she'd last seen him, he was a skinny boy with sticking-up hair and a face of freckles. She imagined him as just a bigger version of that. In her last letter, she'd sent him a photo of herself that she had taken at the mobile studio that sometimes came to take pictures of people as they left Ireland. She hadn't looked too awful in it, she hoped.

Sitting comfortably in the Queen Anne chair, the afternoon sun warming her through the glass, she quickly checked through the first two letters, saving JohnJoe's until last. The first was from a recent guest excitedly telling her about their first day in America, and the second was from Eleanor Kind, an elderly lady who had been summoned to San Francisco by her brother because he decided she could no longer live alone on her County Sligo farm. Eleanor had been heartbroken at the thought of leaving her animals – she had a special way with them – and in the end decided she would defy her brother. She gave her ticket to Molly O'Brien and stayed in Ireland to run a little veterinary surgery.

Finally, she opened JohnJoe's unusually bulky letter and realised to her delight that it contained a photograph. It must have been of him, but it showed only the faintest trace of the JohnJoe she knew. It was black and white, so she couldn't see his exact hair colour, only that it was fair and cut in a very nice style, longish on top and neatly trimmed at the sides. He still had his freckles but they seemed less obvious now, and his teeth were perfectly white and straight, not crooked as she remembered. He wore an open-necked shirt and he'd filled out. She thought he looked really handsome. No wonder Erin O'Malley had eyes for him. She wondered if he'd kissed her. Probably. America was much more easygoing about things like kissing, she decided. She gazed at his mouth in the picture, his perfect Cupid's bow lips, and found herself wondering what it would be like to kiss him. Though she was alone, she blushed, hardly the reaction of a modern woman who only moments ago had scandalised her mother with talk of Fanny Hill. But books were one thing; real life was something entirely different.

She reluctantly put the photo down and read. His handwriting was still childlike, despite years of writing to her, but it made her smile.

Dearest Harp,

Wow! You've grown into quite the dish, as they say here. It came as a surprise, I can tell you, since you are still twelve in my mind. I guess, like, I'm fourteen in yours, huh? I don't know if I look much different. Sometimes I think I am, and then other times I'm the same dumbass kid who landed here four years ago.

I thought you were lovely then, and I think it even more now. So thank you. Auntie Kathy saw I had your picture framed and put it on my dressing table, and she was teasing me about my Irish girl. She's happy I never got along with Erin O'Malley, mainly 'cause I think she hates the idea of me ever leaving, so a nice faraway girl would be just the ticket as far as she's concerned.

So turns out my friend is this gorgeous Irish girl, who isn't just the smartest person I ever met, but she's a bit of a maverick too, going off to university in Dublin!

I think doing it your way is right. Get your exams – we both know you'll ace them – and then apply without telling anyone. Your mom will probably be crabby about it for a while as she'll miss you, but I bet deep down she's real proud too. And in the very un-likely event of you not getting in, then by not saying anything, you're saving her all that worry.

I saw Molly last week. She wrote and asked me to stop by the convent, so I did. I hadn't been to see her for a while 'cause I'd been in Atlantic City. Uncle Pat's got some business interests down there, so I was sent to check up on them. It was fun, I guess, but it would make a sailor blush to see the girls on the beach, wearing almost nothing, and the bars and the clubs. Well, it's not like anything in Ireland, I can tell you that.

Anyway, when I got back to Boston, I went over to the convent, and I gotta tell you, Harp, she's not doing so good. She's lost a lot of weight and looks sick. The doctors are doing lots of tests. She wanted to see me and gave me a lecture on being a good boy. You know Molly. She still talks to me like I'm a kid, not a man, but I don't mind really – she's nice. The Reverend

Mother gave me a filthy look when I called her by her name and not Sister Angela as they call her, but she'll always be Molly O'Brien to me, even with that nun costume on. She wrote to her parents but they never replied, so she doesn't really have any family. Auntie Kathy and Uncle Pat donate money to the convent, and they've invited her for dinner too, but she can't really come. I think nuns aren't really supposed to so-cialise – I don't know.

To answer your question about if we knew about the Easter Rising – are you serious? It's all anyone can talk about. I didn't get to go on account of being in At-lantic City, but the others all went to hear Nora Con-nolly speak at Faneuil Hall about the death of her father, James Connolly, who was so injured that the British had to tie him to a chair before they shot him. Everyone was angry about the way the Rising was put down back in April, but after the executions of the leaders, they were furious. Thousands gathered to protest. Congressman Joseph O'Connell really got everyone riled up – he's some speaker, Harp.

Boston feels like a part of Ireland really. James Connolly lived here for a while, so did Jim Larkin and Francis Sheehy-Skeffington. I feel more Irish here than I ever did at home. I guess in Ireland everyone is Irish so it's not a big deal, but over here, Danny was right – you gotta stick to your own and stick up for your own. It's the only way. Even people who followed the Home Rule idea are changing over to support the Rising, and honestly I think they'd lynch Redmond if he came here now. Uncle Pat had lunch last week with James Michael Curley, the mayor of Boston, who is very outspoken on the subject of the Rising and Irish independence. The Boston Globe *put the entire proclamation on its front page in May, when only a few weeks before they said it was an 'insane movement'.*

Danny sends his love. He got in a bit of bother at the protests – he punched a policeman on the nose – so he's lying low right now! Auntie Kathy is trying to get him to settle down, find a girl, but he's got so many on the go, he's not inclined to reduce his options to just one. Still the same old Danny, joking around. He's eight years older than me but he feels like a brother, so I cover for him when girls ask questions. I don't know how he remembers what he's said to each one, though.

Like I told you, I ended it with Erin – well, it never really started, to be honest; I wasn't really interested. I guess my mind is on another girl. One too far away to take for an ice cream or a box of saltwater taffy on the boardwalk in Atlantic City.

Write back soon.

Love always,

JohnJoe xxx

CHAPTER 4

$\mathcal{H}$arp thought that Matt Quinn was looking particularly good that night, even though it was only to eat with her and her mother. His suit and shirt were neatly pressed and his fair hair cut and combed. She hadn't thought about it before, but Brian must have got his height and red hair from his late mother's side. Matt was more blond than red, and although he wasn't a short man, his son was easily three inches taller. The undertaker was slight, whereas Brian was beanpole thin.

Matt ate quietly at first, speaking only to compliment Rose on her cooking. But then Brian started telling Harp about some friends of his from the university who'd joined the Royal Medical Corps and were now working in a hospital in Amiens in northern France.

Matt's knife and fork clattered on his plate. 'I don't know what their parents were thinking of, letting them go. I wouldn't have a son of mine put on an English uniform, doctor or no doctor.'

'Ah, Dad, it's not like that and you know it. They're only helping the injured, and plenty of the wounded are Irish.'

'Cannon fodder for the British,' said his father, his pleasant face darkening with frustration. 'Getting young Irish men killed to maintain their notions of empire.'

'Well, to be fair, the Germans are riding roughshod over small nations – what about poor Belgium and the Low Countries?' began Brian, but his normally mild-mannered father stopped him again.

'What about *this* small nation, their next-door neighbour that they've brutalised and tormented for centuries? Where was all the defending small nations talk when they were doing it to us? The English don't give a damn about anyone but themselves – never have and never will. So we'll have no more of this at the dinner table please.'

'But –' Brian tried again.

This time both Harp and Rose jumped as Matt

shouted, 'Enough! Even Redmond knows now he set us on the wrong path completely, saying if we sent our sons as cannon fodder, we'd get our independence as a reward. The cheek of the English – how dare they!' A vein in Matt's temple pulsed, and his fingers gripping his knife and fork were white. He glanced at Rose, whose eyes were on her plate. In the silence, the clock ticked loudly from the dresser. 'I'm sorry, Rose. We shouldn't speak of such things after you cooked such a lovely meal for us. We're sorry, aren't we?' He glared at his son across the table.

'Yes, Mrs Delaney, I'm sorry,' Brian said, and Harp felt sorry for him. He was red in the face, clearly embarrassed to have been so publicly admonished in front of Rose and Harp.

But Rose smiled at both men and said, 'Brian has his opinions, Matt, and I know from my daughter here, it's hard when you raise them to be intelligent and opinionated and then those opinions don't align with your own. But you did a great thing, raising a strong moral boy who has turned into a man with his own mind. If he has opinions you don't agree with, you've no one to blame but yourself.'

Harp felt a rush of love for her mother. She didn't know how Matt would react, but then he said, 'I suppose you're right, Rose. My father would never countenance us having a thought on anything. His word was law and that was that. I swore I'd be different, and this is the price we pay.' He favoured his son with half a smile, but Brian was seething still and refused to meet his father's gaze.

Harp nudged her old friend. 'The Ancient Greeks were forever giving out about their children, saying that they had terrible manners and no respect for their elders, always contradicting their parents and a trial to their teachers, so it's nice to know we are behaving exactly as we're supposed to, isn't it, Brian?'

But even she couldn't raise a smile from him. Instead, he stood up abruptly. 'Thank you for dinner, Mrs Delaney. I'll be off now. It was lovely.' And within seconds he had left the room.

Matt stood up to follow, but Rose put a hand on his arm. 'Leave him, he needs to cool down. If you go out there, you'll just argue again.'

'I'll go,' Harp offered, and her mother nodded.

She hurried through the kitchen. As she entered the garden, Brian was already disappearing through the side gate to the Smuggler's Stairs. The evening was warm so there was no need of a coat, but she was only wearing her house shoes and could feel the sharp gravel through the thin soles. Just this year her mother insisted she begin dressing like a lady as opposed to a girl, so she now wore blouses and floor-length skirts. Rose also exclaimed in horror if Harp appeared downstairs without having her hair neatly pinned. Harp couldn't care less about such matters, but her mother resolutely refused to accept anything but full attire as befitting a young lady.

'Brian, wait!' she called, hobbling awkwardly over the painful stones.

He stopped and turned in the gateway, and she could see he'd been crying. 'Harp, I'll see you tomorrow...' he began, clearly desperate to get away.

'No, wait. Come with me.' As she reached the gate, she took his hand and led him to the garden bench, which her mother had asked Matt to make after Henry died. The plaque on the seat read, *In memory of Henry Devereaux, who was loved very much by Rose and Harp.* Such a frivolity would never be allowed in the churchyard where his body lay these last four years, so when she or her mother wanted to feel close to him, they often came out to the bench instead.

'I'd rather just be alone...' He tried again.

'Sit down,' she ordered, and Brian did as he

was told. 'Now, look,' she said, sitting down beside him. 'I know you're cross with your father. My mother annoys me too, with her dresses and hairdos, as if I give a hoot. But they love us and want the best for us. Your father adores you – you know he does.'

'But in his eyes, I'm just a silly boy...'

'He doesn't think that. He just wants you to be safe, and he's terrified you might get hurt if you follow your friends,' she reassured him.

He stared at the ground between his feet, his arms resting on his knees. She put her hand on his shoulder. 'I don't want you to go to France either, you know.'

'Don't you?'

'No!'

Suddenly he sat up, turned and leaned in. Before she knew what was happening, he kissed her, not a chaste brotherly kiss on the cheek as he'd done before, but on the lips, pressing his mouth to hers, his opening slightly.

She recoiled, jumping to her feet, and stood gazing at him, stunned.

'Harp, I'm sorry...' He looked confused. 'I didn't mean to alarm you...'

'I... Well, yes... But I...' She could hardly get the words out. 'I just wasn't expecting...' Her normal eloquence had deserted her; she felt completely out of her depth. She knew about kissing and romance, but it was only from books. The idea of ever engaging in such activities in real life was unfathomable to her.

He stood up as well and tried to take her hand. 'I like you, Harp – well, more than like really. I think I love you. And I know we're young and all of that, but would you...would you consider being my girl?' His face was open and honest.

Her heart ached for him, but she also had to be honest; to do otherwise would be cruel. 'No, I won't, Brian,' she said, gently pulling her hand away. 'I like you very much as a friend, but I can't...'

'Harp, please.' Now he looked very young and unsure and vulnerable. 'I've liked you for ages, and I was waiting. And when you said you didn't want me to go to France, well, then I thought...'

'But what I meant was I think the same as your father. I don't want you to get hurt, and I especially don't want you to put on an English uniform. Why should you shed your blood for them?'

Brian's eyes flashed with hurt and anger. He drew himself up tall. 'Goodbye, Harp. I have to go.' And he walked with long strides out of the garden. She could hear his feet running down the steps.

'Brian, come back…' she called, but he was gone.

Sighing, she walked slowly back to the house. She wished she'd handled that more like the heroine in a book. But was there a better way in real life? She had no idea. She felt awful that he had been so crestfallen, but she was sure he would come down tomorrow and they would either laugh about this or never mention it again. Either way they'd solve it.

She decided to enter the dining room through the French doors rather than through the kitchen, as it meant walking across lawn rather than the hard stones. She slipped off her house shoes and held them in her hands, not wanting to soak them on the grass; there had been a summer downpour earlier. The fresh damp greenness tickled her toes as she crossed the lawn. The French doors were rarely used, but as she rounded the corner, she saw that this evening they were standing open, the gossamer-thin silk curtains billowing in the soft summer breeze. The scent of roses was on the air, the oils from the large blooms on the bushes warmed by the evening sun.

In the dining room, Matt Quinn and her mother were clearing the table, and something about the scene made Harp pause before she entered. She noticed the casual way Matt placed his hand on the small of her mother's back as he opened the door. The two of them seemed utterly comfortable with each other, as if they'd been doing domestic chores together all their lives. Instead of interrupting, Harp slipped quietly away. Were there other romantic feelings in the air that she hadn't noticed? Matt Quinn was a nice man, and he'd been so kind to them since Mr Devereaux died. Did he hope to become more than just a friendly neighbour?

She crept up the stairs, the events of the evening confusing her. What on earth was happening? First JohnJoe writing to say she was a dish, whatever that was, and saying he was thinking about a girl too far away to buy her an ice cream. Did he mean her? And if not her, then who?

She entered her bedroom and threw herself down on her bed. Could JohnJoe have meant he liked her in the way Brian had said he did? It was hard to imagine, but her logical mind told her there was no other interpretation. She found herself warmed at the thought. Whatever she might feel for JohnJoe, she certainly didn't for the younger Mr Quinn. Brian was nice and kind and interesting, but she could never imagine wanting to kiss him. Could she kiss JohnJoe? She took the photograph from her bedside locker and looked at it. Yes, she decided. If it had been JohnJoe kissing her in the garden, she would not have recoiled.

Her thoughts turned to her mother and Mr Quinn. Mammy was thirty-four years old; surely she wasn't thinking about romance at that age? And Mr Quinn must be forty something. But if their friendship did turn into a romance, did she mind? She had to ponder the question. It felt peculiar, undoubtedly, but Mr Quinn was a very nice man and Mammy deserved someone lovely, so she decided if it was what her mother wanted, then she didn't mind.

Restlessly, she stood up and opened the window. As the summer sun set over Spike Island, the stone walls of Fort Westmoreland turned a buttery yellow, silhouetted against the setting sun. Leaning against Henry's chair, she wondered what he would have made of it all. He'd probably be heartbroken at the idea of another man loving Rose. He'd never had a relationship with a woman in his whole life, but her mother had confided to her only last year that his final letter to Rose had been one of unending adoration. He'd always loved her mother but never could get up the courage to tell her.

She smiled at the thought of his innocence. 'We're a right pair, aren't we?' she said ruefully into the warm evening air.

CHAPTER 5

'Ah, the waitress!' Ralph boomed as Harp appeared in the breakfast room. 'At long last.'

Her uncle was seated at a table with Captain Pennington, and as she took their order, she tried not to wrinkle her nose at the fumes of stale alcohol and cigarettes rising from their bodies. They had come home in the small hours of the morning, crashing and banging so much that Rose had had to go down and ask them to be quiet. They were both so drunk, it was unlikely they recalled her admonishment.

'Two full Irish breakfasts, lots of toast and coffee, and don't scrimp on the sausages like you did yesterday – I like a nice juicy one.' Ralph winked theatrically at his friend.

Pennington's eyes roamed over Harp's body lecherously, his lips curled in a half smile. 'I'm more partial to tenderloin.'

Ralph wagged his finger mockingly. 'Take your eyes off my niece. She's very innocent – or so she pretends.'

'Pretends, eh?' Pennington smirked.

Harp tried fiercely not to blush; the pair would only enjoy that. She wrote the order in her notebook and turned to serve the three young men who'd just arrived down. 'What can I get you?' she asked as they took the window seat.

'Bacon and eggs, please, and tea for three.' They looked remarkably alike, all sandy-haired and brawny, ranging in age from late teens to early twenties.

'You're going out to Sean O'Sullivan, I believe?' She was glad of the distraction from her odious uncle and his lewd companion.

'We are, and he told us to stay here in the Cliff House and to pass on his regards to you and your mother,' said the middle lad. 'I'm Anthony Foley, and these are my brothers Damien and Ronan.'

'Nice to meet you.' Harp smiled. 'Please tell Sean

and Gwen we were asking about them and hoping all is well with them. He sent us the newspaper article from the *Kentucky Gazette* when his horse won a big race last year. My mother and I were delighted.'

'We certainly will pass on your regards,' said Anthony. 'He's doing great. His parents are going out to visit in September – imagine that! He's paying for them and for the Major, Gwen's father, to come to Lexington. They were none of them thrilled about Sean and Gwen – he told me you all knew the story. The Major nearly went mad when he heard they'd eloped, and Cousin May and her husband were mortified. They couldn't believe Sean would do that and felt the whole place was scandalised, but it's all worked out in the end and they are quite friendly now. Did you know Gwen is expecting a baby? That's why they're all going, to meet their grandchild.'

'No, that's wonderful news. I'm so happy to hear that.' Harp smiled at the memory of the two young lovers from different social classes who had run away together.

'They got married on the ship, you know. The captain married them,' Anthony went on.

'Yes, Sean wrote and told us. It all sounded very exciting,' Harp replied. Sean had also written of how he managed to settle a very distressed and expensive horse on the voyage, which had given him an opening into the equine world of Kentucky. He had never looked back. 'Now I'd better get your order to the kitchen or you'll get no breakfast at all.'

The older couple were finishing their meal – her mother had served them earlier – and there was a young family yet to appear.

Harp went into the kitchen and gave her mother the fresh orders. There were deliveries coming at the same time, and the new kitchen maid wasn't really working out. She was a clumsy girl and so far had broken two bowls and spilled a jug of milk all over the floor.

Mrs Lucey and her daughter Katie arrived; they were employed to do the laundry and were, in her mother's words, a godsend. Harp had to acknowledge that they were good at it, but Katie was doing a line with Emmet Kelly, the boy who'd tormented Harp every moment of school. He was joining the police and had gone to Dublin for training, but they planned to marry, it seemed, just as soon as he was trained and given a position. Harp hoped it was in Donegal. Nowhere could be far enough away when it came to Emmet Kelly.

Katie never said or did anything outright, but

Harp could feel her snide looks and caught glimpses of her smirks as she saw Harp's bedroom, a haven of learning and music. The harp that had been in the Devereaux family for generations was hers now, and Harp loved to play. She sometimes entertained the guests in the drawing room, but mostly she played in her room, for her own entertainment. A girl called Harp who played the harp was ridiculous, she knew, but she had stopped caring about what people thought of her years ago.

She took the hot plates containing Ralph and Captain Pennington's breakfasts and returned to the dining room. Ralph was in mid-flow in his droning irritatingly condescending voice, and Pennington seemed only mildly interested. As Harp lay the food on the table, neither man even acknowledged her. She turned, and as she did, Ralph snapped, 'Coffee.'

'I'm sorry. I'll get it now.'

Ralph rolled his eyes at the captain, a gesture that said, *How irritating to have to endure this simpleton serving us.* 'Well, run along then.'

Harp longed to walk out without getting him the coffee, but maybe her mother was right – it was easier to endure him for a week or so twice a year and maintain a semblance of cordiality than have an all-out war with him. The idea that he was her father filled her with disgust.

'Are you still at school?' Captain Pennington asked her as she returned with the silver coffee pot.

'Yes, I matriculate next year.' She hated the oily feel of his gaze.

'And then what? Marriage, I suppose?'

'Oh, my niece has ideas above her station, Robert. She thinks a life of academia is her due.' Ralph sneered.

'What, she's to be a blue stocking, is she?' Pennington drawled. 'Rather a waste, don't you think? That's the life for a plain spinster, and Harp is definitely not plain. Unusual looking, certainly, but she has a certain…charm.'

Ralph glanced critically at Harp, then shrugged. 'Can't see it myself. Anyway, as I was saying, the Kaiser is really on the back foot now and…'

Harp withdrew, feeling dirty. How dare they discuss her like that, as if she weren't even there.

When she returned to the kitchen, Katie and Mrs Lucey were upstairs doing the rooms and Eithne, the new kitchen maid, had been sent out to gather the eggs from the chicken coop.

'I cannot bear Ralph and now that Captain

Pennington. They are so…just *urgh*,' she complained to her mother, who was scrambling some eggs.

'What did they say?' Rose looked worried.

'Just talking about me like I was a piece of meat, and Ralph being all superior and trying to show off. I know why we can't turn him away, but honestly, do we need to put up with him all the time?'

Rose spooned the eggs onto three plates beside slices of crispy bacon. 'You stay in here. I'll bring these out.' She deftly untied her apron and quick as a flash was out into the dining room and back again.

An hour later, after the flurry of breakfast was over, mother and daughter sat down to have a cup of tea together. 'So how did you get on with Brian last night?' asked Rose. 'I didn't see you come back in. Did you manage to calm him down after the blow-up with his father?'

'Oh, Mammy, it was awful.' Harp blurted out the whole thing, and Rose looked genuinely shocked.

'I knew he liked you, but to try to kiss you, without any warning… Well, I would never have thought him that kind of a pushy boy. You're barely sixteen, and he had no right to –'

'I'm all right, Mammy. I told him I wasn't interested, and he accepted it right away. But he was very upset and I felt terrible. Especially after the row he had with Matt.' Harp sighed.

'I know, and he's usually a nice boy. But don't worry. He and Matt will patch things up – they always do. Matt adores Brian. When his wife died, he put every ounce of energy he had into raising that boy. They could never stay cross with each other. Matt lives for his son. He promised his wife on her deathbed that he would care for their child, and he takes his role as Brian's father as seriously as I take raising you.'

'I hope so, and I hope Brian forgives me too,' Harp said dolefully.

'There is nothing to forgive on your part!' said Rose with surprising intensity. 'You must never feel sorry for rejecting a man's advances. You owe no man anything. He made an advance, you didn't want it, and you told him so – that's the end of it.' Rose took Harp's hand and her brown eyes locked with Harp's grey ones. 'No man has a right to make a woman feel responsible or bad for not wanting him. That is the nonsense some men go on with, but we must rail against it. You were perfectly within your rights to reject him, and if anyone should be apologising, it should be him.'

'But he looked so forlorn.' Harp was confused. Her life was being turned on its head, and she felt like she was being thrust into a world of things about which she knew nothing.

'That's as may be, but that is not your concern. Harp, I know it feels strange now and you like Brian as a friend, but believe me, there will come a time when you won't feel indifferent or re-pulsed by someone, and then it is the time to ask yourself, "Is this man worthy of me?" Don't make the same mistakes I did, Harp, giving way to a cad and a liar. Brian is a good person, I know he is, but men are men, and they often have more...' – her mother searched for the word – 'base desires than we do. And some will stop when you tell them to, but others won't stop no matter what you say or do, so a girl needs to be on her guard. Do you understand what I mean?'

Harp knew what rape was – she'd read enough to understand the concept of a man's un-wanted attentions – and now she was sure this was the warning her mother was giving her. 'I think so. But Brian would never...'

'Oh, I know that. He's not who I was referring to. But types like that Captain Pennington behave as if the normal rules of society don't apply to them. I don't want to frighten you, but at the same time, you need to be on your guard.' Rose reached over and placed her hand on Harp's cheek. 'My darling girl, I wish I could keep you safe, keep the ugliness of the world away from you, I really do. But you are growing into a beautiful woman, and men are beginning to notice you.'

Harp protested. 'I don't think so, not seriously...'

'They do, Harp. You are perfect, and so pretty and clever. Men will clamour for your attention as you get older, mark my words, and I just need you to enter this world with your eyes wide open.'

Harp doubted her mother was right. She had tried to examine her features and her figure objectively. She was small and slight, and her grey eyes and red-blond hair were an odd combination. She knew the likes of Emmet Kelly and the other boys at school ran after girls like Katie, whose breasts were bigger than Harp's and who gave them coquettish glances and giggled when they walked by. Even Brian had probably just mistaken their mutual friendship for deeper feelings. It had always been her mother who was beautiful, not her. She said softly, 'I saw you and Mr Quinn last night.'

Rose gave her an uncertain look. 'Of course you did. He came for dinner.'

'No, afterwards. When I came back to the house, I went round by the French doors and I saw you two, together.'

'Oh.' Rose seemed nonplussed. 'You saw us clearing the table?'

'Yes.'

'And?'

'It just seemed to me that he makes you happy.'

Her mother's eyes widened. 'What on earth do you mean?'

'Nothing. Well, I just wanted to say… Well, I mean…if he does make you happy, I don't mind.' She looked into her mother's bright dark eyes. 'Does he make you happy, Mammy?'

Rose hesitated for a moment, then nodded slowly, her cheeks flushing pink. 'I think maybe he does.'

CHAPTER 6

The next morning, the odd couple who seemed so furtive were in the dining room five minutes before breakfast was officially served. He was nondescript, balding with a slight paunch. She too was a very ordinary-looking woman, with salt-and-pepper hair and a slightly lumpy figure – not unpleasant looking but someone one would pass on the street without taking a moment's notice.

Harp approached them. 'Good morning! What can I get for you?'

'We'd just like some scrambled eggs and toast please, and tea for two,' the man said.

'Certainly.' Harp wrote the order on her notepad. From the corner of her eye she saw her uncle appear, and her heart sank. But at least Pennington wasn't with him today. 'So you sail on Saturday?' she asked the couple, just to make conversation. She knew they were on the New York sailing of the White Star ship that weekend.

'Yes,' said the man. His companion looked weepy.

'Are you excited?' It was a question she often asked; it seemed to illicit a more interesting response than 'What are your plans in America?'

Yet the simple question seemed to stump them. 'Ah, well, yes, I suppose...' the man answered.

Ralph clicked his fingers to gain her attention, then noisily unfolded his newspaper.

'I'll be right back with your breakfasts,' she said, and with her stomach churning in dislike, she approached her uncle's table.

'Are there kippers today?' he asked in his bored voice.

'Yes, there are...er...' She couldn't bring herself to call Ralph Devereaux 'sir', and 'Uncle Ralph' felt out of the question, so she never called him anything if she could possibly avoid it.

'Then bring me some porridge with honey and cream, followed by the kippers – and Pennington will have the same. And make it quick.

We're getting a quick round of golf in before the sailing this afternoon. I joined Cork Golf Club last week, and the captain is coming as my guest. Oh, and Pennington will have lapsang souchong and I'll have coffee. And tell your mother to make us a picnic with a bottle of wine – you can put it on my bill.' Ralph went back to his paper without uttering a 'please' or 'thank you'.

On her way back to the kitchen, Harp passed Pennington in the hallway. As usual he tried to flirt with her, but she flatly ignored him. She was fuming. How dare Ralph Devereaux add a picnic to his non-existent bill. Was he trying to bank-rupt her and her mother? And it wasn't like he was broke – if he had joined the golf club, he must have some money; the membership there was very expensive. Her heart sank suddenly. Did this mean her uncle wasn't going back for ages? Surely he wouldn't have spent such a lot of money if he didn't intend to stay around for a while. Could he be planning to move back to Queenstown? He had a house in Calcutta, she knew; he was forever blowing to the British offi-cers about his fine estate and his servants and all the rest of it when he came over. Enduring him for a week or two twice a year was one thing, but him moving to Queenstown permanently was a terrible thought.

Once she and her mother were finished serving breakfast and all the guests had gone back to their rooms or out exploring, Rose sent Eithne to the Devlins for some provisions.

In the yard behind the guest house, Harp tossed the bucket of scraps into the chicken coop for the hens, then walked slowly back down the side of the house. She hated the chickens, with their beady eyes and jealous ways. An old lady out at Belvelly had died and left her hens without care; Matt was the undertaker and had brought them to the Cliff House coop. But the Cliff House hens weren't having it and savaged the poor bereaved hens. It was a bloodbath of feathers and horrid prehistoric-looking chicken feet. Matt had had to intervene and nearly got pecked to death himself. Harp knew how the guests loved the free-range eggs for breakfast, but if she could shoo the whole flock out the gate, she would do it happily.

As she came around the side of the house, she spotted the middle-aged pair she'd served at breakfast. They were deep in conversation, sitting on Henry's garden bench beside the wall, the very one where she'd rejected Brian's advances only last night. The woman was crying, and the man was trying his best to comfort her.

As she passed them, a carriage came into view, the horse struggling to make the climb up the steep driveway. The odd couple suddenly stood and ducked out of the side gate onto the Smuggler's Stairs. Harp glanced towards them as she passed the gate, and the couple peered back at her through the bars with stricken faces.

'Please don't say we're here,' the man hissed. The woman huddled up close to him, clearly rigid with terror.

Harp carried on around the front of the house, where the carriage had now come to a halt. A man and woman climbed out and hurried to the front door; the man pressed his finger to the bell.

'Hello? Can I help you?' she asked, approaching them from behind.

The pair spun around, and to Harp's surprise, the man looked like a younger, slimmer version of the man hiding on the steps.

'I'm looking for my father and her mother.' The young man jerked his head at the woman, who had an unpleasant pinched face. 'Michael McGrath and Joan Coakley. They're staying here?'

'Sorry, I don't believe we have any guests of that name staying here,' said Harp, doing her best to make her grey eyes look innocent. The couple had not checked in under those names, so she wasn't telling a lie.

'Well, they wouldn't use their own names, of course,' the woman chided her companion. She scowled at Harp. 'They're both in their late fifties. He's bald and fat and she's small and timid looking.'

Harp took an instant dislike to this sharp-featured woman and thought that whatever the older couple's reason, hiding from this pair seemed like a very good idea. 'No, I'm afraid nobody answering that description is staying here,' she said with conviction.

The woman, who was in her mid-twenties, exhaled in frustration. 'Well, if they do appear, can you tell them that Ann, Sean, Maura, Patrick and Benny said they are to come home immediately and not to be disgracing us and scandalising the parish with their carry on. And that Patrick had to come home from Maynooth in disgrace, so they have that on their conscience as well.'

The young man looked awkward. 'Well, Maura, to be fair, this girl can hardly deliver that message. And besides, they aren't here.'

Maura didn't seem to think him worthy of a reply; she stalked back to the carriage in high dudgeon.

'I'm sorry for disturbing you, miss.' The man sat into the carriage, the woman reluctantly following, and clicked the reins to urge the horse forward, back down the driveway.

Harp hurried to the top of the Smuggler's Stairs and stuck her head around the gate. The couple were still huddled in the shadows under the ivy. 'They're gone,' she said, and the two of them visibly relaxed. 'Would you like some tea? You look like you could use it.'

The woman, clutching the man's hand, beamed with gratitude. 'That would be lovely, and thank you. I think we owe you an explanation.'

'Yes, thank you very much,' the man added. 'I know it must have been difficult lying to them for us, but honestly…'

'It wasn't difficult at all,' Harp reassured them. 'And I didn't lie. They gave me names of people who were not on our register, and I couldn't recognise either of you by the description they gave.'

'I can just imagine how she described us,' the woman said darkly.

Smiling, Harp left them at the little white wrought iron table and chairs on the patio and went inside to make some tea. It felt good to have finally made a connection with the unusual couple, and she was looking forward to hearing their story. She entered the kitchen to find her mother baking.

'I'm just making tea for Mr and Mrs Keane,' she said.

'Very well. I thought we might take a walk up to Henry's grave later on?' Rose asked.

They went up there together at least once a week and laid flowers. It felt like a little respite from the relentless comings and goings of the guest house, and it reminded them both of the years when it was just Rose and Harp and Henry living happily and peacefully together in the Cliff House.

'Lovely. I'll just take them the tea, and once the bread is out of the oven, we'll go?'

Back in the garden, Harp set a tray of tea and scones on the table.

'Thank you so much, Harp. Whatever must you think of us?' Joan asked, her brow furrowed with concern.

'I don't think anything, Mrs Coakley,' Harp replied honestly. 'But I don't blame you for trying to avoid that pair, if you don't mind me saying.'

'The man is my son Sean, and the woman was Joan's daughter Maura,' Michael explained. 'Please join us. We owe you an explanation.'

Harp sat down. She was used to people confiding in her, so this wasn't unusual. Henry had always told her that something about her demeanour suggested she was trustworthy.

Joan started telling the story first. 'My late husband, Simon, was Michael's best friend. And Michael's wife, Betty, passed away two years ago after a long battle with illness. We four were friends for years, and our children grew up together. When Betty became very ill, Simon and I stepped in to help.'

'They were the best friends anyone could want,' Michael added. 'Simon helped me in the business any chance he could – I'm a cabinet-maker by trade – and Joan became a mother to my sons.'

'When Simon was killed in an accident at work – he worked on the railway – we were devastated, and then it was Michael's turn to help me. So he did. He did all the odd jobs around the house, and he...' Joan coloured. 'Well, over time, we became close.'

Michael reached across the table and squeezed her hand. The unspoken conversation of love and gratitude between them was clear to see. 'We didn't intend for anything to happen,' he explained. 'We'd both been happily married, but our spouses were gone and we didn't honestly see the harm. But our children, who never really got along with each other, seemed to be united on this subject alone, that Joan and I having a relationship was a scandal and they would never allow it. We tried to explain that we both would love their mother and father forever, but that they were gone and why shouldn't we find comfort and happiness together – we weren't doing any harm to anyone – but they were having none of it.'

'They ranted and raved,' Joan said, and the pain she felt was plain for anyone to see. 'Saying we were a disgrace and how they'd never be able to show their faces in the town again, how everyone was sniggering and jeering and how we were to stop it immediately or risk never seeing any of them again. We have grandchildren as well – Maura had twin boys and Benny and his wife are expecting their third child next month.'

Michael took up the tale. 'And then they even got my son Patrick, who is training for the priesthood in Maynooth, to come down and say how it would look very bad for him if Joan and I were to continue, though don't ask me why. I told him we were both widowed and we wanted to marry, but he nearly ran all the way back to the seminary shrieking at that.' The beginnings of a smile played around his lips, and Harp found herself warming to him.

'So what will you do now?' she asked.

Joan shook her head. 'We're going to America. I've a brother in Phoenix, Arizona, and he'll put us up and give me a job until we get settled. He knows about us and is happy for us both and wants to help. The children will never accept us, and we decided if they can't see past their prejudices and understand that we make each other happy, then maybe we're better off with an ocean between us. But it's hard, the idea of never seeing any of them again, even if they are being dreadful. We don't know if we can do it. But we can't stay here and be together – they would plague us day and night. And we can't give each other up, and we shouldn't have to, so really America seems like the only option.'

Harp observed them. They looked so right together. What was wrong with their children that they couldn't see how their parents were happy?

She thought of her mother and Mr Quinn. Yes, she supposed it would be strange to have someone else in their family of two, but Harp was going off to university the year after next and the idea of her mother having company and someone to love cheered her. She couldn't care less what anyone thought about it. 'But Ireland is your home, and you were here before they were even born. You're the reason they exist at all, so it seems very unfair that you have to leave because your children say so. Surely it's up to you to decide that, not them.'

'Well, it should be, I suppose, but I can't help feeling like I've let them down. They are good girls, really, Ann and Maura, and they loved their father so much. I think they can't bear the idea of him being replaced. But I'm not replacing Betty nor is Michael replacing Simon – I just wish they could see that.'

Harp thought of the Cervantes assertion that no parent can see their own child as ugly, whether in looks or in spirit, but what she saw of Maura today was exactly that. Her mother was trying to see the good in her, but that young woman was full of bile and nastiness. 'They got to choose their own husbands and wives, didn't they? They didn't consult you? So why should you have to get their approval?'

'No, but I suppose they just feel embarrassed – we're not supposed to have feelings like this at our age,' Michael said ruefully. 'I wish we knew what to do for the best. It's so hard to leave and we really don't want to, but we don't know what else to do.'

The two seemed taken aback by her forthrightness. Harp did try to temper her directness these days, but in this case she wasn't feeling able to make such an effort. Why couldn't people just leave others alone? Why did people have to constantly stick their noses into other people's business? 'I think you should tell them exactly what you've told me,' she said firmly. 'Then go ahead and do as you please. As you say, you are not hurting anyone. And if they can't accept it, then fine, but don't throw your chance of being happy away because someone else has some problem with it. Tell them you will marry and you'd like them to be there, but if they can't or won't, you'll be doing it anyway and refuse to put up with their nonsense.'

CHAPTER 7

The full moon shone its silvery rays through the window, and between that and the light of the candle by her bedside, Harp was able to read. Her mother worried she'd ruin her eyesight by such strain, but Harp didn't think that was scientifically correct. She'd researched it in a copy of the *Scientific American Supplement* she'd found in the library in Cork. A study the previous year had found that no adverse effects occurred in the eye from excessive reading.

For now, she was deep in an article about the Peloponnesian War in *Classical Philology*, a quarterly periodical her mother had bought a subscription for as a birthday gift. She read each magazine cover to cover several times before the next one arrived. It was such a broad-ranging publication, covering aspects of language, literature, history, art, philosophy, social lives and religions of the ancients, but it felt like she was alone in the world in its appreciation. When she was younger, she had Mr Devereaux to discuss such matters with, but whenever she raised these subjects with anyone else, even her mother, their eyes seemed to glaze over. Harp had learned to keep her thoughts on the Peloponnesian War to herself. Though the notion presented in one article that the battles between Sparta and Athens were like an elephant fighting a whale was really intriguing, she appeared to be the only one who thought so. She'd ordered a book from the library on the Oracle at Delphi, and old Mrs Byrne, the librarian who was slightly hard of hearing, had produced a book of miracles instead. Not wanting to hurt the old lady's feelings, Harp had taken it home and never opened it. She kept it until it was time to return it and try again to get the book she wanted.

If Mr Devereaux were still alive, she would have had someone to talk to about the things she learned from the journal, but he was four years dead. Her mother listened, but Harp knew it was more out of kindness than interest. Her friend

Brian cared nothing about such things – that is, if he was even still her friend; he hadn't shown his face since the previous evening. And she was worried that JohnJoe thought she was boring when she wrote to him about the Greeks and Romans, even though he never complained in his letters.

When the moon had sunk and the candle burnt down and she could no longer see the words, she reluctantly placed the magazine on her locker beside the ten-inch-high marble replica of the *Venus de Milo*. Cissy and Liz Devlin had given her the statue when she was thirteen years old. It had sat in the window of their shop all her childhood, and one day Harp realised they didn't know what it was. Someone in their family had been a scholar – an old uncle, they thought – and had brought it back from 'out foreign' to the Devlins' parents as a gift. The sisters listened carefully as Harp explained how it was in fact a depiction of Aphrodite, the Greek goddess of love, and had most likely been carved by Alexandros of Antioch. It was named *Venus de Milo* for Venus, the Roman goddess of love, and Milos, the Greek island where it was found. The sisters thanked her for the enlightenment, and the following week when she went for the groceries, they handed the statue to her all wrapped up beautifully. She'd protested – it was a really lovely copy – but they insisted it was better in her care.

Now she snuggled down under the blankets and quickly dropped off. It felt like only a few moments before she woke, and she wondered at first if she was still asleep and having a nightmare. There was a weight on her, an oppressive, stifling weight, and she struggled to breathe because something was over her mouth and partially blocking her nostrils. She tried to push the weight off, but it was too heavy. Her eyes adjusted as she fully woke. It was a man. She realised it was Pennington.

'Shush now,' he whispered in her ear. 'There's a good girl, nice and quiet. I won't hurt you.'

She tried to scream but couldn't. She panicked, hardly able to breathe.

'I'll take my hand away, but you must promise not to scream, all right?' His moist breath on the side of her face stank of cigarettes and whiskey. 'Do you promise?' His demonic dark eyes bored into hers.

Terrified, she nodded, and he removed his hand, allowing her to take several gulps of air. His body was still on hers, pinning her to the bed.

He slid off her and in one deft movement

pulled the bedclothes away, revealing her in her nightdress. She tried to scream but couldn't; it was as if her throat was constricted. He opened his dressing gown, and to her horror she saw he was naked. As he bore down once more, she saw it out of the corner of her eye. Without thinking, she grabbed the marble statue and swung it with all of her strength, connecting with his temple with a sickening crack. He went down with a thump on the rug, a trickle of blood running from where she'd struck him.

She stood there, frozen, the *Venus de Milo* in her hand. He wasn't moving. Was he unconscious? She made herself nudge him with her foot, but nothing happened, no reaction. The trickle of dark blood dripped from his face to the rug. He was slumped half on his side, half on his stomach. Could one blow kill someone? Feeling curiously calm, she tried to remember what she'd read about the subject – as if she could argue her way out of the situation. A hard enough blow could fracture one of the thin bones of the skull and lacerate the artery…

Stop. She couldn't intellectualise her way out of this horror. Then what was she going to do? *Mammy.* She needed her mother. Harp stepped around the body quietly and went to her mother's room and woke her.

'Come with me,' was all she said, leading Rose, blinking sleep from her eyes, to the bedroom.

'What on earth?' In horror Rose took in the scene, bending to place her fingers on Pennington's neck. Around and around the area she felt for a pulse but eventually gave up with a frightened groan.

'Is he? Oh, Mammy, is he dead?' Harp was shaking now, and tears began to flow down her cheeks. 'He tried to attack me, so I hit him with the *Venus de Milo*. I didn't mean to… I just wanted him to stop…' She felt her mother's arms around her.

'It's all right, darling. It's all right.' Rose held her, soothing her. 'It's all right.'

'But is he dead, Mammy?'

'Just take some deep breaths and stay very quiet, and we'll sort this out.'

They stood together for a few moments until Harp's sobs quieted. Then Rose placed her hands on her daughter's shoulders and locked eyes with her. 'I'm going to get Matt. We'll need him and he can be trusted. You go to my room. We'll lock this door as we leave, and you go and get into my bed.

I'll be back soon. Do not open the door or answer to anyone but me, do you hear me?'

Harp nodded, feeling a curious mixture of panic and numbness. They crept out of the room, turning the key in the lock as they did, leaving the slumped body of Pennington on the rug. Rose put the key in her dressing gown pocket. They returned to Rose's room, where Rose dressed quickly and Harp got into her mother's still-warm bed.

'Will they send me to prison?' she whispered.

'You are going nowhere.' Rose's eyes flashed with determined fury. 'You did nothing wrong. Now, please, Harp, just stay here, lock the door after me, and I'll be back as quickly as I can.' She left the room.

Harp sat up in the bed, her eyes locked on the door. Had she just killed a man? Really? Was it a nightmare? Would she wake any moment, realise it was just a bad dream and go down to help her mother serve breakfast?

The minutes ticked by painfully slowly. Had someone stopped her mother? The police? There were RIC patrols out all the time now, and a woman wandering around Queenstown at night would surely arouse suspicion. But it was lashing rain, so perhaps they'd stay in their barracks.

Mammy could get to Matt Quinn's house via the steps, and the patrols would be less likely to be there. Had someone heard Pennington fall? Were the British looking for him already? What was Mr Quinn going to be able to do? Maybe he would think she should go and confess. What would happen then? Would she be arrested?

Round and round the thoughts went in her head, all arriving at the same conclusion: There was a dead man on her bedroom floor and she was responsible.

The black door handle turned silently, and then her mother and Mr Quinn were in the room. Wordlessly Harp got out of bed and followed them to her bedroom, the only other bedroom on the attic floor, where her mother opened the door with the key.

Matt got on his knees to check for a pulse, then looked up at their frightened faces and shook his head.

Harp shuddered. 'I didn't mean to, Mr Quinn... He was trying to...'

'He knows,' said Rose quickly.

Matt stood up, crossed the room and placed his arm around Harp. 'I know, love, your mam told me. Don't worry. We'll sort it out. He's no loss to the world, that fella.' He nodded at the crumpled body on the floor. 'He and his kind have no business here, and he's the worst of the worst of them.'

'Shouldn't we call Inspector Deane?' whispered Harp.

'No. Deane will have the British swarming all over us before the sun is up.' He turned to Rose. 'Right, how about this? Old Mrs Duggan out the Belvelly road is being buried later today. I'm collecting the body at eleven. The grave is dug and the last one in there was her husband, but that was thirty-odd years ago. I'll wrap him, throw him into the Duggan grave and cover him, and I'll put Mrs Duggan in on top. Nobody will be any the wiser.'

Rose nodded. 'Yes. We could just say he checked out, clear his room of all his belongings. I mean, how are we to know where he went? We could say he skipped out without paying his bill?'

'Good idea, a motive for taking off,' Matt agreed. He started pulling the sheets from Harp's bed. 'I'd go and fetch Brian to help me, but he went out this evening and didn't come back yet...'

'I'll help you carry the body down to the car,' said Rose. 'Harp, go back to bed.'

'But...' Harp was consumed with guilt. She had blood on her hands, and now they were

burying a man in an old woman's grave and letting his family think he'd just disappeared? 'Supposing he has a wife and children? I can't just...'

'Harp, listen to me,' said Matt in a low, firm
voice. 'A British officer is dead in the house of an
Irish woman and her daughter. They're trigger-
happy now anyway after the Rising, and this will
not be treated as an innocent girl being attacked
by a brutal predator. They're only looking for ex-
cuses to wreak havoc, and all they will see is a
British officer being killed – the circumstances of
what he was attempting to do at the time of his
death won't bother them. They'll be all over this
place and you will hang, and I won't have that so
we're doing this my way. There was some reason
for a drinking session in the barracks this
evening, and between that and the weather, we've
a good chance of not being spotted. I'll put a
lookout on them anyway to warn us if they stir
out. Now, Rose, get some old sheets and a roll of
twine to wrap him and help me to bury the body
before the sun comes up. And, Harp, go to your
mother's room and forget this ever happened.'

CHAPTER 8

*S*erving breakfast the next morning, Harp tried her best to look normal, though what that was supposed to be, she had no idea.

She had waited in her mother's bed as instructed, and her mother came home shortly before four in the morning, washed herself and her clothes and got into the bed beside her. She told Harp it had all gone fine. Pennington was in the Duggan grave; she and Matt had lowered him down and shovelled a layer of earth on top of him. Rose had assured her nobody would suspect a thing.

Harp hadn't slept but rose with her mother at six as usual and mechanically went about preparing breakfast as they always did. She tried to do as Matt had told her – forget the previous night had ever happened. She was just a girl, planning to go to university, to live her life.

Was she really going to university, though? The chilling reality of the previous night should mean she was going to spend the rest of her life behind bars for murder. Or worse, at the end of a rope. She felt dizzy, and cold sweat prickled on her skin. How could she walk around with plates in her hand, chatting to the guests at the breakfast tables, when the reality of her life was so horrifying?

Her uncle snapped his fingers at her, and she topped up his coffee for the third time.

'Are you all right, love?' Joan asked her, concerned, as she passed their table.

'Yes, thank you. I'm just a little tired. I read too late, I'm afraid.' She gave a small smile. 'Now everyone is served, I'm off to sit down for a moment.' As Harp headed for the kitchen, she tried not to stumble. Images of Captain Pennington slumped on her bedroom floor kept flashing before her eyes. Her mother and Mr Quinn had wrapped him in the rug before tying the sheets around him, and now her floorboards were bare. She made it to the kitchen and stood there swaying.

'Harp!' Rose came to meet her, panic in her voice. 'What? Are you all right? Has someone said something?'

Harp shuddered uncontrollably as her mother hugged her. 'No, I just… It just hit me…'

At that moment, Ralph stepped into the kitchen without knocking. 'Ah, the perfect domestic scene.' He managed to sound pompous and disdainful simultaneously.

'How can we help you, Ralph?' Rose stepped back from Harp, amazingly calm again.

'Captain Pennington didn't come down for breakfast, and we were to play golf again this morning. I knocked but there's no answer at his door?' He stood there expectantly.

'Perhaps he's having a lie in?'

'No.' He sounded exasperated. 'Can you let me into his room? I'm concerned he will miss our tee time.'

'I don't think that would be appropriate, Ralph. He's a guest, so allowing another guest into someone's bedroom…' Rose's voice trailed off.

'Well then, let Harp go and check on him.' Ralph sighed impatiently. 'He was most anxious to play again today. We had a few drinks last night, so perhaps he didn't wake.'

'No, I'll do it. Harp can you go and feed the hens, please?'

'Of course.' Harp grabbed the pail of scraps as her mother followed Ralph from the room.

There was nothing to worry about, she told herself over and over as she hurried to the back yard. She knew that Mr Quinn had come back after the impromptu burial and taken the captain's personal effects and got rid of them. The room would be empty of everything personal to Robert Pennington. But as she fed the hens, her hand shook dreadfully. And after nearly a quarter of an hour, she had to force herself to go back into the kitchen. Her mother was already there, clearing way the last of the breakfasts. Through the open doorway, Harp could see Ralph lingering in the hallway, checking the post.

'Captain Pennington's room is empty, all his belongings gone and his bill unpaid,' Rose said to Harp indignantly – clearly for Ralph Devereaux's benefit.

'But he was here for four days,' Harp replied loudly, taking her cue from her mother. 'His drinks bill alone would have been large. I can't believe it. What will you do? Report him to the barracks?'

'I doubt they'd care. He wasn't attached to the

barracks here. He told me himself he was just on a fortnight's leave from his regiment in France.'

'But that's not fair.' Surprisingly, Harp found she meant it. None of this was fair.

Before Rose could reply, Ralph called from the hallway. 'I'm expecting a telegram. Please notify me immediately when it comes. I won't play golf now, so I will be reading in my room.' He turned on his heel and walked off.

As soon as he was gone, Harp collapsed, shaking, into a chair.

'Come on.' Rose helped her to her feet and out the back door; they slipped through the side gate onto the steps. Wordlessly they climbed upwards and turned right at the top, walking towards the Protestant churchyard where Henry Devereaux lay. The sun was shining but the downpour of the previous night had evaporated in the morning heat, and though the exertion of climbing the steps should have meant she was hot, Harp was shivering. She pulled her thin cardigan around her.

Rose shoved at the rusty old gate, hanging drunkenly from its ancient hinges. As always, the base caught on the rough stones, but it gave way eventually. They picked their way across the cemetery, not laid out in neat rows like the

Catholic one but with headstones and tombs scattered all higgledy-piggledy around the little hill leading up to the church. The Devereaux tomb was easily found, marked by a seven-foot angel, one wing outstretched.

Harp sat down by the stone that bore the names of her ancestors and hugged her knees to her chest, only then allowing the sobs to come. Rose sat on the kerbstone of the large grave beside her.

'I killed a man, Mammy. He's dead and I did it,' Harp gasped through racking breaths.

'Harp...' Her mother shushed her. 'You were an innocent girl in her bed, set upon by a monster. You defended yourself, and you did the right thing. Please, Harp, calm down.'

But she couldn't. The images went round and round in her mind. His artery being lacerated by bone, his parents grieving forever, never knowing, her arrest, the court, the judge passing down a sentence. Could she really hang?

'Will they execute me, Mammy?' she gasped, barely able to get the words out.

Rose gripped her shoulders and gave her a shake. 'Harp!' she said, louder and more forcefully than before. 'Stop it. You are not going to be executed or arrested or any of that. Matt Quinn has seen to everything. You will drive yourself mad if you keep going over it and over it. It happened. It's finished. We've dealt with it.'

'But they'll come looking for him,' Harp protested.

'They will, and we'll tell them what happened, what Ralph saw with his own eyes. That when we went into his room, his things were gone and there wasn't hair nor hide of him. He left a big bill, and we are most put out.'

'And will they believe it?'

'Of course they will. Why wouldn't they? The only other person who knows what happened is Matt Quinn, and we can trust him entirely.'

Suddenly Harp wanted to talk to that dependable man. 'Can we go to see him? The Duggan funeral should be over by now.'

They stood and turned and faced the grave. *Henry Devereaux, 1860–1912* were the last lines added.

'Henry, if you are up there, or somewhere, look after us, please. Keep us safe, please,' Rose whispered.

Then mother and daughter linked arms and left, walking the short distance to the Quinn's large terraced house overlooking the town. The arc of three-storied Georgian houses was a desirable location in Queenstown, commanding views of the entire harbour.

Rose knocked on the front door using the large brass knocker, but there was no answer. The latch was off, so after waiting for a few moments, she pushed the door inwards. Matt's coat and hat were on the hallstand in the tiled hallway.

'Matt!' Rose called. 'It's Harp and me. Are you there?'

There was no sound or sign of life, so they walked down the hallway to the kitchen. The stained glass of the door obscured the room beyond, but Rose turned the handle and there they found him, sitting at the kitchen table, his head in his hands.

'Matt!' Rose rushed to him, and he looked up, his face tearstained.

Harp was shocked. Matt Quinn was the most stoic man she'd ever met. As an undertaker, he dealt kindly and fairly with everyone in the town and surrounding area when they came to say the final goodbye to their loved ones. He was gentle and respectful, quietly spoken, always neatly dressed and universally liked, and to see him looking so distraught was shocking. What had happened? Had someone found Pennington in

Mrs Duggan's grave? She stifled a scream of panic.

Matt pushed a note across the table to Rose, who scanned it.

'Oh no… Oh, Matt, I'm so sorry…'

'He's gone.' His anguish was painfully raw.

Rose passed the note to Harp, and she recognised Brian's sloped handwriting immediately.

Dad,

I'm joining up with the Royal Army Medical Corps and going to France. They'll take me even though I'm not yet qualified. I feel like I have to do what I can to help out. They are woefully short of medical people. Dad, I am so sorry to disappoint you. But I'm a grown man now, and I have to make my own decisions. I will always admire and respect and honour you, and I will write as often as I can.

Your loving son,

Brian

Harp felt the crushing weight of responsibility. Another crime chalked up to her account. Brian would never have run away to war if it weren't for her rejecting him. He'd almost said as much. And now Matt had lost his son and it was all her fault. 'Mr Quinn, I'm so sorry. I should have stopped him…'

But Rose caught her eye and shook her head.

Now was not the time to tell Matt about Brian trying to kiss her.

Matt Quinn sat, shaking his head. 'It's not your fault, Harp. Please don't think that. There was nothing you could have done to stop him. He was going to go, whatever happened. He is a grown man now, and neither I nor you nor anybody else can tell him what to do any more. We just have to pray he'll survive and come home safe.'

'He will come home, Matt, I know he will,' murmured Rose. 'And he'll be behind the lines, in a hospital or whatever they have for treating the wounded, so not in the line of fire.' She moved close to the grief-stricken man and put her hand on his shoulder with deep tenderness. Reaching up without looking, Matt placed his broad hand over hers.

CHAPTER 9

*H*arp sat at Henry Devereaux's old bureau, which now occupied one corner of her room. Another letter couldn't hurt. She would keep writing until she got a reply. It was all she could think of to do. She'd written to Brian every day for the last two weeks, as she knew his father had, but nobody had yet heard a word.

She pulled a sheet of paper towards her and screwed the top off her pen. She only ever wrote letters with her monogrammed fountain pen, the one Henry Devereaux had given to her on the day he died. She wished Henry was here with her now; he was the only person she'd ever met who thought about things the same way that she did.

It wasn't just that she was more intelligent than other children – that wasn't vanity on her part, merely a fact – and it wasn't just that she was a voracious reader. It was that, like Henry, she reacted differently to other people. Sometimes a very sad thing, something she knew would move others to tears, wouldn't touch her at all, while something trivial, something meaningless to everyone else, could cause her throat to constrict and words to become stuck. A passage from a poem had had her in floods of tears recently, and she couldn't really explain why. It was from Walt Whitman's 'Song of Myself'.

I celebrate myself, and sing myself,
And what I assume you shall assume,
For every atom belonging to me as good belongs to you.

She wished for that connection, that sense of belonging. She loved her mother with all of her heart, but she knew her mother didn't understand her in the same way that Henry had understood her.

Only last year Harp had said to her teacher, Mr Barry, that she agreed with Oscar Wilde about education being an admirable thing but that nothing worth knowing could be taught. She'd assumed Mr Barry would understand what

Mr Wilde meant – that the real lessons of life, the ones worth knowing, have to come from experience. Mr Barry didn't even give her the chance to explain; he just slapped her hard with the switch for being cheeky. It was at moments like that that she missed Mr Devereaux the most; he would have known what she meant.

She began to write.

Dear Brian,

I don't know if you are getting these letters or not. I hope that you are. I'll keep writing until I hear from you anyway. I wanted to write to say how sorry I am about everything. When you left, it was under such circumstances that I can't even express the tumult of emotion, but please, Brian, know this: You are loved and missed, and even the briefest of communications would ease my worried heart.

I feel so responsible. That night when you kissed me, please do not think I was repulsed or that I don't...

She paused. What should she say? That she loved him? She did, but only as a friend, and that would be hard to say. That she greatly admired him?

...care for you. I really do. I just had never been in that position before, and I didn't know how to react.

She scribbled the last part out. She couldn't let him think she had romantic feelings towards him; that wouldn't be right. Then she took the whole sheet and scrunched it up and threw it in the wastepaper basket and began again.

Dear Brian,

I am so sorry for everything. Please write to me, even just one line, to let me know you are all right. I check the post every single day, hoping to hear from you.

Love,

Harp

She'd post it that afternoon.

She took another sheet; there was another letter she had to write.

Dear JohnJoe,

Thank you for your latest letter. It arrived yesterday morning, and I was so happy to get it. In fact I got two together; there must have been a delay with the post. It sounds like life is treating you very well. The picture you drew of the Statue of Liberty was wonderful. I know you said you had to go to New York on business, but I'm glad you got some time to see the sights. I'd love to go there sometime. Perhaps I'll meet you there and we can climb up the statue together. Wouldn't that be something? And you could draw my picture at the top.

She tapped her lip with the pen; she longed to ask JohnJoe if she was the girl who was too far away for him to buy her an ice cream. But how could she ask a boy if he liked her, when only two weeks ago she'd killed a man? He might hate her if he found out. Her throat tightened.

I wish I could come to see Francis O'Neill playing the flute at your uncle's fundraiser. Is he still the police chief of Chicago? Mr Devereaux loved Irish music and bought all of the chief's collections of tunes. Thank your aunt so much for the kind invitation that we would visit. I said it to Mammy, but it's so busy here that she can't possibly leave and she says I can't come to America by myself even though I know you and your family would take good care of me. Besides, I can't leave even if she'd let me because things here are...

Again, she felt a terrible urge to confess about Pennington. Perhaps JohnJoe would understand. But supposing he didn't?

...strange. R is still here, and he's making lots of friends with the British officers who drink in the Queen's Hotel. He swans about the place making demands and never putting his hand in his pocket. He's awful.

I'll finish now as I want to get to the post office before it closes for lunch. I have a letter for Brian Quinn to post too; I told you he joined up and his father is heartbroken. Mr Quinn and I are writing to him every day, begging him to get in touch. He left in rather a bad way – he had an argument with his father – so I'm worried he's ignoring us.

Or maybe it's because communications from the front are awful. Mrs O'Callaghan in the dairy was telling me that her brother is in the Munster Fusiliers and his wife got a letter the other day, sent last February. They'd not heard anything for months, and when she enquired at the barracks, asking that they try to locate him, they said he couldn't be found. Then two days later she got a telegram from someplace in France where he was stationed for rest after a stint at the front. It's like the right hand doesn't know what the left hand is doing...

She stopped, feeling dishonest; she should tell JohnJoe the whole true story. Or should she? Would he think she was trying to make him jealous if indeed she was the girl he was referring to in his letter? It was all so confusing. She needed to tell someone other than her mother, who just went on about how no girl should be forced to do anything she didn't want to. She knew that, of course, but this was a bit more complicated. She decided to tell him.

You see, the thing is, I feel responsible. The night before all this happened, he tried to kiss me. I was shocked and told him I didn't love him. He was very upset then, even more than before, and the next day he left and went to be a doctor in the war. So I'm trying to explain to him that I like him, just not in a romantic way, more like a brother or a cousin or something. I'm not very good at things like that; I always seem to get it wrong.

So that's my news.

Your sad friend,

Harp xx

She folded the sheet of paper and placed it in the envelope, addressing it to him at his uncle's house in Boston, stuffed both letters in her pocket and ran downstairs.

CHAPTER 10

*A*s Harp opened the front door ten days later, she found a tall moustached man standing on the doorstep, getting ready to knock. He was a British officer, and his uniform was resplendent, khaki green but with the cuff insignia of a high-ranking officer. The buttons shone on his chest pockets, and his shirt and tie were perfectly neat. He wore the tan breeches of the top brass, and his leather boots gleamed; his stiff peaked cap was under his arm.

'Good afternoon, miss.' His voice was gentle yet commanding, an intriguing combination.

Harp found herself staring.

'Major Charles Grant,' he introduced himself.

Then when she still didn't speak, he prompted, 'And you are?'

She cast her eyes down. 'Miss Harp Devereaux.'

'A relative of Mr Ralph Devereaux? A popular man about town, I believe. I've heard the name often from my colleagues at the Queen's Hotel.'

'Yes, Major, he's my uncle.'

He took a box of matches from his pocket and lit a cigarette. 'So you and your mother run this house, I understand?' He paused for confirmation, and Harp inclined her head. 'Indeed. Well, I understand a Captain Robert Pennington was here until recently. I'm sorry to say he has failed to return from leave.'

Harp didn't reply. She couldn't. It was happening. And this was the man they had sent to convict and hang her.

'So have you any insight into where he might have got to?' asked the officer, smiling.

She opened her mouth, praying sound would come out. 'No, sir. I just know he left without paying his bill,' she managed.

'Hmm.' The major nodded briskly. 'Well, that won't do. Is your mother in?'

'No, sir. She's gone to the draper's for some material.'

'Then I'll call back this evening to apologise to her and settle Captain Pennington's bill. We can't have people saying that British officers don't pay their way, now, can we? Good day, miss.' He bowed smartly, turned on his heel and was gone.

Harp felt dizzy and sick. She had to run away. No, she had to find and warn her mother and they both had to run away. By the time she'd reached the foot of the Smuggler's Stairs, she could hardly think what she was doing, and when she saw the major walking ahead of her in the street, she turned into the Devlins' shop and stood panting just inside the doorway.

Cissy and Liz were busy counting money and locking up the till; it was closing time and the shop was empty of customers.

'Ah, Miss Devereaux, how are you? We were hoping you'd come by for a chat,' Cissy said with a smile.

'I'm sorry, I can't stop,' gasped Harp. 'Mam sent me out for a bag of sugar, so if you're still open...' Harp lied badly, but she needed to get in off the street in case the major turned around. She was panicking.

'Of course.' Cissy passed her a bag of sugar, but it slipped from Harp's fingers, exploding across the floor.

'Oh, I'm so sorry...' Harp tried to scoop it all up, but her hands were shaking too much and suddenly she was crying. 'P-please, p-p-put it on our b-b-bill.' She tried to stop – the Devlins would think she was mad – but she couldn't. She tried to breathe, but each breath was a rasping gasp.

Cissy bustled out from behind the counter. 'Come inside, Harp love, come inside and settle yourself. Don't worry about the sugar – we'll clean it up.' She put the closed sign on the door as Liz led Harp through the door at the back of the shop into their sitting room.

Harp had never been in the Devlin sisters' home before, but it reflected them perfectly, she thought. Bright and spotlessly clean, there was a range, polished black and cold now that it was summer. Beside the range were two fireside chairs; on one was a half-finished knitted jumper, the needles jutting out at odd angles, and on the other lay a book, face down.

'Sit yourself down, love, and we'll make you a cup of tea. You look like you've seen a ghost.' Cissy fussed over her while Liz quietly removed the book from the chair and tucked it into a shelf of bright romances, its spine facing inwards.

Harp had thought for a moment she recognised the cover from Henry's collection – *Labour in Irish History* by James Connolly. But she dismissed the idea; a little old spinster would hardly be reading a socialist book.

'I shouldn't stay. I have to go and find my mother...' she began. Yet she sat down anyway, and when Liz handed her a cup of hot sweet tea, she sipped it and it warmed her shivering bones.

'What has given you such a fright, Harp?' asked Cissy, moving the knitting and sitting down in the other chair.

'Nothing...nothing really. A Major Grant came looking for a captain who stayed at our house, and he wanted to know where the captain was and...' The tears came again. 'I just don't want them around. My uncle is friendly with the English, but my mother and I try to keep out of their way. We don't want any trouble.'

'You're right – no good can come of being overly friendly,' said Cissy calmly. 'Sure what on earth would you or your mother know about Pennington anyway, and he going off without paying his bill? The downright cheek of him.'

Harp looked at her, confused. How did Cissy know she'd been talking about Pennington?

Liz perched beside her sister on the arm of her chair. 'If the English give you or your mother any more trouble, Harp, be sure to come and tell us.'

'Tell you if they come to our house?' Harp asked, still puzzled.

'Yes, be sure to tell us whenever they come to the Cliff House,' said Liz. 'And tell your mother I said it.'

'I will,' Harp replied, though she didn't understand why the sisters wanted to know. Maybe they were just being nosy, she thought, but then dismissed the idea. The Devlins were not ones for gossip. She drank her tea and the conversation slowed to a trickle. She found situations such as this excruciating; she had no ability to make small talk about the weather or whatever a pair of ageing spinsters liked to talk about.

'And will your uncle be staying with you long?' Liz asked.

'I don't know. He never says when he's coming or going. He just arrives and stays as long as he wants.' She thought she caught a subtle glance between the sisters.

'That must be difficult for your mother, what with the guests and everything,' Cissy remarked.

'We've no choice,' Harp said with a sigh. She

was past caring who knew that she couldn't bear her uncle. Her mother wouldn't approve of her speaking about Ralph outside of the home, but she felt so full of everything, all the secrets, that if she didn't release at least some of it, she would go mad. 'He's mean to my mother and me and we can't stand him, but as I say, what choice do we have? And he's on such good terms with the British – the last thing we want is to be drawing them on us.'

'Yes, we hear he likes going to the Queen's Hotel with the officers from Spike and some from here and from Cork too.' Cissy still kept the tone light and conversational. 'Sure, why wouldn't he, working for them in India as well as being educated over there and all the rest of it.'

'The Devereauxes always thought of themselves as being British,' agreed Liz.

Harp flushed hotly. 'My father was as Irish as anyone. He was a supporter of people like Michael Davitt and James Stephens, and he had many of the writings of the Fenians.' She needed them to understand that Henry was not in his heart one of the ruling class who wreaked such havoc on the population for centuries.

'But his brother? Is he of the same mind?'

Cissy asked with a smile that belied any trace of accusation in her voice.

Harp shook her head sadly. 'I doubt it.'

Liz said quietly, 'Be wary of your uncle, Harp. He's a slippery one, always was. Even as a young man, he was in debt and involved in things he shouldn't be. That's why old Mrs Devereaux put the run on him, sent him away to India, though it broke her heart. She had no time for the brother at all, your Mr Henry, 'twas all Ralph this and Ralph that. But she knew he'd disgrace them for a finish, and a leopard never changes his spots. He's in with the British now, and both sides are bene-fiting from it. He never stands his round but the British keep him in food and drink, so you can be sure he's giving them something in return. The forces of occupation don't make friends – they cultivate informers. The British have no business here, and sooner or later we'll all have to stand up and be counted, every last man and woman on this island, and they will either be with us or against us – it's as simple as that.'

Harp had never heard Liz Devlin come out with so many words in her life – and what words! It was clear the sisters had wanted to see her for a lot more than a cup of tea and a chat about the weather. And everything Liz had said about

Ralph was correct. He had asked Harp to pick up his boots from the shoemaker, and of course they had not been paid for. He never had any money but still lived and mingled with the gentry and the officer class. 'You're right – he's up to something,' she said angrily. 'I wouldn't be one bit surprised if he was an informer. Though from what I read about the Volunteers so far, they don't give anyone helping the British much quarter. Hopefully the local republicans will see what Ralph is and deal with him. I know I shouldn't think that about my uncle, but I hate him, I really do.'

'Don't worry, Harp, the day is coming. They struck such a blow on Easter Sunday. It was not enough to send the whole rotten Empire crumbling, but it will happen. They lit the spark. Now all that's needed is to fan the flames.'

'Do you think something else will happen? I would love to think it could, but would people not be too scared after what they did to the leaders?'

Liz fixed her with a steely gaze. 'I don't *think* something else will happen – I *know* so. Nineteen sixteen was just the beginning. And the women of Cumann na mBan acquitted themselves admirably. They didn't get their chance down here, but they will, mark my words, and when they do, they'll strike a blow for Ireland, for women, for the vote, for workers' rights, that the British will never forget.'

'I would love to be part of Cumann na mBan!' Harp was fascinated. She'd read a lot about the women's army, the female wing of the Irish Volunteers who had bravely stood on the steps of the General Post Office last April and declared that Ireland was free. Inside the occupied buildings, the women fought alongside the men and took on dangerous delivery jobs, keeping communication lines open between the various garrisons. She would never forget the opening words of that proclamation: *Irish men and Irish women...* The fact that women were acknowledged, that they were so integral to the fight that they were mentioned in the first line, stirred her heart. She'd copied it out and pinned it over her writing desk.

Cissy and Liz exchanged another subtle glance. 'Very well. If you'd like to join us, we'd be happy to have you,' Liz said decisively.

Harp sat bolt upright in the chair, her mouth open. 'I... You...' These tiny apple-cheeked sisters were as far away as she could possibly have envisioned from the Amazonian young women of her imaginings, standing tall on the steps of the GPO. 'But...what do you do?'

Cissy laughed then, merrily. 'Oh, there's plenty for us to do. We're working to support the families of the men locked up after the Rising, so we're sending them what food and clothes we can and whatever few shilling we can spare. They are destitute without the men and the wage they brought in, and the British would love nothing better than to see those patriots' families starve. There is money being raised in America as well.'

'My friend JohnJoe is involved in fundraising in Boston! Do you remember him from four years ago? His uncle is Pat Rafferty, and his Aunt Kathy even invited me to the concert with Francis O'Neill! Shall I write to him about what we're doing? Perhaps he can arrange for more money to be sent?' The idea of JohnJoe knowing she was doing her bit on this side of the Atlantic was a heartening one.

The sisters exchanged a quick mysterious glance. 'Say nothing to JohnJoe about what we have said to you,' warned Liz. 'But come back and talk to us again tomorrow.'

'Can I tell my mother?'

'No, Harp. The less your mother knows, the safer she will be. You have to stand on your own two feet now.' Liz stood up herself, barely five feet tall and thin as a greyhound. 'But you should go and find her and warn her to expect a visit from this officer you told us about. And you should tell Matt Quinn too.'

'Oh, Mr Quinn doesn't know anything about Pennington,' Harp said hastily, standing up as well. 'I mean, about him going missing...'

'Even so, tell him about this Major Grant,' said Liz, ushering her out. 'And keep your ears and eyes open, Harp. If any more British officers come to your house, or if you overhear your uncle saying anything about plans they might have, then that would be useful. We are trying to build up a full picture on the personnel stationed here and their movements.'

Harp was thrilled and terrified at the same time to have what felt like such an important job. 'I'll come back tomorrow and tell you what I've found out.'

'James Connolly said that the worker is the slave of capitalist society and the female worker is the slave of that slave,' said the tiny woman as she unlocked the shop door and let Harp out. 'The independence struggle goes hand in glove with the fight for equality. Until women can vote, how on earth can we expect representation?'

'You're right, Miss Devlin.' Harp felt upbeat for the first time since that awful night. Ireland needed to be free, to be a place where the Robert Penningtons of this world held no authority. Things had to change, and she was going to be a part of it.

'Keep watching and listening, Harp, and we'll be in touch.'

CHAPTER 11

*H*arp climbed up the Smuggler's Stairs, her mind shooting off on a thousand different tangents. Was being a revolutionary heroine her destiny? She so admired the women of Cumann na mBan, and of the Irish Citizen Army, the labour movement that welcomed females from the start, Countess Markievicz, Hanna Sheehy-Skeffington and Nurse O'Farrell.

She'd read only yesterday a scathing piece in the newspaper about the exploits of Winifred Carney from Belfast, who James Connolly requested specifically come to Dublin just before the Rising. She'd arrived armed with a revolver and a typewriter, and she'd worked as Connolly's secretary for Easter week and was currently in prison. Though the article's intention was to show Carney as a brutal, unfeeling, unnatural woman, Harp thought she was marvellous.

But as she entered the garden, reality hit her and she was overcome by that familiar feeling of dread and foreboding that had been her constant companion since the night she killed Captain Pennington. What was she thinking, allowing such flights of fancy to take over her mind? A revolutionary heroine indeed. She was a silly girl with no experience of anything, and she was probably going to be arrested soon for murder.

She went around the back to the kitchen door as she always did. As she entered, she was startled to find her uncle there, standing beside her mother with his hand on her elbow, talking in a low voice. Clearly Harp had interrupted something.

The moment he saw Harp, Ralph dropped her mother's arm and said more loudly, 'I'm going down to the Queen's. I'm meeting a Major Grant. He's newly arrived from London and would like a tour of the town, so I volunteered. I'll eat there, so don't worry about my dinner tonight.' Passing Harp on his way out the door, he added in an oily voice, 'Ah, my dear niece! Every time I see you, it's like I'm looking at my dead brother. Most disconcerting.' He himself looked nothing like Henry; his perfectly coiffed hair and immaculately pressed suit, with scarlet silk pocket square, served to make him more like a mannequin in a shop than a real person.

Harp waited until she heard the front door slam, then moved to the westerly window of the kitchen that looked over the front lawn. He was gone. 'Was he telling you about what any of the other British officers are doing, or just this Major Grant?' she asked.

Rose sighed. 'He wasn't talking about any of them.'

'Then what was he...?'

'He was just talking a lot of nonsense about how happy he was staying in Cliff House. I suppose he thought he was being charming – you know the way he likes people to like him. But I hate it when he tries to charm me, as if he thinks I might still...' Rose shuddered.

Harp turned from the window and hugged her mother, knowing how badly Rose felt about having allowed Ralph to seduce her all those years ago. 'It's all right, Mammy. You were my age, just a girl. And he was... Well, we know what he's like, but you're not his servant any more, you're a businesswoman, and it's 1916 not 1816.'

'Still, I don't like him coming near me.'

'You're right, Mammy, and you should always be careful of him. He's very pally with all the British officers. I think he might be informing on people for money.'

'Why do you think that?' Rose looked shocked. 'What have you heard?'

'I… Nothing. It's just a feeling I've got. But, Mammy, there's something even more important. That Major Grant who Ralph was talking about came to the house this afternoon, and he was looking for Pennington – he'd been sent over to find him. He said he's going to call on you later to ask you about it.'

'Oh, Harp…' Rose's hand flew to her mouth. 'Oh no…'

'I'm going to go and warn Mr Quinn.'

'Yes. And tell him to stay away from us for a while. He can't ruin his life on our account.' Rose was pacing, agitated, and Harp was alarmed at how panicked her mother seemed. The only thing that had been keeping her calm in this whole mess was Rose's assurances that it would all be all right. The words of Epicurus sprung to her mind.

The just man is most free from disturbance, while the unjust is full of the utmost disturbance.

How right those ancient Greeks were about everything. She was unjust, she'd killed a man, and her mother and Matt Quinn had helped her by getting rid of his body; she didn't deserve a peaceful mind. She took a deep breath and steadied herself. 'Don't worry, Mammy. I'll warn Mr Quinn. And what could Ralph say to this Major Grant, even if he is an informer? Apart from me and you, it's only Mr Quinn who knows the truth, and no one is more reliable. Look, let's get the interview with Grant over with, stick to the story, and then we'll worry about Ralph. What's the worst thing that could happen?'

Her mother looked at her in admiration. 'Harp, you are so brave for such a young girl.'

'It's not just me. Women all over the world are standing up for themselves. As Anne Elliot in *Persuasion* says to Wentworth, "I hate to hear you talk about all women as if they were fine ladies instead of rational creatures. None of us want to be in calm waters all our lives."'

Rose laughed, and Harp felt relief to see her mother relax once more.

'You've had a quotation for every situation, ever since you were little.' Rose hugged her and stroked Harp's hair. 'You are a wonderful girl, Harp, and I'm so proud of the woman you are becoming. You're brave and strong and so intelligent. And Henry would be so incredibly pleased and full of joy at seeing you blossom – I know he would.'

CHAPTER 12

Matt Quinn was not at home, and Harp couldn't find him anywhere around the town, not even in the graveyard. In the end she had to go back to help with the dinners without having spoken to him. But the moment she and her mother had finished clearing the tables, he came to the back door. He looked flushed but happy, with a torn and stained letter in his hand.

'Brian wrote to me at last! He's still alive and not too near the front, thank God. I've been lying awake every night, imagining all sorts.'

'I knew he'd write,' said Rose, setting down her tray. 'Brian is a kindhearted boy, always was. I told you he wouldn't leave you to suffer. The two of you love each other so much.'

He went to her, and Harp saw the adoration he had for her mother in his eyes. 'You're right, Rose. And I don't know what I'd do if anything happened to him. When his mother died, they wanted to take him from me. Her sisters in Waterford were offering to have him, and even the priest called to me and urged me to let him go, saying a man couldn't raise a child alone. But I promised Bessie I'd take care of him and I couldn't let him go. He was just a lad and God knows I didn't know much about child rearing – I left all of that to Bessie– but I learned and we were so close. As he grew I could see he was bright, and so getting him to university was the goal, and we did it. I couldn't bear to lose him now, and to an English war…'

'You won't lose him, Matt.' For a brief moment, Rose held his hand.

The silence was shattered by the sharp rapping of the brass fox-head knocker on the large teak front door. Harp whispered urgently, 'That must be Major Grant. I'll go and hold him at the door. Tell Mr Quinn what's happening, Mammy.'

Rose pushed Matt towards the garden. 'Matt, you should go. There's a British officer looking for Pennington, and I think it's better if you're not here.'

The undertaker looked alarmed but shook his head. 'I'm not going anywhere, Rose. But I'll pretend to be fixing the drain.' He went outside the back door, leaving it open, and got on his knees beside the drain. With a deep breath, Rose took the baking bowl with the ingredients for scones already dry and mixed and removed the teacloth covering it. They had to make it look as if it were just another evening at the Cliff House, not that they were waiting with dread for their visitor.

Harp answered the front door, and to her dismay, Grant wasn't alone. Ralph was beside him, slightly flushed in the face. He'd clearly been drinking since he left them earlier. Grant was still in uniform, and once again he had removed his hat and wedged it under his arm. His silver hair was cut short in the military style, and his green eyes were the colour of the sea.

'Ah, Major, allow me to introduce my dear niece, Harp Devereaux. Harp, this is Major Grant,' Ralph said with a sloppy flourish, slurring a little on the major's name.

'We've already met.' Harp extended her hand, trying to sound more confident than she had earlier.

The major took it. 'Indeed we have, Miss Devereaux, indeed we have.' His tone was as before, light and jocular. 'I'm sorry to disturb you. I had intended coming earlier, but I was waylaid in the hotel, I'm afraid.' He glanced at Ralph.

What did that mean? Harp wondered in fright. 'That's fine, Major. My mother is here now. Would you like to come in?' She spoke as lightly as he did and hoped the inner turmoil she was feeling wasn't evident on her face or in her voice.

'Lovely, thank you,' he replied, as if it were a tea party he'd been invited to.

'Follow me,' she said with a smile, and led him towards the kitchen.

'Surely we can do better than entertaining our guest in the servant's quarters, Harp?' Ralph asked, outraged. 'Major Grant, come through to my drawing room and Harp will bring coffee – or would you prefer a real drink?'

The major demurred. 'Not at all. I won't stay long. Wherever Mrs Delaney is, is fine with me.'

'No, I insist. A guest of the Devereaux family has never yet been entertained in the kitchen, and we shan't start now,' Ralph insisted expansively. 'I and my...my dear Rose will entertain you in the drawing room.' He was definitely drunk, behaving as usual as if the house were his.

His whole being infuriated Harp. She drew herself up as tall as she could for a small girl. 'My mother has no time for entertaining. She owns this business and has to make sure it runs smoothly every hour of the day. But she can spare you five minutes in the kitchen. Please follow me, Major.' She could see the glint of fury in her uncle's eye at being overruled, but she didn't care; she was sick of him.

'Lead on, Miss Devereaux,' said the major politely. He followed her through the door into the kitchen, firmly closing the door behind him.

As Harp made the introductions, Rose calmly washed the flour from her hands. 'Welcome to Queenstown, Major Grant.'

'Mrs Delaney, I am so sorry to barge in like this, and you are clearly busy. I promise it won't take a moment. I just wish a few words in private, if you don't mind.' He glanced towards Matt, who was visible on his knees through the open door, poking around in the drain.

Rose looked in the same direction, with an air of indifference. 'Oh, that is only Mr Quinn. We employ him to do odd jobs around the house.

Our drain is blocked, so he is trying to free it for us.'

'Ah, yes, and Mr Quinn is also the local undertaker, I understand? I hear he is a busy man, with his finger in a lot of pies.'

Without looking up, Matt suddenly did a very convincing job of pulling something disgusting out of the drain. Immediately a rancid smell filled the kitchen. 'Apologies, Mrs Delaney,' he called over his shoulder. 'I found the blockage. The smell will clear in a moment.'

Wrinkling his nose, Major Grant nudged the back door closed with the tip of his polished boot. 'So, Mrs Delaney, I'm sure your daughter mentioned I called earlier to inquire after the whereabouts of a Captain Robert Pennington. It seems nobody has had sight nor sound of him since he stayed in your house.' His tone suggested Pennington's disappearance was nothing more than a mild inconvenience, a lost hat or scarf, rather than a missing brother officer.

'Indeed,' said Rose, equally smoothly. 'And when you do find the captain, could you point out to him that he left here owing for two weeks' accommodation and quite a considerable drinks bill?'

'I am most sorry for that – that kind of behaviour is simply not acceptable. Please furnish me with the bill. I'm staying at the hotel, and I will see that His Majesty's Government reimburses you in full on his behalf.'

'Thank you, Major,' Rose replied coolly. 'That would be much appreciated.'

'Not at all. Now, can you tell me the last movements of the elusive captain, as far as you remember them?'

Rose shared a look with Harp. 'Well, he stayed here for most of his two weeks' leave, and he was due to go back to his regiment, I think he said on the first of August. The last time we saw him was the morning of the thirtieth of July. He went out and never came back. He had friends in Queenstown, and he often ate with them or at the hotel, so we weren't worried. But he never came back to the house.'

'And when he left, did he have any luggage with him?' the major asked, and despite the gentle conversational manner, Harp detected an edge of steel. 'He must have had a considerable amount of luggage to carry away.'

Rose's eyelids fluttered. 'I didn't notice him leave. We'd served breakfast and cleaned the rooms, and then as usual a local woman, Mrs Lucey, and her daughter came to do the laundry, so I went down to the town to run some errands and replenish supplies.'

The major turned to Harp. 'What about you, Miss Devereaux? Did you see Captain Pennington leave the house that day?'

Harp wrinkled her brow as if in deep thought. 'No, I don't recall seeing him at all after breakfast. He had porridge and cream, and kippers, and Chinese tea, which my uncle ordered for him.'

The major looked steadily at her. 'I believe your uncle played golf with him all morning, they ate lunch at the golf club, and then they went sailing, after which Mr Devereaux went on to see another friend and the captain returned here to wash and change. Why are you so certain Captain Pennington never came back to the house?'

Harp glanced at her mother in a moment of panic. 'I...I don't...'

'Is there any way he could have come back without you realising it?' asked the major.

Rose interrupted smoothly. 'I suppose it's possible. My daughter and I went to bed around 10 p.m. and he wasn't back by then, but if guests are out late, I leave the front door on the latch so they can just push it open.'

'So when did you first realise he had actually left?'

'The following morning. Ralph asked my daughter if she'd seen the captain, as they'd made plans to play golf again. She said she hadn't, and once breakfast was over and there was still no sign of him, I went up and knocked on his bedroom door. Ralph was with me. When we got no answer, I opened the door and found the room completely empty of any of his things.'

'Had the bed been slept in?' the major asked.

'There was no sign of it,' said Rose firmly.

The major smiled slightly. 'Captain Pennington is proving himself to be quite the Scarlet Pimpernel, isn't he? Now, might I trouble you to see his room? And then I will leave you two ladies in peace.'

'Of course.' Rose lifted her chin and smiled bravely. 'As luck would have it, the blue room where Captain Pennington stayed is vacant. We are rather empty tonight, as there won't be a ship going for another two days.'

'But other guests have stayed in the room since he was there?'

'Yes, of course. Why not? Harp, will you finish the scones while –'

'Please, Mrs Delaney, I would be grateful if you would allow Miss Devereaux to accompany us,' interrupted the major. 'You never know – if we all look around the room together, your daughter might remember something important about what happened on the thirtieth of July.'

Trying to appear as calm as her mother but with her heart beating painfully in her chest, Harp followed the major and her mother up the stairs to the second floor. She had a dreadful thought that when Rose opened the door, the captain would be lying across his bed, blood pouring from his head. But the room looked as it always did, with eau de Nil wallpaper, a walnut chest and wardrobe and a Belleek china dish and jug on the nightstand. She and her mother had embroidered the pillowcases and bedspreads last winter, and everything looked clean and welcoming.

'What a lovely room, and the view is spectacular.' The major walked in and stood with his back to them, facing the large window overlooking the harbour. 'You can see everything from up here.'

'Yes, the guests always remark on the view from the Cliff House. Cork is the second largest natural harbour in the world,' Rose said as if she were showing off the house to a paying guest.

'Is Poole the largest?' Grant asked.

'No, Port Jackson, Sydney, Australia,' Harp replied without thinking.

'Ah, really? How interesting. It is a lovely place you have here, Mrs Delaney, really quite charming. Makes me wish I was booked in here rather than the hotel, if I'm honest. But now' – he lowered his voice to a theatrical murmur – 'I must continue the quest for the missing Captain Pennington.'

On their way back downstairs, they passed the guests' drawing room on the first floor. Ralph was there, helping himself to a drink from the decanter. The Cliff House operated an honesty box, and when it came to drinks, the people were usually very fair. If they had a drink, they put the money in the discreetly placed mahogany box on the sideboard. Everyone, that was, except Ralph, who treated the shelf of whiskey and brandy like his own private bar.

'Been visiting the scene of the crime?' he asked loudly, coming to the door of the room with a cut-glass tumbler of whiskey in his hand.

Rose said coldly, looking at the whiskey, 'The major wanted to see Captain Pennington's room. The one he left without paying for.'

'Would you like my input, old chap?' Ralph asked, taking another deep drink of spirit.

The major smiled. 'I thought you'd told me

everything you know, Mr Devereaux? About the golf and the sailing?'

'But I think I've just remembered something else. Ah...what was it now? Didn't I mention something about it to you, Rose... About...I seem to remember...'

Harp stood frozen, hardly able to breathe. It took all she had not to seize her mother's hand like a frightened child. Did Ralph know something? How could he know? Had he heard something?

'Perhaps you can tell me over a drink at the hotel later on, Mr Devereaux,' said the major, moving on, with Harp and her mother on his heels.

But Ralph followed them all down the stairs, staggering slightly and waving his glass. 'No, wait, I have it!' he boomed. 'He said something to me about going to America, and Rose, you were surprised when I told you, because he'd said to you he was going back to France at the end of his leave...'

The major stopped in the hall and turned with a frown. 'Captain Pennington was due back in France on the fifth of August. If he went to America instead, that would mean he'd chosen to go AWOL, and that is a very serious accusation indeed, Mr Devereaux.'

'Don't you remember, my dear Rose?' Ralph swayed against Rose, grinning and breathing alcoholic fumes. 'Don't you remember?'

The major said angrily, 'Mrs Delaney, *do* you remember anything about this?'

'I...' Rose looked utterly miserable, as if she actually regretted the help that Ralph Devereaux was offering, as if she would have denied it if she could. But instead, to Harp's secret relief, she said, 'Oh...yes, I do remember. America... Ralph, you said Captain Pennington was on his way to America.'

The major stood staring at the three of them, flushed with annoyance. Then he clicked his heels. 'Good evening, sir. Miss Devereaux, you have been most helpful. And please, Mrs Delaney, do send the captain's bill to me.' He bowed politely and replaced his hat before opening the front door and striding off down the avenue.

CHAPTER 13

*H*arp couldn't wait to see the Devlins again, to tell them as much as she could about Ralph and Major Grant and the way the smooth British officer had hid his iron fist in a velvet glove. She'd spent the evening reading about the women of Cumann na mBan, and she was determined to be a part of the struggle in some small way.

The Cliff House had been quiet since breakfast. Rose had gone to the hair salon recently opened on the promenade to have her hair done; it was a rare treat for her. The place was still relatively empty before the crowds expected for the bank holiday weekend, and Eithne could manage any queries for a short while. Harp put her light summer coat on – it was still very warm – and let herself out. As she emerged into the bright August sunshine, she saw Matt come out of the sheds, which were once the stables, behind the house.

'Good morning!' she called.

'Hello, Harp. Nice morning, isn't it?' he called back, wiping his hands on a rag and shoving it into the pocket of his trousers. He was dressed as he normally was when not directing a funeral, in dark-brown moleskin trousers and a soft and well-worn checked cotton shirt. Harp always liked the smell of him, of soap and something else, a spicy woody aroma. A cologne, she assumed, but thought it was odd, a working man taking such pains to smell nice. The farmers who came to town stank of sour milk and dung, the workmen on the docks usually smelled of oil, and the fishermen smelled of salty fish guts, but Matt Quinn was different.

He wasn't like the local men in a lot of other ways as well. He was well read and thoughtful, not unlike Henry in some ways, though much more sociable of course. His strong solid presence at every funeral in the area was a source of comfort to the grieving, and he was an egalitarian. Every family got the same respect and treatment, whether the body was coming out of one of the big detached houses up on the cliff or the small terraced homes down by the Holy Ground. And he never harassed people for payment either. People paid him on time because it was the right thing to do, but if families couldn't afford it, he was happy to take instalments or even waive his fee altogether in extreme circumstances. The Quinns had been in Queenstown for generations, Matt's father and grandfather the undertakers before him. He knew everyone and everyone knew him, and not one person in Queenstown ever had a bad word to say about Matt Quinn.

'It is a lovely day. Mammy's gone to get her hair done, if you're looking for her. You should take her out to dinner someday.' Harp nearly bit her tongue off, instantly knowing she'd said the wrong thing. She berated herself. This was typical; she was too blunt sometimes. But Matt just smiled.

'I'd love nothing more than to show your mother off to the whole town, Harp. I'd be the proudest man in Cork,' he said quietly.

'So why won't you?' Harp asked, all thoughts of speaking too directly forgotten.

'You were down with Liz and Cissy Devlin

yesterday, I believe?' he asked, changing the subject.

Harp nodded, surprised. 'I was. And I'm going to go down to them now, actually. They have some interesting ideas, and I enjoy talking to them, especially Liz. We are aligned on lots of things.'

Matt put his hands in his pockets and observed a thrush building a nest high up in an oak tree in the garden. The feral cat that had taken up residence in the shed and was mother of all the kittens was circling below. The cat was an expert catcher of mice and rats but also of birds, and left several at the back door each morning as a gift that made both Harp and her mother shudder.

'The thrush will survive but only if it manages to stay out of the clutches of the cat there,' he said, lighting a cigarette. 'And that takes intellect, skill and a lot of luck.'

Harp looked at him. He had an inscrutable look on his handsome face; he clearly meant something more than the chat about cats and birds, she was sure of it. 'Are you warning me about something, Mr Quinn?' she asked quietly.

He took out a packet of cigarettes, lit one, and took a long pull on it, exhaling a thin plume of blue smoke slowly. Then he offered her his arm, and she took it. Together they walked to the garden seat, the one dedicated to the man she thought of as her father. The morning sun was high in the sky, and small puffy clouds scudded across the blue. The honk of a large fishing trawler rippled over the sea as it approached Queenstown, ready to take on supplies for another few weeks at sea and disgorge its cargo of herrings and mackerel.

Matt finished the cigarette and ground it out with the heel of his boot, tossing the butt into the bushes rather than have it on the pathway where guests might see it. 'I want to talk to you,' he began quietly, his blue eyes resting on hers. 'But I need your word that anything I say will stay between us.'

'You have it,' she said solemnly.

'I trust you, Harp. But if you are considering working with Cissy and Liz Devlin, then you'll need to know what you're getting yourself into.'

It was obvious he understood what was going on, and she trusted him as much as he trusted her. 'I do know, and I want to do what they do. I want to help set Ireland free.' She hoped her words were strong enough to convince him that she wasn't just a silly schoolgirl looking for a heroic cause. Killing the captain still gave her terrible nightmares, but she also knew that if she hadn't fought back, nothing would have happened to Pennington, whatever he'd done to her. The British officers in Ireland were above the law. It wasn't right. The treatment of the Volunteers earlier this year, executed in cold blood for having the audacity to declare their independence, was abhorrent to her. The way the British had sailed the gunboat, the *Helga*, up the Liffey and blasted the heart out of Dublin and then blamed the rebels for the damage, as if the Irish had drawn that misery on themselves for being so uppity...

'I also want to see my country free.' Matt Quinn rested his hands on his knees, and she noticed his fingers were long and the nails cut square. 'Cork was to take part in the Rising last Easter, but we were stood down, sent home and told it was off. There were mixed messages coming from Dublin – a command was issued and then countermanded – and the result was we didn't do what we intended. But that was only day one, week one. For centuries, Irish men' – he paused and looked at her – 'and women have struggled to release our country from the stranglehold of British imperialism, and in each generation they failed but the spirit of revolution was kindled again and again. And we were battered, bruised, beaten down, but once we could rise again, we did. Time and again, we rose and fought, and this time, Harp, this time we'll do it. I know we will. But we need to be clever. We can't take on the British in pitched battle – the odds are stacked too high against us – but we can fight a different kind of war, one where we use what we have and they don't. We can use our intellect, our spirits, our country, the loyalty of our friends and neighbours, and we can win.'

'What can I do to help?' she asked eagerly.

'You'll need to discuss that with Cissy and Liz.' He smiled.

'Liz Devlin said I was to tell you about Grant. Are you involved with the rebels?'

'I am more than involved,' he answered slowly. 'I'm the Volunteer commander of this section and the British are after me, except they don't know who I am. They know there is an active unit in the area, and that more and more people are flocking to the cause, not just here, but all over the country. That's why there's been such an in-flux of military since the executions last May, be-cause they knew they made a mistake. They made martyrs of those men, and that action has sent up the cry, Ireland calling her sons and daughters to her flag. People like us, who are sick of it, tired of fighting for equality in our own country, men and women who don't want the signatories of the Proclamation to have died in vain.'

'Does my mother know you are the commander?' Harp asked.

'No. The less she knows, the safer it will be for her, Harp. Now I've to get back to work.' He stood, and Harp stood up with him.

'I still think you should take her out to dinner,' she said. She knew Rose would be angry with her for badgering him, but she wanted Matt to understand that he made her mother happy.

He smiled and it crinkled his eyes. 'And as I said, I'd love nothing better, but because of who I am, what I do, I need to keep a low profile. And I certainly don't want her name up with mine – it would be too dangerous.'

'So will it just be this, then? You and her being friends and you saying nothing to her about the way you feel?' She knew she was being impertinent, but the way he spoke sounded to her too much like Henry Devereaux, who had only revealed his love for her mother after he'd died.

Matt looked sad. 'I know it's hard. I didn't want this to happen. My life is too complicated to involve anyone else in it, to endanger anyone. But I...I couldn't help it.'

'Then what will you do?'

'Harp, I will always be there when your mother is in the slightest danger. Yesterday I waited until the major was off the property before I left the house. But while we are still fighting for freedom, that's all I can do.' He patted her shoulder and walked away.

CHAPTER 14

*L*ater, on the way back from the Devlins', Harp rounded a corner on the Smuggler's Stairs to find her mother deep in conversation with Ralph again. His head was close to hers, and Rose looked decidedly uncomfortable. The exchange, whatever it was about, wasn't the usual sneering with a veneer of friendliness. This time he looked threatening.

'Mammy, I've been looking for you everywhere!' Harp called, and instantly Ralph turned and stepped back a pace.

Rose looked relieved. 'Ah, Harp, I was just on my way home. Can you help? This bag is rather heavy.' She passed Harp a shopping bag full of flour and butter.

'Hello,' Harp said to Ralph, though her tone was cold.

He cast a glance over her, didn't reply and walked quickly down the steps. Wordlessly the two women climbed up to the garden. Whatever Ralph had said must have shaken Rose; she was pale.

'Mammy, are you all right?' asked Harp as they reached the kitchen door.

Rose said faintly, 'Of course I am. I'm just a little breathless from the climb.'

'Are you sure? Did Ralph say anything about Major Grant and Pennington...'

'Not at all. He was just telling me that he'd bought a season ticket to the golf club. And I'm thinking he's going to be taking up our best bedroom for a month at least.'

Harp dropped the shopping on the kitchen table. 'Oh, I'm sorry – I meant to tell you about Ralph and the golf club. I was worried it might mean he was staying longer than usual. Is he?'

Rose sighed. 'Yes, which means we're going to be very short of space because we've been booked out by the rest of the Clancys for all next week.'

'Oh, Mammy...'

Harp understood exactly what Rose was saying. The entire extended Clancy family had been making the voyage to America over the last few years. The older brothers had gone to Philadelphia in 1910 and were systematically bringing members of the family over, having set up a large building contracting business. They were the loudest bunch of people Harp had ever encountered, and while they were perfectly friendly, whenever they stayed, they had a habit of taking over the whole house. Last time, she'd had to intervene when two little boys were plucking the strings on her harp while another was scribbling on the wall with a pencil. The last of the clan, elderly and babies and a lot of women, were arriving on Monday and planning to sail on *RMS Langton* next Saturday. Ralph would do nothing but complain while cluttering up the place himself.

'You should get rid of him, Mammy,' she said impatiently. 'Just put your foot down and tell him he has to stay at the hotel with all his friends.'

But Rose, still pale, shook her head. 'I can't turn him out of his old family home, Harp. And he was very helpful to us about Pennington, even you have to admit. So I'm grateful to him.'

Harp nearly stamped her foot. She wanted to tell her mother to stand up to Ralph and never be grateful to him. She thought that it was probably true about Captain Pennington planning to go AWOL, and that Ralph had only said it to the major because he was drunk, not because he was trying to be helpful to Rose. 'Well, at least I can solve the problem of you not having enough rooms. I'm going to America this Saturday. I've bought my ticket with money JohnJoe sent me for it, and I'm going to see Francis O'Neill. You can use my room.' She nearly frightened herself by the way she blurted it out; she hadn't meant to say it all out at once, not all of it and all of a sudden. She'd been going to break it to Rose gently that she was determined to go to see Francis O'Neill, that she'd never have such a fine chance again, that Henry would have wanted her to go and that JohnJoe's aunt would be there to chaperone her.

'To America all on your own?' Rose was aghast. 'To stay with people I've never even met? Absolutely not, Harp! I've already told you no. It's too far and too dangerous. Look at the way the Germans sunk the *Lusitania*.'

'That was over a year ago, Mammy, and they thought there were munitions on board. They've not sunk any passenger ships since then – you know they can't or the Americans would join the war. So I'll be fine,' Harp said firmly. 'You know I love Francis O'Neill's collections so much – I play those tunes all the time – and I'll only be gone a month.' Her heart was beating quickly, and she was desperate for her mother to say yes. Yet she was going anyway, whatever her mother said. As the Devlin sisters had explained when she went back to see them, she was the perfect person to fetch the money collected at the massive Boston fundraiser; nobody would suspect a sixteen-year-old girl of having wads of dollars stitched into all her clothes. The local Cumann na mBan had held a secret meeting the previous night, and apparently the women had decided she should do it. It was money from the Cumann na mBan that had paid for Harp's last-minute ticket, not JohnJoe at all.

Rose was adamant. 'No, you can't go.'

'But, Mammy...'

'Let her go, Rose.' It was Matt, who had suddenly appeared at the open kitchen door. He caught Harp's eye, just a flicker of mutual understanding that let her know he understood about the plan. 'It's an adventure for a girl her age, and it might do her good. I'll give you any extra help you need around the house and garden, and that Katie Lucey can carry a few dishes in between doing the laundry.'

Rose spun to face him; her eyes pleaded with him. 'Why are you on her side, Matt? She's only sixteen, and she's never been anywhere without me.'

'I know, but she's got more brains than most men I know, and she's got a loyal friend in JohnJoe O'Dwyer. He'll meet her off the boat and take care of her. We'll see she has her own cabin, and she'll be safe.'

Harp was breathless with happiness. If Matt was speaking up for her, then surely Rose would agree. 'I can do this, Mammy, and I promise I'll be very careful.'

Rose's eyes glittered with unshed tears. 'You're my precious girl. I can't bear the thought of you travelling all that way on your own.'

'I won't be on my own on the boat. It will be full of families – the entire boat will be full of the Clancys, for one thing. And in America I'll be with JohnJoe's family. I'll be back here in a month and be able to tell you all about it. The only thing is…' – she glanced at Matt anxiously – 'I'd be worried about whether you'll be safe here when I'm gone.'

Matt seemed to understand right away what Harp was saying. 'I'll be here every day, so don't worry, Harp. There will be no end of jobs needing doing around the Cliff House over the next while. I won't leave your mother out of my sight by day, and by night she'll have a house full of guests to keep her out of trouble.' He smiled and squeezed Rose's hand.

'Oh, Matt.' Rose sighed and looked down at her hand in his. The sight seemed to make her both happy and sad. 'I know Harp is clever, but I don't know if you're right about her being sensible. Maybe you are, but all I know is sixteen is so…young and very foolish.' She blushed and with her free hand brushed the tears from her eyes.

CHAPTER 15

'Well, isn't this nice?' Ralph exclaimed. His ebullience was unbridled since Rose had agreed to his taking the two of them out to dinner in the hotel. Harp couldn't understand why her mother had gone along with it, but she knew Rose didn't like the town to think she was at odds with Ralph Devereaux. Besides, Harp was so happy about going to America that she was prepared to put up with anything on her last night.

The dining room was busy; the ship leaving the following day was full. Harp had one of the last tickets. All around the three of them, people milled, and the excitement at the impending voyage was tangible. The décor was heavy and dark, the burgundy carpet and heavy teak furniture giving the place an air of sumptuous decadence. The crystal glasses on the tables shone, and the candlelight and murmur of conversation made Harp feel like she was in a play.

A waiter approached the table. 'May I get you a drink, sir?'

Ralph smiled. 'Just a jug of water please,' he said, just loud enough for fellow diners to hear.

There was a table of British officers in the corner, with one vacant seat. One or two gave Ralph a discreet nod and a wave.

'Major Grant said he'd look in. He's dining with his fellow officers this evening.' Ralph shook out his carefully folded napkin with a flourish.

Harp said nothing but observed him and her mother. Rose looked beautiful, even more than usual. She had made herself a dusty-pink dress in velvet, and it set off her dark looks to perfection. It was cut a little lower than her mother normally wore – she hardly ever showed any flesh except her face and hands – but the soft neckline of this dress showed the curves of her throat. Her hair was done in a new style too. She'd invested in the latest Hump hairpin, which claimed in the advertisement in the new salon to 'lock the locks', and it really did make her look very elegant. She usually wore her hair tied back in a low bun, but tonight the natural waves were not free exactly but pinned loosely with some tendrils framing her face. The overall effect was dazzling. As they'd entered the dining room, a hush had fallen, and even the normally arrogant and pompous Ralph had known he was not the centre of everyone's attention. He made a great play of seating Rose but of course left Harp to fend for herself.

Harp also had dressed as nicely as she could, in a copper-coloured silk dress that her mother had made from a pattern. The top had short sleeves and a square neck and was overlaid with cream lace. It was cinched under the bust and fell to just above her ankles, and she felt quite grown up in it. Her mother had set her hair as well, and the result had astonished Harp. In preparation for the big trip to America, Rose had made sure that Harp had a full wardrobe thoroughly befitting a young lady, altering some of her own dresses to fit the tiny frame of her daughter.

'He's not had any luck whatsoever locating the whereabouts of the mysterious Captain Pennington.' Ralph carried on the conversation, and to Harp's surprise, Rose and he shared the briefest of glances.

'Really?' Rose replied with a charming smile.

Then she turned to her daughter. 'What do you think you'd like to order, Harp?'

Harp read the menu. She had never dined in the hotel before and didn't want to make a fool of herself, especially in front of the dreadful Ralph. The waiter appeared again, and Rose ordered fish while Ralph ordered an omelette; Harp ordered fish as well.

Mr Bridges, the owner of the Queen's Hotel, appeared. He was a slight dapper man, grey haired with a beautifully waxed moustache. His hair and clothes were always perfect, and Harp thought his voice sounded like a cat purring. 'Ah, Mr Devereaux and Mrs Delaney and young Miss Devereaux, how lovely to welcome you to the Queen's.'

'Thank you, Edward.' Ralph loved that he was on first-name terms with anyone worth knowing in the town. 'And how is the lovely Mrs Bridges? I hear she is fast becoming a rival to Dorothy Campbell on the golf course?'

Mr Bridges smiled. 'Yes, Angelica certainly knows her way around eighteen holes, and she's actually going to play at the Royal Portrush in the autumn, weather permitting. She and her sister Emily – you know, Brigadier General Potts's wife – are quite the duo. It would be a brave or a foolhardy man who would take them on. I certainly wouldn't anyway – she'd beat me out the gate.'

'Oh, come now, Edward, I'm sure that's not true. While some ladies might enjoy a stroll about the course, hitting an odd ball as they go, golf is a man's sport.' Ralph's supercilious nasal drone caused some diners to look.

'Mary, Queen of Scots played golf. It was she who coined the term "caddy", actually,' Harp said. 'And Dorothy Campbell, who you mentioned yourself, won ten national championships all over the world in the last ten years.'

Ralph sent her a look of pure loathing. Harp knew he disliked her, but the sheer venom in his expression actually frightened her.

Rose jumped in, speaking soothingly, while her eyes shot Harp an almost imperceptible warning. 'Harp dear, I'm sure Ralph knows more about golf than we do. After all, he plays and neither of us has ever so much as set foot on a golf course.'

'Too busy running your fine establishment, Mrs Delaney,' said Mr Bridges with a little bow. 'Now, please, I have matters I must attend to, but tonight's meal is on the house. Just a little gift of congratulations to a fellow business owner in the town. Enjoy.'

Mr Bridges left, stopping at a few tables to say hello, while Ralph called the waiter again. 'Change my order to the chateaubriand, and we'll also have a bottle of Moët and Chandon 1912.'

The waiter never flinched, but Harp's toes curled in embarrassment. Now that it wasn't going to cost him anything, Ralph was going to take it for all it was worth.

'So, Harp, how are you feeling about your big voyage tomorrow?' Rose asked. 'I can't believe you're really going. I want you to remember everything to tell me when you get home. I can't imagine my little girl in Boston, as I sleep here and you over there.' She was putting a brave face on it, trying to be calm despite her obvious anxiety.

Harp smiled at her. 'I'm so excited. I can't believe I'm going to see Chief Francis O'Neill in the flesh.' She hoped she sounded sincere. The real reason for her journey was to collect the fundraising money from the Raffertys, but it was important that her mother and Ralph thought she was just keen to see the famous musician. 'And I'll visit Sister Molly a lot as well. JohnJoe says she's been very ill.'

'I hope you won't be disappointed. America is

very big and noisy and lacks class or dignity,' Ralph pronounced.

'Disappointment is the gap between expectation and experience,' Harp replied. 'And I have no expectation but to go to a concert and visit an old friend, so I'm sure I won't be disappointed.'

'Yes, well, someone such as yourself, such a...' – he struggled to find the word – 'bookworm, will no doubt consider it a cultureless wasteland of loudmouthed ignorance.' He turned to Rose, clearly bored with Harp. 'Now, did I mention how ravishing you look this evening, Rose?'

Harp saw her mother flinch as Ralph's oily gaze lingered on the modest neck of her dress. Harp worried for her mother, having to put up with her uncle's lecherous behaviour, but Rose had assured her she would make sure never to be alone with him. The only reason she'd accepted dinner with him that night, she told Harp, was because Harp was going to be there too. And besides, Matt would make sure she was safe.

'Have you been to America then, Uncle Ralph?' Harp addressed him by his title for the first time in her life.

He turned to her once more and sighed as if her question were tiresome. 'What?' he asked, clearly bored.

'America. I was wondering if you'd been since you know so much about it?' She tried to keep the contempt from her voice.

'No, of course I haven't.' He tutted. 'What on earth would someone like me want to go there for? I've travelled to many areas of our vast and glorious Empire but never had the inclination to visit there.'

Harp could tell that the mention of 'our vast and glorious Empire' set a few teeth on edge around the room. Though the hotel was frequented by the officers from the base on Spike Island, and the sister-in-law of the owner was married to the brigadier general, that did not mean that all the patrons saw the British Empire as either glorious or theirs. The resentment at the occupation of Ireland for nearly eight centuries may have been expressed more vocally in the past by the lower classes, yet many of the diners at the Queen's Hotel still rankled at such a blatant display of loyalty by an Irishman.

Harp said quite loudly, 'Well, I think the nation that brought us the first flight and the mass-produced motor car, and that dug the Panama Canal, should not be dismissed so easily. It is also the country that produced Abigail Adams, Benjamin Franklin and George Washington, and it is the birthplace of the notion that it is an inalienable right for each person, regardless of station, to life, liberty and the pursuit of happiness –'

'Thank you, Harp, that will do,' Rose interrupted.

Harp flushed. Her mother hated her to rile him up like that, and she knew it.

'I'm sure there is an apology coming for such impertinence.' Ralph raised an eyebrow. 'Really, Rose, that girl needs to learn some manners. I appreciate that raising her alone must have been difficult, but she needs a much firmer hand. Had I been here when she was younger, I would have seen to it. Spare the rod and spoil the child.'

Harp couldn't believe him. He was speaking about her as if she weren't even there, the ignorant buffoon.

'Harp, please apologise to Uncle Ralph,' Rose said evenly.

Exhaling to calm herself, Harp did as she was asked. 'I'm sorry.'

'Yes, well, you'll do well to mind your tongue, young lady. Someone in such a situation as yourself cannot afford to be too…presumptuous.' His words were weighted heavily with an inherent threat, as if he imagined he had some power over her. It turned Harp cold; she was frightened for a moment that he might know that she was travelling on behalf of the Cumann na mBan. But how was that possible? Surely no one would have told him.

She was spared answering by the arrival of their food, which they ate mostly in silence. Rose tried to begin conversations about the weather or the food, but Ralph was in murderous form and Harp was miserable. The food tasted of nothing as she cut and swallowed. She was nervous about the voyage the next day, far more frightened than she was letting on to her mother, if she was honest, but she hated more the idea of leaving Rose with this monster. What if he forced himself on her, as he had when she was seventeen? Harp realised that as much as she was determined to help the cause, the sooner she could get back from America, the better she would feel about her mother.

CHAPTER 16

It took all of Harp's powers of persuasion to stop Rose asking a pair of spinster sisters whose other sister ran a department store in Chicago to watch over her for the whole voyage to America. They were a right fussy pair, and Harp knew they would drive her mad if given free rein over her. And even Rose knew the unruly Clancys, who were also travelling, would be more likely to draw her into trouble than steer her clear of it.

In the end, Matt was her ally, convincing Rose that Harp was sensible and well able to mind herself. She'd hugged him on the quayside as she left, something she'd never done before, and he held her tight in return. Ralph by contrast had barely managed a goodbye that morning as she'd served his breakfast.

'I'll send a telegram from Boston the moment I arrive, I promise,' Harp told her mother, who was clearly already having second thoughts about the entire plan and probably worrying about the *Lusitania* again. 'And I'll be back before you know it.'

Rose opened her mouth to speak but no words came out. She nodded. Her eyes were bright with unshed tears. Harp could see how Matt longed to comfort her but didn't dare do so in such a public place – as he'd said, he didn't want Rose's name to be linked to his if there was even a hint of suspicion about him, now or in the future.

Harp took Rose's hand. "'Goodbyes are only for those who love with their eyes. Because for those who love with heart and soul, there is no such thing as separation,'" she said quietly. It was the same game they'd always played. Harp had no end of quotations for every occasion, and her mother would try, usually in vain, to guess the source.

'Mm. Let me think…' Rose smiled through her sadness. Matt bent his head and whispered in her ear. 'Rumi!' she said triumphantly.

'That's cheating.' Harp chuckled. 'That's two against one.'

'What?' Matt feigned innocence. 'I don't know what you're talking about.'

* * *

ALTHOUGH HARP'S ticket was paid for, ostensibly by JohnJoe though actually by the Cumann na mBan, Rose had had enough money to upgrade her daughter to a private cabin, and though it was tiny, Harp was glad of the solitude. It felt so incredible to see her hometown become smaller and smaller until the whole place looked like a child's toy set. Even the huge cathedral that dominated the town seemed tiny as they sailed out of the mouth of Cork Harbour. She'd been nowhere really – to Cork sometimes on the train, but that was it. And yet every day in the guest house, her life was populated with people coming and going to America, Canada, Australia. There were even a couple of men last summer going to farm sheep in New Zealand. Now she was the one seeing the view that every departing Irish man or woman had witnessed as they set out for adventure in new lands.

Eventually there was no more to see and the

wind up on deck cut through her jacket and shawl, so she went down to her cabin. Matt had advised her to lie flat if she felt queasy and to eat in small quantities. So far, though the sea pitched a little at the mouth of Cork Harbour, once they were out on the open ocean, she felt fine. It was mostly calm, and she found she enjoyed the beauty of the Atlantic.

The food was tasty, though not a patch on her mother's cooking, and while her fellow passengers were polite whenever she encountered them, she was left to her own devices. She read a lot and walked on the deck in the afternoon sun. She tried to imagine the reunion with JohnJoe. Was the intimacy of their letters going to be repeated in real life, or would they be awkward with each other? He might have an American accent by now. Would he think her very parochial by comparison to the Bostonian girls he met? She certainly didn't feel very sophisticated, though her mission was a grown-up one. She could hardly believe it when the Devlins had suggested it. The idea that the local branch of Cumann na mBan had decided to invest their hard-raised money in her was such an enormous honour, but Liz had explained that she was the perfect person. She had a reason to go to

Boston that would withstand scrutiny if she was questioned, she had people to take care of her there, and the Raffertys were involved with funding the Irish cause anyway and had been for some time. She had a long-standing association with them through JohnJoe, so her visit would raise no eyebrows. Besides, she was just a girl, and a small, innocent-looking one at that. As far as the Devlins were concerned, it was too good an opportunity to miss.

They'd assured her it would be a simple matter of doing whatever JohnJoe's aunt and uncle instructed as far as concealing the money. And that was all she had to do. The bonus for her was seeing Francis O'Neill play and meeting JohnJoe again. If only it hadn't meant leaving her mother in the clutches of the repugnant Ralph, it would have been a dream trip.

Apart from the occasional nightmare in which Pennington loomed over her in the bed, blood dripping from his face, the voyage passed uneventfully. At last, on the fifth day of sailing, the noticeboard in the passenger area proclaimed the ship would be docking in Boston at five in the evening the next day. It was an hour and a half later than planned because of headwinds, and

Harp hoped JohnJoe wouldn't get too bored waiting for her.

By early the next morning, she was already washed and dressed. She had a light breakfast of porridge and toast with tea and noticed some of the Clancys in the dining room looking considerably the worse for wear. It had been a rough night, and they were known for carousing. *Too much porter and a tempestuous sea do not good companions make*, she thought, hiding a smile as one of them passed her looking positively green.

She decided to wait and read in her cabin until the purser called them. She could have gone up on deck and watched the approach to Boston, but she'd tried to get her hair to curl and had pinned her hat on neatly and didn't want to risk looking like the wreck of the *Hesperus* when meeting JohnJoe.

Her mother had packed each outfit carefully, with tissue paper between each dress to stop it getting wrinkled because she knew Harp couldn't iron to save her life. Today Harp had chosen a powder-blue skirt and jacket, under which she wore a navy-blue silk blouse. Her hat matched the dress and her mammy had made lovely dark flowers for the brim, so all in all, she thought as she looked in the tiny mirror over the sink in her cabin, she looked all right.

She knew JohnJoe had changed; she'd seen the photo and he looked much more sophisticated and grown up than she was. He was two years older, but she hoped America hadn't made him so worldly that she'd seem like a silly schoolgirl to him. Would he see her as a young lady? She hoped so. She had no idea about boys really, apart from what she read in books and overheard at school, and up to very recently had never envisaged herself having the slightest interest in them. But JohnJoe was different. He was her first best friend. And now that he was grown up, a man of eighteen, she found herself hoping he would see her as an equal, not a child.

As they approached the dock, she went up on deck and finally got to watch the ship's approach to the port. Boston was so exciting, but she was sad not to be sailing into New York; she would have loved to have sailed right up to the Statue of Liberty.

From the many letters she'd been sent from those who'd done it before, she was familiar with all of the processes she would need to go through once she disembarked, and while this terrified her the most, she would get through it. She would have to present herself at immigration, be checked for disease and have her papers stamped and signed, and then hopefully she would be through. She would set foot on the New World, the United States of America. It was still hard to believe.

The arrivals hall was the noisiest, busiest place she'd ever been in her life. There were people wearing all sorts of outfits, and several of the languages she heard, she didn't recognise. Everyone seemed to be in a hurry and to know exactly where to go. She was glad her suitcase was not too heavy because she'd had to carry it a very long way before being instructed to place it with a whole line of other cases and join a queue of women. Her mother had insisted on her taking a hatbox as well, and though it wasn't heavy it was very cumbersome.

She endured the questions and answers as best she could, deliberately attempting to sound more authoritative than she felt. She tried not to cry out when they used the button hook to pull back her eyelid to test for trachoma, and when the physician gazed at her from top to toe, even circling her and making her feel like a beast at the mart, she stared ahead and did not meet his eye, standing tall and straight.

'You have a return passage booked two weeks from now?' another man in uniform asked. He spoke slowly and loudly, as if she were either deaf or mentally impaired.

'Yes, it's a quick visit,' she said clearly.

'You came all this way for two weeks?' The doctor raised a suspicious eyebrow.

'Yes, I have a friend here who is ill. She's a nun,' Harp replied. That was the cover story she had agreed to give to the American authorities. The Devlins feared Pat Rafferty might be well known and wanted her to distance herself as much as possible from the Boston Irish republican community and their fundraiser. She'd only known Molly for a couple of days four years ago, but they'd written to each other often since and it was the best reason she could come up with.

The doctor shrugged and nodded, and the uniformed man directed her to another booth. More questions, but eventually she was given a stamped piece of paper and told to collect her suitcase from a pile by the huge doors that led to the outside world.

All around her, the languages of the world mingled noisily. She saw the most extraordinary clothes, women in colourful robes with matching headdresses, men wearing what looked like nightgowns, under which they wore wide-legged trousers. There were Asian people, with their almond-shaped eyes and straight jet-black hair; she'd never met someone from that part of the world before, and she had to try hard not to stare. One family who were gathering to her right were all dressed in black, and the man – the father, she assumed – wore a high-crowned hat and had the most interesting ringlet curls growing almost to his shoulders from his temples. They spoke a guttural language that she thought might be German, but she wasn't sure.

To her left an enormous Italian family were gesticulating and arguing passionately as they retrieved their bags from the pile. Everyone was shouting, and one woman even slapped her husband across the face, which horrified Harp but didn't turn a hair on the family. Babies wailed, children ran riot and adults looked extremely harassed. The cacophony was deafening.

With relief she removed her single case; it was an old leather one that Matt had lent her. Brian had used it to go to university. His initials were engraved on the straps. As she stood in line to shuffle out, she wondered about him for the millionth time. She wished he would write to her as well as to his father. Brian had been like a big brother to her; he'd looked out for her in school, protecting her from bullies like Emmet Kelly, and then spent the summers with her walking or talking about books. He didn't find it peculiar that she was so well read, or that she could quote so many authors at random, or that she played the harp and was called Harp. He accepted her and liked her for who she was. That wasn't something she took for granted, yet she could never feel anything for him but sisterly affection. The idea that her rejection of his advances played a part in his departure still tore at her heart.

Eventually she was outside. There were throngs of people behind a barrier waiting. The yelling from the Italians, which she could not have imagined could get any louder, suddenly amplified when they were enveloped in hugs and kisses from another group at least as big outside.

She watched as reunions happened left, right and centre. The man leading his dark-clad family walked purposefully towards what seemed to be a bus stop, the tails of his floor-length coat flapping, his ringlets dancing in the breeze. Sweethearts were reunited, kissing and hugging. A man wearing working clothes went down on his hunkers and held his arms out to greet three little children, who ran to him with squeals of 'Papa! Papa!' as his wife struggled to carry all the bags.

Then she saw him. He was waving and beckoning to her while trying to ignore a policeman who was asking him questions. Skirting around various groups of excited people, she finally reached him.

'See, I told ya,' said JohnJoe to the policeman. 'I'm here picking up my friend Harp Devereaux all the way from Ireland, so, Officer, if you wouldn't mind? We got stuff to do.'

Harp was shocked at the way JohnJoe spoke to the police officer, that he was so cheeky.

'All right, Rafferty, but just you remember, your cousin has to show his face sometime.' The police officer scowled and turned to walk off.

'What was all that about?' Harp asked warily, conscious she was there on a secret mission and not happy about meeting a cop first thing.

'Him? He's the fellow Danny popped on the nose at the protest, and he's still giving out about it.' He seized her bag and offered her his arm, beaming. 'Oh, Harp, it's so good to see you! I can't explain how excited I was when you telegrammed. Aunt Kathy is in such a tizz getting the house ready, you'd think it was a queen or somethin' comin' to visit.'

Harp laughed. 'Your Irish accent is completely gone! You sound like you've lived here your whole life. And are you called Rafferty now?'

'Yeah. I kinda feel like my life started here. I dunno – Boston feels like home more than anywhere back there does any more. And I've changed my name to Rafferty because that was my mother's maiden name and Uncle Pat's name. It's easier and better. I don't want anything of my father's, not even his name.'

'And have you heard anything from your father?' Harp asked diplomatically. JohnJoe's father had put him in a borstal when his mother died and shipped his two sisters to England to their aunt.

'Ha, no.' JohnJoe laughed bitterly. 'I don't even know if he's still alive. He took the money from Danny that day, as payment for me when Uncle Pat decided to adopt me, and that was the last I heard of him.'

They crossed a busy street, and JohnJoe had to yank her back so she wouldn't get hit by a streetcar – she'd forgotten the traffic went the other way in America.

'Careful, Harp. Everything is faster and louder here, and people don't care the way they do back home.'

'I can see that.' She enjoyed the comforting feel of his arm around her as they crossed the street. The buildings, the teeming hordes of people, the noise, the heat, the smells – everything was different from home and she loved it. To their left she spotted a post office.

'Could we go in?' she asked. 'I promised my mother I'd send a telegram when I got here. She was really worried letting me go.'

They entered the lovely corner building. It had high ceilings, and each teller was behind a dark wood-carved desk. She dictated the telegram to the clerk, and JohnJoe insisted on paying. She had some American money, but he wouldn't hear of it.

'You're my guest, and the first and best and only visitor I've ever had, so please, don't insult me by putting your hand in your pocket. I might only have you for two weeks, but we are gonna have the best time. Molly wants to see you as well, so I wrote her and said we'd take a drive over there one of the days next week and have tea. Like I told you, she was really sick the last time I saw her. I guess she'd love to see someone else she knows from home.'

'Poor Molly. I'd love to see her too.' Harp felt slightly guilty at having used Molly as an excuse to the customs officers; of course she should go and see the courageous young nun who had defied her family to join a convent.

They walked out into the sunshine again. JohnJoe whistled, a piercing sound, and a yellow motor car pulled up to the kerb. To Harp's astonishment, JohnJoe opened the door of the vehicle for her. 'Louisburg Square,' he instructed the cab driver, throwing her bag in the boot. Harp climbed in, and he settled himself in beside her.

CHAPTER 17

*I*n the close confines of the car, JohnJoe felt bigger than outside. His thigh up against hers was strong and thick, and while JohnJoe wasn't particularly tall, he was broad and muscular. She glanced sideways, not wanting to be caught looking at him. His jaw was chiselled and freshly shaved, and his hair was cut in a proper style, not just short like most men at home; someone had taken time with JohnJoe's. Gone was the spiky red-blond hair of the child he had been, and in every way, that boy had been re-placed with a man. A handsome, charming, confi-dent man. But for all his change, he still seemed the same – confident not arrogant, funny not cocky, good-looking but not vain. She felt she could trust him and was eager to talk to him about the real reason for her visit, the money. But the cab driver would be able to overhear them, and so she tried to think of something ordinary to say.

'Is Louisburg Square in South Boston?' she asked, knowing that most of the Irish lived in that part of the city.

JohnJoe turned to her and smiled. As she'd seen in his photograph, his crooked teeth had been straightened. 'No, it's about three miles further into the city, and about a million miles away in every other sense.'

'But I thought your Uncle Pat lived in South Boston?'

JohnJoe shook his head. 'No, his office is there and it's where he does his business – he's very connected to Southie – but he don't wanna live there and Aunt Kathy hates it. So we talk and act like people from Southie, but we actually *live* in one of the best addresses in Boston. Don't tell anyone, though.' He winked.

'Don't worry, I won't.' She smiled. He spoke with the broad vowels of that city, pronouncing Boston like 'Bahston'. She racked her brain for more small talk; as always, she found it hard. 'Where is the statue of Paul Revere?' she asked suddenly, wondering if they would pass it on the way.

'Who?' JohnJoe's brow furrowed.

'The midnight ride of Paul Revere?' Harp prompted, wishing she'd not asked. She wasn't trying to sound superior; she'd assumed Paul Revere to Bostonians would be like Daniel O'Connell or Wolfe Tone to Irish people. Perhaps she was wrong.

'The guy on the horse?' JohnJoe asked.

Harp grinned. 'Yes, I believe he was on a horse when he went on his famous midnight ride to alert the colonial militia to the approach of the British in 1775, before the battles of Lexington and Concord.'

'Oh, yeah. Some old guy wrote a poem or something? That really happened, huh? I thought it was made up for the poem.' JohnJoe was unperturbed by his ignorance of the history of his adopted country.

'Longfellow, yes.'

'I remember it from school. Not back in Ireland – that was just a bunch of Christian Brothers beating the living daylights out of us – but school here. Aunt Kathy sent me to St Kevin's, a posh boys' place – I wrote to you about it. And though they were nicer than the lunatic priests back in Ireland, I still couldn't grasp most of it. I was too late trying to catch up despite all you taught me. I'll tell you, Harp, if I hadn't spent that summer with you learning to read, I'd have been a total dunce. Poor Aunt Kathy was distraught – she thought she might make a doctor of me or something – but Uncle Pat was fine about it. He's not a big one for the books either. He was kind of relieved, so he made a builder of me instead, and I've managed to make a decent job of it.'

'They probably didn't teach you properly,' Harp said, then realised how rude that sounded. 'I don't mean that they were…' She coloured, trying to correct herself.

JohnJoe laughed. 'You were the only one that could ever teach me. I always say that if there's something I really need to learn and I can't do it, there's always Harp. She can get anything into even this thick head.' He knocked his skull with his fist theatrically. 'Anyway, I'll show you the sights, including your guy on the horse, one of the days. But tonight it's the fundraiser for the Volunteers back home, and you and me can go with Uncle Pat and Aunt Kathy. Your hero Captain O'Neill is in town, so he's the star attraction. There'll be lots of people there, and it should be nice.'

The car took a corner quite fast, and she was thrown against him.

'Hey,' JohnJoe admonished the driver, 'take it easy, buddy! We ain't in the Indianapolis 500.' He lifted his arm and placed it across the back of the seat behind her head. She found herself sitting closer to him, and it was nice. 'That OK with you?' he asked gently.

'Yes, fine, thank you.' She hoped he didn't think she was being too forward.

'I'm so happy you're here, Harp. I kinda can't believe it. I told Uncle Pat and Aunt Kathy so much about you. They are really excited to meet you. I was so nervous this morning, thinkin', I dunno...that you'd be so sophisticated by now – and you are, so smart and everything – but it feels just like before, that summer I spent at your house when we planted the garden and cleared out all the old stables.'

Harp laughed. 'Yes, and Mammy and I were so glad you didn't mind the rats in the sheds as much as we did. We missed you and Danny a lot when you left. It was so lonely. I'd never had a real friend before.'

'Me neither. And now, well, I got my cousin Danny and the guys we work with, but I don't really got friends either. There were some guys at that school – they used to give me a hard time about my accent and stuff. That's why I sound so American now, I guess. I had to get rid of my Irish accent quick. I didn't fit in. Like, I have the Rafferty name and all, and the nice house and the money, but inside I was still the same kid, y'-know? And after school I just went to work, and I'm the boss's son in their eyes. They're OK, nice guys, but they stick to themselves. You think back in Ireland it's all about place in society – rich, poor, educated, not, Catholic, Protestant – but at least there they are open about it. Here things are just the same, even within the Irish. We're one kind, and there are some other Irish families like us at the top, but the ones on the bottom, they work for us but they don't trust us and don't mix with us. And then there's the lace-curtain Irish. They don't want nothin' to do with Ireland and want to forget they ever came from there.'

'Do you see Erin any more?' she asked, trying to keep her voice light.

JohnJoe shook his head. 'No, there was no point.' He didn't elucidate further, but she knew he was telling the truth.

The car drove more slowly now through leafy suburbs. The tall buildings, bigger than anything in Ireland, seemed to almost radiate heat. There were people everywhere, men in business suits, ladies with parasols, nannies pushing babies in very fancy prams. Everyone looked so well dressed and clean and shiny.

'And how is Danny?' she asked, relaxing a little.

JohnJoe rolled his eyes. 'He's OK, doing fine, but, er...he's kinda laying low these days. My uncle and aunt think it would be best if he wasn't out and about much for a while, just until everything settles down. So he won't be able to come tonight, though you'll probably see him in the house.'

'Is your home near here?' she asked. Once they got to the house, it sounded like there would be a lot to do, and she might not get time alone with him again until goodness knew when.

'Sure, it's four blocks away,' he replied.

'Could we walk the rest of the way?'

He answered by tapping the driver on the shoulder. 'Here will do. Thanks, pal.' He took some coins from his pocket and paid the fare, then helped her out and collected her case from the boot. This time, he noticed the initials embossed on the leather. 'BQ? What's that?'

'Oh, it's Brian Quinn's initials. I didn't have a case of my own to bring.'

They were standing on a street with several tall brownstone homes, and on their side of the road was a small railed garden. In it, women were pushing prams and several children were playing. JohnJoe once again offered her his arm. She took it, and together they walked along the edge of the green park. There was a bench under a huge chestnut tree, and without discussing it, they sat down together, side by side. Harp sighed.

JohnJoe turned to look at her. 'Is everything all right, Harp? Your mom? The house?'

Harp was touched by his concern. 'We're all fine.' But as soon as she said it, she knew she wasn't fine. What she really wanted to do was tell him all about Pennington and that terrible night. Maybe that's why she'd wanted them to spend more time alone together, so she could confess to him. But if she did tell him everything, how could he ever look at her the same way again? She didn't want him to think of her as a murderer.

'Harp.' He lowered his voice, though nobody was near them.

The laughter of children playing, distant traffic rumbling on the street and the murmur of conversation from a group of women having a picnic on the grass twenty yards away were the only sounds. The hot sun beat down, and she was glad of the shade of the tree, though she could feel the perspiration trickling down her neck.

He moved slightly closer. 'Harp…I know you just got here, and I don't want to put any pressure on you, but do you think you might like to stay on a little longer, now you're here?'

'But I'm here for a reason,' said Harp softly, 'not just a visit. You know that, don't you?'

'Yes, Uncle Pat told me, of course. And I think you're amazingly brave. But two weeks seems such a short time. Can't they wait for the money just another couple of weeks?'

'I don't think they can. And it's not just that. I have to get back to my life, and my mother…'

'And Brian?'

'Brian?' She was confused. 'He's not in Ireland. He's in France.'

'But you're always writing to me about him and worrying about him, and now you have his case…'

Harp was incredulous. 'JohnJoe, no. Brian is like a big brother to me. I'm really fond of him, but that's all.'

'So you and him ain't, y'know, sweethearts or nothin'?'

'Definitely not.' Harp had a fleeting image of Brian the night she rejected him.

JohnJoe's face split into a big grin. 'No kiddin'? Brian is like a brother, huh? That's great news, really great. Well, that's just swell.' He looked so pleased, she had to laugh.

'Did you think I was lying to you when you wrote and asked? I told you then I didn't have any romantic feelings for him.'

'Not lying, just…I thought you might change your mind, that's all. What with him bein' so smart and studyin' to be a doctor and all.'

'Anyway,' she teased, 'why do you care about whether I have a sweetheart or not?'

'Well, now, I think I'd have to be very careful about answering that question in case you find a reason to laugh at me.' JohnJoe grinned. Getting to his feet, he said, 'Come on. My folks are only dying to meet you, so I can't keep you from them any longer. You'll love them – you don't need to be shy of meeting them.'

She stood up as well. 'I'm not shy.'

'Good, because I thought you used to feel awkward about meetin' new people at first. Anyway, my aunt and uncle are just swell. Aunt Kathy is as nice as pie, and Uncle Pat's a good guy. He tries to help people out – he's decent. The people he represents – he sits on the Boston City Council – the poor Irish in Southie, he's their champion. They love him 'cause he cares about them and fights for them. The law, the cops, they don't do nothin' for those people, and without Uncle Pat they'd be much worse off. The cops know that if they take them on and treat them bad, then they'll have Uncle Pat to deal with, and so they don't. The law here supports those that make the laws, people that only want to look out for themselves, and to hell with the little guy. They don't give a curse for immigrants or poor people. It's different in Ireland, I know, but not as much as you think. '

'People crushed by laws have no hope but to evade power. If laws are their enemies, they will be enemies to laws, and those who have much to hope and nothing to lose will always be dangerous,' said Harp, half to herself as she thought about Ireland – and Pennington.

'See? You are so smart. That's what I was trying to say, but you say everything so much better than me.' He held her hand as they walked, and though she could never have countenanced such familiarity with a boy at home, she found that here she liked it and didn't care who saw her.

'That's as may be, but it was Edmund Burke who said that, not me.'

'Who's he?' JohnJoe asked, guiding her through the traffic once more.

'You've heard of him surely? The Irish statesman and politician? MP for Bristol? Wrote *A Vindication of Natural Society?*'

JohnJoe laughed. 'Harp, you know it's not me but you that's peculiar right? Nobody knows that guy, I swear to you.'

'Of course they do.' But she joined in with his good-natured laughter.

CHAPTER 18

The Raffertys' house took her breath away; it was so large outside and inside so beautifully and tastefully decorated. JohnJoe's uncle and aunt came to meet them in the vast hall, already in evening dress for the fundraiser.

Pat Rafferty was nothing like the way Harp had pictured him. She'd imagined an avuncular man, bald and rotund. Someone with a benevolent love for JohnJoe and his wife, a sort of Robin Hood and Friar Tuck character combined. But she could not have been more wrong.

He was, she guessed, only in his late forties. His eyes were the most unusual colour, amber like a cat's, and they seemed to see right through her. He was tall and well built, and though he was a businessman, he looked like he could do very well at any manual job. He reminded her a little of Martin Powell, the blacksmith in Queenstown, a powerfully built man who could calm any horse with his gentle hands and voice but was also quite capable of stopping one with sheer brute force. But unlike Martin Powell, Pat Rafferty was clean; his fingernails even looked manicured, and his dark-red curls were oiled and combed perfectly. His tailored suit hugged his lean, muscular frame.

His wife, the much adored Aunt Kathy, was also like nobody she'd ever seen. She'd imagined the wife of the jolly old uncle as a sweet old lady, with a floral dress and grey curls, but again she was so far wide of the mark, it was laughable. Aunt Kathy had flame-red hair, which was cut in a sharp bob at her jawline. Harp had never seen a lady with short hair before and could only imagine the fluttering it would cause were she ever to wander down the promenade of Queenstown. She was dressed in a scarlet gown, daringly off the shoulder, baring pearly skin, and her red lipstick matched her outfit perfectly. But despite the very stylish look, she seemed very kind, and when she looked at JohnJoe, the pride she felt in him was plain to see. She adored her adopted son, nothing less, and the feeling was clearly mutual.

Harp had barely time to be introduced and say hello before a maid with very dark skin and very curly black hair led her upstairs to a pale-pink room with a large four-poster bed to change for the party.

Harp tried not to stare, but she'd never seen a Black person before in the flesh. 'What's your name?' she asked the girl, who looked to be only a little older than she was herself.

'Celia, Miss Devereaux.' The girl smiled to reveal even white teeth.

'Oh, please, call me Harp. Back at home in Ireland, I do your job, so I'm the same as you.' She feared she'd said the wrong thing because the look the girl gave her was fearful.

'No, Miss Devereaux, Mrs Rafferty wouldn't like that. She's a nice lady, but she runs this house properly, so you call me Celia and I'll call you Miss Devereaux.'

'Very well,' Harp agreed, not wanting to upset anyone. 'But if you ever get to Ireland, my mother and I run a guest house and you can be Miss... What's your surname?'

'Surname... Oh, you mean my last name? It's Williams.'

'Well then, if you ever get to visit, I'll wait on you and you can call me Harp then and I'll call you Miss Williams.' She smiled and hoped she hadn't said the wrong thing.

The girl grinned again. 'I don't think travelling the world is in my future, Miss Devereaux, but you never know.'

'You really don't,' Harp said. 'My life has taken so many twists and turns already and I'm only sixteen, so you're right – we have no idea what's round the corner.'

She was glad her mother had made her so many lovely dresses, even altering some of her own. She selected an emerald-green one, feeling it was fitting for the occasion. She washed and dressed quickly, but her hair needed to be set properly. She was despairing of it when Celia came in with the most amazing contraption. She called it a curling iron, and using a pungent spray, bent metal wires that she called bobby pins and the hot metal pole, she arranged Harp's hair into a very sophisticated style. Celia even suggested Harp wear a little make-up. Harp didn't own any, but the maid returned within moments with a large velvet box in which several compartments offered any number of paints and powders.

However her mother might feel about curls,

Harp knew she would be horrified to see her daughter with a painted face, but Harp had to admit the effect was lovely. Her grey eyes were ringed with a suggestion of black kohl, and black powder was brushed onto her eyelashes. It stung for a second but was amazing. Harp had always seen her odd-coloured eyes as a liability, but tonight they looked lovely. A faint brush of rouge on her cheeks and lips and she was ready.

'THIS WAS one of the first buildings in Boston to get electric lights,' Pat explained to Harp as they entered Young's Hotel on Court Street for the evening's event.

Uniformed staff showed their party through to a huge dining room, which had a low ceiling and pillars dividing the space into three areas. A long marble fireplace dominated one wall, and the wainscotting was mahogany red. There were glittering chandeliers, and the columns were carved with griffins. In the centre of the room on a brass table was a fern and flower arrangement that was the hugest Harp had ever seen, and the whole room was decorated in Irish flags, perhaps to make people feel a stronger connection to that little island so very far away.

The place was already full when they entered, and everyone seemed impossibly well dressed and shiny. Ladies in gowns of every hue, their hair set perfectly, smiled coquettishly at the men in black tie who held cut-glass tumblers of whiskey and puffed on cigars. The combined aromas of cigar smoke and perfume made Harp's eyes water for a moment, but she decided on the spot that she loved it all.

As Pat Rafferty, with Harp on his arm, made his way to the table reserved for his family, there wasn't exactly a hush, but certainly his arrival was noticed by everyone; Harp had never seen a person command such respect just by his presence alone. Even the brigadier general, who sometimes left his barracks to walk down the street of Queenstown, didn't seem to have the same impact as Pat Rafferty did.

He spoke to a few people, then paused to introduce Harp to a pair of distinguished men in their fifties. Both were silver-haired, and one sported a very impressive moustache and lamb-chop sideburns. 'Alderman Collins and President Cleary, I'd like to introduce you to a very impressive young woman, all the way from Queenstown, County Cork – Harp Devereaux.'

'Ah, the lass from the old country,' the alderman said with a flourish. 'And what do you make of our city so far, young lady? A long way from the Emerald Isle, I guess?'

'It is, and it is very different,' Harp agreed, unsure of how to answer.

'Different good, I hope!' the other man boomed.

'Yes, different good...' She rather liked these Americans and their direct way of speaking. It suited her own outspoken style.

'Look, Harp!' JohnJoe pulled her aside and pointed at the stage at the end of the room. There was a large green flag that said 'Erin go Bragh', and the Irish tricolour and the Star-Spangled Banner were entwined. In pride of place was a beautiful Irish harp.

'Harp plays the harp, Uncle Pat, did I tell you? She's amazing at it.' JohnJoe was bursting with pride, and Harp felt the men's eyes upon her.

'You did, about twenty times. I doubt there is anything Kathy and I don't know about you, Miss Devereaux. JohnJoe has one topic of conversation these days, and one only.' Pat's amber eyes twinkled merrily, and JohnJoe didn't seem to mind a bit.

As they passed another table, JohnJoe stopped to greet a man with a very full but well-groomed moustache. He had burning dark eyes under straight heavy brows. 'It's very nice of you to come and help my uncle raise funds for the cause, Mr O'Neill. Everyone is looking forward to hearing you play.' JohnJoe shook the older man's hand. 'I'm JohnJoe Rafferty, and this is Miss Devereaux, who has come all the way from Cork.'

'So we are both Corkonians?' The former police chief of Chicago rose and extended his hand to Harp. He made a commanding figure, well built, straight as an arrow, although his voice was much softer and gentler than his appearance would suggest.

Harp was completely awestruck. Nobody had done more for Irish music than Francis O'Neill, gathering tunes and dances and recording them for all time. Music that would have been lost to the mists of history was now preserved for future generations to play and enjoy, all because of this man's efforts.

'Yes, I'm from Queenstown,' she said, 'and it is a great pleasure to meet you. My late father collected your books and urged me to play the tunes on my harp, so thank you for writing them all down and preserving so much Irish music for future generations.'

He smiled at her earnest enthusiasm, then answered gravely, 'Thank you for the kind sentiment, Miss Devereaux, but I only collect the tunes – I do not write them down. I have to learn them by ear, and a friend in Chicago transcribes them for me. It's a skill I wish I could master. Why only today I was on a streetcar and I heard a slip jig I'd never heard before – a man was whistling it – and I had to ride six extra stops just to make sure it was implanted in my brain. I must have looked an odd sight indeed, standing on a street corner playing my whistle, trying to commit it to memory. I have to hurry back to Chicago tomorrow. I have three tunes in my head at the moment – that slip jig, a hornpipe and a lovely air I got from an elderly lady from mid-Cork who's been here in Boston for fifty years – and I'm desperately trying to keep them all straight in my head.'

'I could write them down for you now if you'd like?' Harp offered impulsively. At once, she could have kicked herself for being so direct, but the former police chief seemed delighted.

'Could you really? That would be most helpful, Miss Devereaux. Here…' He pulled a sheaf of blank manuscript from his inside pocket and winked at her. 'I'm always ready. Mr Rafferty, please allow me to detain this excellent lady for a brief while.'

'My pleasure, Chief O'Neill. She is a very talented harpist and very clever about music altogether,' said JohnJoe proudly. 'Harp, I'll be back in just a minute.' Pat Rafferty was beckoning his nephew, and JohnJoe crossed the room to his uncle's side.

Francis O'Neill led Harp to the end of the room to an empty booth. The cacophony of the crowd was less here, and she could hear him much better.

A waiter hovered, inquiring what she would like to drink. She had no idea what to order so just asked for a glass of water.

'Seltzer or still, miss?' the obsequious waiter asked, an eyebrow raised.

Harp shot an anxious look at Francis O'Neill. She had no idea what he was asking her.

'He means do you want it with bubbles or without?' The former police chief smiled.

'Er…without bubbles.' She felt distinctly foolish.

'Still. Very well, madam. And a slice?' There

was a hint of bored impatience in the waiter's voice now.

'She'll have lemon,' said Francis O'Neill. 'And an Irish for me.' The way he spoke to the man dismissed him, and Harp was glad to see the back of the waiter with his puzzling questions.

Francis O'Neill handed her a stubby pencil, then took a tin whistle from his inside pocket and played a hornpipe slowly and softly, bar by bar, as everyone around them strained to listen and Harp transcribed it note by note.

'Marvellous. That's called "The Fisherman's Lilt".' He took the paper from her. 'Now the old lady's song is a lovely one called "Cath Chéim an Fhia, The Battle of Deer's Leap".' And he played the haunting melody on the whistle, slowly enough for her to get it all in the first go. She handed him the finished sheet.

'This is so helpful, Miss Devereaux. Thank you so much. What talent you have to be able to hear and write the dots so well. This is clearly as natural to you as breathing. Please be sure to use your God-given talent – do not squander it.'

Harp glowed under his approval and took a sip of the lemony water that the waiter had placed at her elbow.

'Now this last one, this slip jig...' His brow

knitted as he recalled the tune, and with extreme concentration he brought the whistle once again to his lips and began to play softly at a fast pace. It was a beautiful melody, light and cheerful, and Harp just listened, not writing anything.

'It would make you want to dance,' she said, smiling. 'I thought at first it was the "Foxhunter's Jig", but it's not. The first section has some similarities, but the turn is quite different.'

'Indeed it would,' the police chief agreed. 'I was entranced when I heard it, and you're quite right – the ornamentation is similar to the "Foxhunter's", but it's a different tune definitely.'

'And how will you find out what it's called?' she asked, taking a third sheet of paper, her pencil poised.

The man paused, his whistle halfway to his mouth, and gazed at her. 'What's your first name, if you don't mind me asking, Miss Devereaux?'

'It's Harp,' she said, colouring slightly. 'I know, a girl called Harp who plays the harp is a bit silly probably, but my mother loved the name.'

'It's a beautiful name and suits you perfectly.' He put the whistle to his lips and played the melody bar by bar, pausing as she wrote the notes. This, like the hornpipe, was a complicated tune with a lot of ornamentation. When she had finished, he took the manuscript, examined it with pleasure and then rolled it carefully with the others before placing them all in his inside pocket. 'Thank you very much, Miss Devereaux. This is a wonderful help to me, and I will always remember you when I think of these tunes. This last one especially. It's such an uplifting tune, 'twould make your heart sing and your feet tap, wouldn't it?' He smiled.

'It really would,' she agreed.

'And since we don't know what the name of it is, we can, in the grand old tradition of our homeland, rename it for ourselves. And so this tune will henceforth be called "Harp Devereaux".'

Harp was so flattered that she didn't know what to say.

Up on stage, Pat Rafferty was calling the crowd to attention. All eyes turned to him as he stood at the podium beside the harp.

'Aldermen, Mr Mayor, Monsignor O'Donnell, Reverend Fathers, ladies and gentlemen, thank you all for coming this evening to this, the third annual Irish American Association Gala evening. It is so heartening to see so many patriots here, willing to give up not just of their valuable time but also their dollars to assist our brothers at home.'

A rumble of applause and nodding heads meant he held the room in the palm of his hand. His tone was so commanding, Harp could never imagine anyone refusing him anything. He wasn't good-looking in the traditional sense, but there was something powerful about him; compelling was the word. He was at home in front of these people. They were his tribe, and no matter what the ballot box said, Pat Rafferty was their chief.

'Boston is 5000 miles from Ireland's shores, but in our heart and mind and spirit, it is a part of the home country. We salute Pádraig Pearse, James Connolly, Joseph Plunkett, Éamonn Ceannt, Seán Mac Diarmada and Tom Clarke. Some of those brave men were, as you all know, at one time or another of this very parish. When the old enemy coldly and with malice afore-thought slaughtered our brothers last May, they did not, as they hoped to do, dampen the spirit of rebellion within the heart of every Irish man and woman. No, they strengthened us, steeled our de-termination to free our homeland. They have not weakened us but emboldened us still further to march relentlessly to victory.'

The rapturous applause and drumming of feet on the floor caused the entire room to re-verberate.

He projected his voice over the cacophony of applause and stamping of feet. 'Freedom, total and complete freedom, will have to be forged. They will not give it willingly, as we know. It will have to be fought for inch by inch, drop by precious drop of Irish blood. But we will never stop, never give in, never lie down. And when we win – and note I say when, not if – when we gain freedom for our beloved homeland, only then can the Irish Republic be born.'

He raised his hand for silence, and to Harp's astonishment, he got it. A faint murmur of conversation was all that remained. 'Now, we promised you a great night, and a great night you shall have. Chief Francis O'Neill is here to play you the music of Ireland, which will delight you, and there is also a very, very special guest. She arrived only this evening, all the way from Queenstown, County Cork.'

He held his hand out, and Harp found the light that had been on Pat suddenly on her. The crowd clapped and cheered. She tried to swallow, but her mouth was dry; she would have given anything to slink away.

JohnJoe appeared beside her. 'My uncle is hoping you will say a few words to the crowd,' he said. 'To talk about the cause from first hand and encourage the people to put their hands in their pockets.'

'Oh!' She didn't know what to say; she had never spoken in public and was sure she wouldn't even know where to start. 'I don't think I...'

But he was offering her his hand to accompany him to the stage. 'You're so clever, Harp. I know you can do it.'

To her relief, just as he had done with the waiter, Francis O'Neill came smoothly to her rescue. 'Mr Rafferty, this is a remarkable young lady, with a very special musical talent. And like myself, I am sure she feels that music is the best way to people's hearts and through there to their pockets and is far better than making another speech. Miss Devereaux, perhaps you will accompany me on the harp and we will entertain the audience.'

The suggestion was hardly any less frightening, but JohnJoe's face lit up. 'That's a wonderful idea, Chief O'Neill. Harp, they will love you – you're amazing. You were so good four years ago, and I know you play every day, so I can only imagine how good you are now. Please, will you do it?'

Something about his face, the pleading look, made her realise that what was at stake was more important than her fears. If it meant that much to him, she could do it. 'Very well, I will.'

Nervously, she allowed JohnJoe and Francis O'Neill to lead her up to the stage. The clapping became deafening as she took her seat at the harp. She prayed it was in tune. As Pat silenced the crowd once more, she ran her hands over the strings, and to her relief it was.

'What will we play, Harp?' asked Francis O'Neill, and the room was suddenly quiet.

'Could we try "The West's Awake"?' Harp suggested, her voice so quiet only he could hear her.

'Ah, wonderful.' He turned to the audience. 'This song was written by the Young Irelander Thomas Davis and refers to the Williamite War of the 1690s, when the Catholic James II with the assistance of the Irish took on Protestant William of Orange.'

Pat Rafferty took up the story. 'The Battle of Aughrim and Battle of the Boyne were unsuccessful, as we know, but each rebellion, each insurrection in the centuries since that first treacherous invasion of 1169, has edged us closer to freedom. So we must never call our efforts in the past failures. They were anything but. They were steps on the path to victory. And the "west" in this song refers to the province of Connaught.

Many's the man in this room has Connaught blood in his veins, but tonight the West is truly awake. Not just the west of Ireland but further west, across the Atlantic to this, the United States of America. And by God we are awake and will, as the song says, "fight till death, for Erin's sake".'

He'd deliberately misquoted the last line; Harp was sure of it. He left the stage to rapturous clapping, people congratulating him as he went.

Harp inhaled deeply, then exhaled through her mouth, steadying her nerves. She flexed her fingers and then, as if she were at home in her own drawing room, she seemed to hear Henry Devereaux's voice. *Feel the music, Harp, heart to fingers, bypass the brain. It is in you already – just let it out.*

Francis O'Neill had exchanged his tin whistle for the flute, and he was already playing the opening melody. Harp joined in, running her fingers over the strings, and then, with a volume that surprised her, she sang. She closed her eyes. Her voice was clear and true, and the crowded room, the weight of expectation, the strangeness of it all dissipated, and it was just her and the flute and her harp and the song.

As she sang the last verse, she heard a man's voice join in, in perfect harmony, and when she opened her eyes, JohnJoe was standing beside her, singing. And in the room, the crowd also sang along, softly.

'And if, when all a vigil keep,
The West's asleep the West's asleep,
Alas and well may Erin weep,
That Connaught lies in slumber deep.'

Then like a wave gathering momentum and power, the choir of voices sang out, strong and passionate.

'But hark, a voice like thunder spake,
The West's awake, the West's awake,
Sing oh hurrah, let England quake,
We'll watch till death, for Erin's sake.'

The melody ended, and Francis O'Neill laid down his flute and offered her his hand. 'Take a bow, young lady – you deserve it. That was beautiful.'

'More, more!' chanted the crowd, their eyes on her.

She looked anxiously at JohnJoe, who grinned back at her. 'It's you they want, Harp. The brave young girl all the way from the home country. Play something else!'

'By myself?' It was a terrifying thought.

'Do you want me to sing with you?' he offered, and she nodded in relief. Years ago, as children, they had sung and played the famous song 'I Dreamt I Dwelt in Marble Halls' from the Balfe opera *The Bohemian Girl*. She struck the opening chords, JohnJoe stood close beside her, and together they sang.

'I dreamt I dwelt in marble halls,
With vassals and serfs at my side.
And of all who assembled within those walls,
I was the hope and the pride.
I had riches too great to count, could boast,
Of a high ancestral name.
But I also dreamt, which pleased me most,
That you loved me still the same,
That you loved me still the same...'

As they came to the chorus, she was conscious of JohnJoe gazing at her as if he was singing to her alone, and she lowered her head to hide her smile. Behind them, Francis O'Neill accompanied them on the tin whistle, and when they had finished, the room erupted again into cheering and clapping. This time the crowd was on their feet, all eyes on her. If someone had told her that the evening would have gone like this, she would surely have bolted for the port and back on the ship, but to her surprise, she found she was enjoying it. She smiled and curtseyed but declined to play any more. It was time for the brilliant Francis O'Neill to take centre stage.

'That was amazing,' she said as JohnJoe led her to his family's table.

'It was, and he enjoyed playing with you as much as you enjoyed playing with him, I think,' he answered.

Up on the stage, Pat Rafferty was back at the podium. 'We have more wonderful entertainment lined up for your enjoyment, folks, but I ask you to remember what it is all about. Remember why that brave young girl there, Harp Devereaux, crossed the Atlantic to play for you, and dig deep, gentlemen, dig deep and make your forefathers proud. They came here, many with nothing but the shirts on their backs, but they built this city, this country, with their toil, and now we will use the fruits of that labour to liberate our homeland from the yoke of British oppression.'

The applause continued while men appeared, dressed impeccably and carrying baskets. Each table was given its own basket, and within seconds each one was overflowing with green notes. Francis O'Neill played several more tunes, including the slip jig, which he explained to the crowd's delight was called 'Harp Devereaux'. And when he left the stage, a band struck up and lively jigs and reels filled the room.

Before he went back to his own table, the former police chief made his way over to Harp and took her hand. 'Miss Devereaux, thank you for your time and your talent. It was such a pleasure to play with you and to avail of your generosity. It has made this trip away from my beloved Windy City worth every inconvenience.' He bent low from the waist and kissed her fingers. His moustache bristled her skin and she blushed.

'I'll always remember this,' she said sincerely.

'As will I, Miss Devereaux, as will I. Perhaps our paths will cross again.' He took his leave and was swallowed up by the crowds of people all wanting to talk to him.

CHAPTER 19

'You must be exhausted. Let's get you inside, you poor girl.' Kathy fussed over Harp as they entered the house. A dark-skinned butler and a lady in her fifties greeted them.

'To be able to perform like that, and having only just got off the boat! Honestly, I don't know how you did it, but I just know your performance really helped the cause, Harp. It really did.'

'Undoubtedly, Harp, they were enthralled by you,' Pat agreed. 'Oh, good evening, Mrs Dennis, Clayton. Thank you.'

The staff took their light summer coats and hung them up. Clayton, the butler in full livery, followed them to the drawing room, where he gave Pat a drink without asking him if he would like one. There were two large chesterfield sofas facing each other across a coffee table the size of a billiard table. The fireplace was filled with a display of dried flowers for the summer months, and the décor of the room was pale greys and blues. It was restful if a little austere. Certainly not cosy.

'Well, look who's here!'

They looked up to find Danny crossing the room.

'Well, Miss Harp, you sure grew up pretty.' He held his arms outstretched. Harp crossed the room and found herself enveloped in a huge bear hug.

Danny looked just the same except for a large black beard. His dark hair was oiled, and his brown eyes were warm with affection.

'The beard is new.' She grinned.

'All part of my disguise, Harp. I'm a wanted man.' He winked and accepted a drink from Clayton.

'Don't listen to him, Harp. He's just showing off. You slug one cop around here and suddenly you're Jesse James.' JohnJoe dismissed his cousin good-naturedly.

'Come sit, darling.' Kathy beckoned him beside her, and he sat obediently, giving her a peck on the cheek.

'So how'd it go?' Danny asked.

Kathy regaled him with tales of Harp's talents and how well Chief O'Neill had been received.

Harp sat on the sofa with JohnJoe beside her. Danny and Kathy sat on the other one facing them, and Pat leaned on the marble fireplace. It all felt so natural, so easy – it was hard to believe she'd just met them. On the mantlepiece, a green glazed porcelain clock with cherubs on it ticked loudly. It was probably expensive and no doubt old, but Harp thought it was the ugliest thing she'd ever seen. It seemed so out of place with the rest of the stunning décor.

'Would you like something before bed, Harp? A drink, a cup of cocoa?' Kathy asked.

Harp found she would love something. She and Mammy had warm milk every night, and she was suddenly overwhelmed with loneliness for her mother, her home. 'I would like a cup of cocoa please,' she answered.

'Of course. What about you, JJ? What would you like, darling?' Kathy asked, brushing a hair from Danny's shoulder.

'I'll have cocoa too please, Clayton.' JohnJoe smiled.

'And you, madam?' the butler asked, his deep voice rumbling.

'I'll have a chamomile tea please, Clayton, and could you bring some of those cookies Mrs Dennis made earlier today? They were delicious.'

'Certainly, madam.' Clayton nodded and withdrew.

'Well, I think the bumper takings tonight can be attributed to none other than our charming little houseguest here, so on behalf of the Irish American Association, we thank you, Harp.' Pat raised a glass to her. 'They loved you, and rightly so. You have a remarkable talent. You should come over here – we'd put you on the stage and you could become famous.'

Harp coloured under the spotlight of his approval. 'Oh, I won't be a performer. I intend to go to university and study,' she said.

Pat smiled and nodded knowingly. 'JJ here told us that you were so smart, but you do have a gift so you could do both.'

He clearly noticed the glance between Harp and JohnJoe and raised an eyebrow questioningly. 'So, Miss Devereaux from County Cork, apart from taking my nephew's mind off everything and everyone but you since he heard you were visiting, we have something we need to discuss, do we not?'

Harp nodded.

'So Kathy and I have been thinking. We need to get that money to Ireland – considerably more than anticipated now, thanks to you – but without raising any suspicious eyebrows, so my wonderful wife came up with this.'

He pointed to a two-foot-square box that was sitting on the floor by the window. Kathy went to it and removed a fur coat. She crossed the room and gestured that Harp should stand. She then helped her into the long coat. Harp tried not to shudder at the idea that this was once on the body of some misfortunate animal.

'Fur is bulky anyway, so nobody will question it,' Kathy said. 'We'll sew the money into the lining – nobody will suspect a thing. You wear it, and once you get to Ireland, have someone who is handy with needle and thread unpick the lining. And there we go.' Kathy smiled as if it were the simplest thing in the world to smuggle lots of money into Ireland under the noses of the British.

'It's a bit long,' Harp pointed out, noting that the coat reached almost to her ankles.

'I'll have it taken up a little,' Kathy said, eyeing her appraisingly.

'But won't that ruin it? It looks expensive,' Harp protested.

'Yes, it's muskrat and racoon, and only because the cause is so deserving am I willing to part with it at all. I can still wear it a few inches shorter. I love it, so maybe I can have it back once it's relieved of its load?'

'Oh, absolutely,' Harp immediately agreed. She wanted nothing to do with the horrid thing. It was heavy and sleek, the fur sitting perfectly, a blend of black and brown, with a double-breasted front and side slash pockets. The collar seemed to be even more furry, and she hated the sensation of it near her face. But Kathy was clearly sad at parting with it, so it would have seemed churlish to appear anything less than delighted. 'I'm sure the Devlins will be able to unpick it, remove the money and stitch it all up so well, you'll never notice anything had ever happened, I promise. I'll take very good care of it in the meantime.'

Kathy smiled. 'I know you will, dear, and if anything happens to it, well, it's just a coat. I'll get over it. But try to take care of it.' She helped Harp out of it. 'Now, you're right – it is a little big on you, so we might need to alter it a little on the shoulders too. We don't want to arouse any suspicions. Mrs Dennis is a dab hand with the needle too, so we'll see what she can do. We can change the bills to the largest denominations, so there will be the smallest amount of cash in terms of volume but with the highest value.'

'Well, the pot was certainly very generous tonight, that's for sure. I'll have it exchanged at the bank into $500 bills in the morning,' Pat replied, then sipped his whiskey. 'It should keep our boys over there in bullets for a while.' He winked at Harp, and then his face turned serious. 'Now, I don't want you to have to do this alone – it would be too frightening for you. As Kathy says, it's most unlikely anything would happen, but just in case, I'm going to send Danny back with you. He'll keep an eye on you and the money. Besides, slugging a cop at the republican rally last month wasn't his finest hour, so it will do us all good if he was out of the picture for the time being, you know?'

'What? I'm goin' to Ireland?' This was obviously news to Danny.

'Well, if you'd prefer Charles Street Jail, be my guest. I hear the food's disgusting, though, and they make you work, something that would be totally alien to you, buddy,' Pat replied sardonically.

'Hold on a minute,' JohnJoe interjected. 'If anyone is escorting Harp back to Ireland, it's me, not Dannyboy here. He can carry the bags if you insist, but I'll be the one taking care of her.'

PAT AND KATHY EXCHANGED A GLANCE, and Harp saw the flicker of worry, of fear, in JohnJoe's aunt's eyes.

'Well, I don't know, JJ,' Pat began. 'Your aunt needs you here and –'

'Let him go, Pat,' Kathy said, her voice steeled against the sadness she obviously felt.

'I'll be back, Aunt Kathy.' JohnJoe stood, walked over to her and perched on the arm of her sofa, putting a hand on her shoulder and gazing down into her eyes. 'Don't worry about me.'

She nodded, her eyes suspiciously bright. 'I know, darling boy, and besides, you're a man now – you need to make your own way. But that doesn't mean I wouldn't rather you tied to my apron strings until you're fifty,' she joked.

Harp could see how much letting him go, even for a short while, hurt her – he was a son in every way – but she loved him enough to let him live his life. She reminded Harp of Rose in that regard, and Harp realised both she and JohnJoe were very lucky in the mothers they got. The idea that the boys would be with her going back was wonderful. She resolved to enjoy her holiday, as now that Danny and JohnJoe would accompany her back to Ireland, she had no need to worry.

'Do you even own an apron?' Danny quipped, taking the tension out of the situation. "'Cause I sure ain't never seen you in it. Oh, yeah, I'm forgetting your peach cobbler and your baked Alaska and that beef thing you do...' Danny teased.

She play swiped him with a cushion. 'They're teasing me because I can burn water, Harp. I'm not exactly domestic, you know. More ornament than useful, if you know what I mean. So of course I don't own an actual apron – with these nails?' She held up a perfectly manicured hand, the nails painted a delicate coral.

Pat stood and crossed the silk oriental rug, offering his hand and lifting her from the sofa. He put his arm around his wife and kissed her head. 'Katherine Mary Rafferty, you are and always will be the best person I ever met. And yes, you are beautiful, but you are also smart and kind and funny, and there is nothing I or either of these two bozos wouldn't do for you.'

Under any other circumstances, such an outpouring of emotional honesty would have been embarrassing to witness, but when Pat said it, it wasn't.

Kathy didn't look coquettish or even flattered. She took the words as they were meant, with genuine love, and Harp marvelled at it. This was true love; she was sure of it. She'd never seen it in her life before, not this raw, this exposed, this unashamed. She was reminded of Jane Eyre's last lines to Mr Rochester: 'All my heart is yours, sir: it belongs to you; and with you it would remain if fate were to exile the rest of me from your presence forever.'

She could never imagine Matt Quinn or Mr Devereaux or the dreadful Ralph ever being so forthright. They might feel it – though in the case of Ralph, the only person he loved was himself – but they could never say it, she was sure of it. That was why literature appealed to people, she thought. Characters could say things normal humans never could.

Pat's pronouncement then interrupted her reverie. 'OK, you can both go, but make sure you come back, you hear me? There's a lot of work on, and I need you two.'

'I can't wait.' Danny looked genuinely thrilled at the prospect of a return journey. 'Ireland is so little and so green, and I'll get to have some of your mom's home cooking – it's the best...'

'Hey, easy there...' Kathy pretended to be shocked.

'Thanks, Uncle Pat, for letting me go too. I'd hate to let Harp go back alone...' JohnJoe began.

'It's your aunt you need to thank. If it was up to me, you'd be staying here, but she's a sucker for a love story.' Pat drained his glass.

Harp stood. 'Thank you so much, Mr Rafferty...'

'Uncle Pat will do, and it's us should be thanking you. You're a very brave young lady, and your country is proud of you.' He smiled.

Clayton appeared with the drinks, poured and handed them to each person and silently left the room.

'No, I mean for letting Danny and JohnJoe come with me. I won't be so nervous if they're by my side.'

'I'd do it for the cause anyway, but I owe you and your mother a debt of gratitude, and I'm sure she'd sleep easier knowing you had these two gunslingers watching over you. Your mother took care of JJ here when he was all alone in the world and she made sure I got this guy back after some clown thought he could make a pincushion of him, so I owe her. And I never forget a debt. This way we're even, your mom and me.'

THEY CHATTED EASILY FOR A WHILE, enjoying the warm drinks before Kathy suppressed a yawn. Pat took his wife's hand and led her upstairs, ushering Danny before them.

JohnJoe and Harp found themselves really alone for the first time since they were children. She felt none of the worries she thought she might, not knowing what to say. It was as if it was yesterday they spent a long warm Irish summer together, when he was fourteen and she was twelve.

She knew they should not be alone together now without a chaperone, but Americans seemed more relaxed about things like that. She knew her mother would expect her to behave with propriety, and she would, but it was nice to be here with him, on their own.

'I couldn't bear it if you left with Danny,' he

said, his voice husky with emotion. He stood in front of her and took her hands in his.

'I'm glad you'll be with me,' she said, meaning it. 'The idea of being caught, being arrested or worse... I really want to do it – the Misses Devlin are relying on me – but I'm not sure I've naturally got criminal instincts.' She chuckled.

'Well, you certainly don't look like a master criminal.' He smiled.

She looked at the man her first real friend had become. His life had been on a totally different trajectory before his uncle asked to have him brought to America. If JohnJoe's father had not been willing to trade his last child for money, if JohnJoe's mother hadn't died, if so many things, then he would probably be a farmer now, working a smallholding in West County Clare, and not an American. But that was not how things turned out, and here he was. He spent the first fourteen years of his life in poverty and now was immersed in wealth and privilege, and yet he was still that sweet boy, gentle, kind and sincere. And despite his American accent, he was so very Irish. He'd been raised in a more Irish way here in Boston than he would have been at home. People in America were so much more aware of their heritage and felt it in their hearts. She supposed it was because there was no effort to be Irish required at home; everyone just was. But here, as so many other nationalities, cultures and languages mingled and fought for their place, a person's national identity meant more. Those people at the fundraiser identified as Irish on such a profound level, it fascinated her. Many of them had never set foot on Irish soil, but that wasn't important.

Aristotle said that poverty was the parent of revolution and crime, and seeing the crowds that night, hell-bent on funding a revolution, it was hard to see how poverty played a role, but it did. Pat Rafferty, like many of the people gathered there, came from humble beginnings. He was from a small farm in Clare and was a self-made man, and now he enjoyed a life of luxury. But it was a crime against his people, the subjugation of his family under the crushing weight of imperial power, that led him to Boston, led him to the life he had, led him to lead his fellow countrymen to revolution. To the British, what they were doing was a crime. They were breaking the law and encouraging sedition and armed insurgence, and she was part of that now. The moment she put on that coat, she would be a revolutionary to these people and to the Volunteers and Cumann na mBan at home, but a criminal to the British. One man's rebel was another man's freedom fighter, she supposed. Crime and punishment, she found, were not as straightforward as one might think.

When the Irish rose again, she and Matt would be seen as outlaws, as would the Devlins and many more people. Were they criminals? Was it wrong to fight, to kill even, to take back what was rightfully theirs? Was it ever justified?

'What are you thinking about?' JohnJoe asked softly. His face was close to hers, but they were not touching.

Another girl might say she was thinking about the party, or how lovely Boston was, or even how happy she was to be there with him, but Harp told the truth. 'I'm thinking about the law, and when, if ever, it is permissible to break it. Aristotle and Plato in ancient Greece and Cicero in Rome spoke often about nature and custom when it came to laws. That for the most part, the man-made law, the custom, was born out of natural law, as in what is morally right or wrong. But there is also the possibility that custom is serving some person or group to the detriment of another, and there it deviates from natural law. And so I was wondering if the breaking of the custom, the man-made law, is sometimes justified if the law itself is in fact unjust.'

JohnJoe smiled. 'I think I understand what you're saying. Do you mean that most laws, like don't murder people or steal their property, are in line with what is morally right, but some laws, like the way the British rule the Irish, are not morally right – they just serve their purposes?'

Harp nodded. 'Exactly. So in breaking those laws, are you in fact behaving morally? As we are about to do?'

'Well, I know my aunt and uncle and Matt Quinn and the Devlins you talk about are not bad people, but if they were to be tried in a British court, they would be convicted.'

'That's the point, isn't it? I'm not a criminal, neither are you, but what we are about to do is, by the standards of the English, a criminal act. But we can't hold ourselves to their standards. Establishing our own Irish court system is a priority – we must be answerable only to ourselves. We have never had justice at the hands of the oppressors, and we should no longer accept their jurisdiction over us. Bombs and bullets are one way of rebelling, but our refusal, our absolute refusal to acknowledge any part of their so-called civilisation is key.' She burnt with the intensity of it all.

JohnJoe stared at her for a long moment and

then he spoke softly. 'Whatever you end up doing, Harp Devereaux, you will be terrifyingly good at it. You are amazing, truly. Not just 'cause you're so intelligent and all of that – that bit scares me a little, to be honest – but the way your mind works. You're unique, you know that? I think there's nobody like you on this earth, and I'm so glad to have you as a friend. The way you sang and played tonight, I was so proud I could burst. I probably shouldn't say this, but you are so special to me.'

The seconds ticked by slowly, the air heavy between them. His face was vulnerable and un-sure. The boy she knew was gone, of that there was no doubt. This man seemed like the boy she knew – there were parts of him still there – but he was a man now.

'You don't need to say anything,' he added, moving back from her a little.

'You're special to me too,' she admitted. Panic gripped her; it was just such a situation with Brian that ended so badly. She felt differently about JohnJoe, she was sure of that, but it all felt too much now, and the rigours of the journey and the excitement of the night were taking their toll. She didn't want to say the wrong thing and ruin everything. She needed time to think, to process all that had happened. The words of Homer slipped from her lips. "'There is a time for many words, but there is also a time for sleep.'"

'What?'

'It's Homer. Odysseus says it to Alcinous,' Harp replied quietly.

He turned. 'Is that a book?' he asked, seemingly deliberately ignoring the relevance of the sentiment to the conversation they were having.

She nodded. 'Homer was a Greek playwright. He wrote two famous poems, the *Iliad* and the *Odyssey*.'

'What are they about?' he asked, sitting down on the sofa again and patting the seat beside him.

Harp sat down, leaving a foot of space between them. Part of her longed to snuggle up to him, to feel his arms around her, but here, in the night, with everyone else gone to bed, it didn't feel right. She tried to imagine what her mother would expect of her, and it certainly didn't involve any impropriety with a boy unchaperoned. 'Well,' she explained, 'the *Iliad* is about the war between the Greeks and the Trojans, when the king of Greece, Agamemnon, was forced by his brother Menelaus to declare war on Troy because the Trojan prince Paris stole his wife, Helen. The idea that she was an independent woman and free to choose her own man was a leap too far for the Greeks, I'm afraid. Helen was his property, and the fact that the handsome young Paris was a more attractive option for her than the warty old Menelaus was beside the point, it seems. The Greeks made a wooden horse and offered it as a peace gift to the Trojans, but inside the horse were Greek soldiers who came out as the Trojans slept and destroyed Troy.'

'I think I heard of that one. Was Achilles in that?' JohnJoe asked. 'I remember a book in the library in school about Achilles.'

'He was, and it was because of his heel that he was killed. That's where we get the saying to have an Achilles heel, a point of weakness.'

'What was wrong with his heel?'

'Well, his mother sought to make him immortal by dipping him in the magical River Styx when he was a baby. But in order that he wouldn't drown, she held him by his heel, and that was the only weak point in his body.'

'Let it be a lesson to us all.' He grinned. 'And what was the other one about?'

'The *Odyssey* is another epic poem, and it is the story of the king of Ithaca, a Greek island, whose name was Odysseus. He went to fight in the Trojan War and never came home. He was a great friend of Achilles, actually. It was Achilles who convinced Odysseus to go to fight in the first place. His wife, Penelope, raised their son, Telemachus, alone but was plagued by suitors who said Odysseus was dead and she should re-marry. It's the story of his efforts to get home and back to his family.'

'Is it good?' he asked.

'Very.' She nodded.

'Could I read it?' he asked, and she heard the uncertainty there. Though he was quite literate now, he still carried the stigma of being a late starter. He still decorated his letters and en-velopes with his drawings, which were excep-tionally good.

'Of course you could.' She stood and stifled a yawn.

'I'm sorry, keeping you up. You must be ex-hausted.' JohnJoe leapt up too.

'I am tired, but it's been a lovely day and evening. Thank you for inviting me, JohnJoe. It's the most exciting thing to ever happen to me.'

He inhaled and concentrated on recalling. '"Good night, good night! Parting is such sweet sorrow, that I shall say good night till it be morrow."'

'Too easy!' She giggled. *'Romeo and Juliet*. "My necessaries are embark'd: farewell."'

His brow wrinkled. 'I'm useless at this, as you know. *Hamlet?'*

'Lucky guess.' Harp winked and went up on tiptoe and kissed his cheek. 'Goodnight.'

CHAPTER 20

*H*arp struggled to breathe. Someone was on top of her, her hands were pinned over her head, and try as she might to move her head, it was stuck. She screamed and then felt other arms around her, softer, smaller.

'Hush now, Miss Devereaux. It was jus' a dream. You was havin' a bad dream. You all right, everything's all right. Wake up now. Wake up. You's safe. Hush now, you's safe.'

Harp opened her eyes to see Celia, her chocolate-brown eyes kind. She was dressed in her nightdress and had some fabric wrapped around her hair.

'There now, y'see? You're in Mr Rafferty's

house in Boston, and everythin' is jus' fine.' She smiled soothingly.

'I was dreaming. He was here, in my room...' Harp was still trying to wake up. The dream had been so vivid, so terrifying.

'It's all right. It was jus' a dream. It's over. You's safe.' Her voice was calming as she rubbed Harp's back.

Long moments passed as Harp brought herself back to the present. 'I'm sorry. I shouldn't have woken you. I'm just being silly...' Harp fought back the tears.

'Is all right. I sleep next door, so I heard you callin' out.'

'What did I say?' Harp asked.

'Just fussin' and sayin' "get off" and "leave me alone", stuff like that.' Celia paused. 'Did somebody hurt you, Miss Devereaux?' she asked gently. 'A man?'

Harp knew she should not discuss that night with anyone – the fewer people who knew about Pennington, the better – but she needed to unburden herself and there was something so comforting about Celia.

She nodded. 'He didn't...he didn't, actually... but he tried to. He came into my room when I was sleeping and...' The hot tears sprang, and the lump in her throat made speaking impossible.

'I'm glad you or someone else was able to stop him,' Celia said quietly.

'I did. I stopped him.' Her voice was unrecognisable as her own. Something about the way she said it brought a sense of understanding to the other girl.

'Good. Men like that, they only understand one thing,' Celia said knowingly. 'In that moment, a girl's gotta do what she can.'

'Did something like that happen to you too?' Harp asked, the intimacy of the situation permitting such a personal intrusion.

Celia nodded. 'Many times.' Sad weariness infiltrated the words. 'The last place I worked was the worst. My mama and me worked in the same place since I was five or six – I ain't got no pa – and she protected me. But she died two years ago, and the master of the house put me out, so I got another position. But the new place, the man, he was like that, like the man you said. He would come to my room most nights, and I couldn't do nothin' to stop him. But one day Mr Rafferty was there, in the house, doin' some kind of business, and the man made some bad remark about me as I served them, something no lady should hear, and he laughed but Mr Rafferty didn't laugh. And that day, when the boss man was gone to the cloakroom, Mr Rafferty asked me if I wanted a job at his house.'

Harp was heartbroken for this girl who had endured so much.

'He's a good man, Mr Rafferty, and Mrs Rafferty too. They good people. I ain't no nice White lady like you – not too many White folks care about a Black girl on her own with no kin to stick up for her – but they took me in and ain't nothin' bad happened to me since that day.'

'I don't have a father either. My mother raised me on her own,' Harp said, to make Celia feel less inferior, to have her understand that Harp was not the young lady of a fine house, that she was the daughter of an unmarried housekeeper, just as Celia was.

'I miss my mama every day. She was a real good lady.' Celia's eyes were bright now too.

'I can't imagine life without mine,' Harp said. 'But you're happy now?'

Celia nodded. 'Oh, yes. He took me from that house that very day, and to tell you the truth, I didn't know why he was takin' me. Part of me was afraid he would be the same as the other one, but a bigger part of me knew he wasn't like that. He loves his wife, and I ain't never seen him even look at someone else. And he was just kind – he is to everyone, to Mrs Dennis and Clayton and even the scullery maids and the house boys. Clayton's mother lived down in Louisiana. His mama was a slave, and Clayton was born a slave, but he was freed with abolition in 1865. He came north, like most young men did. Those Southern owners wasn't givin' up so easy as to let coloured folks jus' go about like free men and women, y'know? So lots of us came north. My mama and her folks did too – they were from Tennessee. But lots of them stayed. Coloured folks down there ain't got no proper doctors, and Clayton's mama was very sick last year. The Raffertys paid for her to go to a real physician in Lafayette, and she's doin' much better now. Everyone that works for them loves them.'

The word rang in Harp's ears: a slave. She'd read about slavery, of course, but the idea that it was as close as the mother of the butler in this house was shocking to her. 'And the other man, who you worked for before here, did he just let you go?' Harp asked, intrigued by the story.

Celia smiled. 'Course. When Mr Rafferty says to do somethin', people jus' do it. Even that man, the old master, he can't say nothin'. He don't want Mr Rafferty as an enemy.'

Harp debated asking the question and decided she could. 'Why is that, do you think?' Harp asked, curious now.

Celia shrugged. 'Mr Rafferty, he's powerful in this town, so it don't do no good to be on the wrong side of him. He knows everyone worth knowin', and the man I worked for, the one who came to my room, he's tryin' to do business in Boston, and bein' an enemy of Pat Rafferty ain't no good for business.'

'I'm glad you're happy here,' Harp said.

'I am. The law says I'm not as important as a White person, and down where my mama come from, in Tennessee, we ain't got no rights at all and that's the law. But Mr Rafferty don't think like that. He was friends with Booker T. Washington, you know? Mr Rafferty's Irish for sure, but he don't got no grudges based on the colour of a person's skin, and that's a rare thing in this country, let me tell you. Mr Rafferty helps them that need it, and he don't bother nobody that don't bother him.'

'But people are frightened of him?' Harp asked. 'If he's such a good man, how does he command such fear and respect?'

Celia chuckled, a deep throaty sound. 'I said he wasn't no criminal, Miss Devereaux. I didn't say he was a saint.'

Celia stood and settled the covers over Harp once more. She went to close the curtains.

'Please, leave them open. I always sleep with them open so I can see the stars.' Harp settled herself back down in her bed. The onyx clock with the mother-of-pearl face glowed in the dark. It was a little after 3 a.m. 'I'm sorry for waking you, Celia. Please try to go back to sleep. I'll be fine.'

'Good night, Miss Devereaux.' Celia withdrew.

* * *

THE FOLLOWING morning dawned bright and clear, the heat intense even at this early hour.

Celia entered Harp's room in her uniform, looking fresh as a daisy, with no sign that she was awake at all hours comforting Harp after her nightmare. Harp sat up.

'Good morning, Miss Devereaux. Breakfast is downstairs in fifteen minutes, so we'd better get you up and ready.' Celia was friendly and smiling, but nothing about her suggested the intimacy of the previous night.

'Thank you. I must have slept late.' Harp glanced at the clock. It was eight forty-five.

'Well, Mr JJ has been pacing outside for an hour, dreamin' up reasons to be on this floor when he sleeps upstairs, hoping for some sign of life from you. He even offered me a nickel to wake you up!'

That information made Harp smile. 'Well, thank you, Celia, you're very good to me. And thank you for last night...' Harp said quietly.

'Ain't nothin', Miss Devereaux. Now, you want help or would you rather dress yourself?'

'I can manage, thank you,' Harp said, and Celia gathered the laundry from the previous day and left with a smile and a wink.

Harp dressed in a navy-blue skirt and a baby-pink blouse and tied her hair back with a navy satin ribbon. She thought she should probably pin it all up in a more ladylike fashion – she was sure her mother would think so – but she wanted to go down. She slipped on her black leather ankle boots and did up the laces.

The house was busy. There were two maids on the stairs using a machine that seemed to be sucking the dust out of the carpet. She'd heard about the machine but had never seen one. She wondered if she could take one back for her mother; it would be such a labour-saving device at the Cliff House. She resolved to ask JohnJoe what they cost. Probably more than she had, but it wouldn't hurt to ask.

'Good morning.' She greeted the maids, and they curtseyed and smiled, keeping their eyes downcast.

Mrs Dennis was in the hallway at the front door, speaking to somebody, and Clayton appeared with a footman behind him, bearing a silver tray with a lid.

'Good morning, Mr Clayton,' Harp said as she descended the last step.

'Good morning, Miss Devereaux. I trust you slept well?' His voice was deep and rumbling but soft, surprisingly so for such a tall and imposing man. His skin was darker than Celia's, and his curly hair was cut short and threaded with silver. He had a broad nose with wide nostrils and full lips. He reminded Harp of a picture in a book of Mr Devereaux's of a Maasai leader. She knew the Maasai were from Kenya and Tanzania and wondered if it would be intrusive or offensive to ask Mr Clayton what part of Africa his ancestors came from.

Harp tried to imagine him being born a slave baby. He was so dignified and noble in his demeanour; the idea that anyone could regard him as inferior was anathema to her. If anything, he looked more imposing, more gracious than the many White men she knew.

'I did, Mr Clayton, thank you,' she replied.

'I'm glad, and it's just Clayton, miss.' He nodded, a small smile playing around his lips, and stood back to allow her to enter the dining room.

'Ah, Harp, don't you look lovely this morning,' Kathy exclaimed as she entered.

Pat and JohnJoe were already seated, and of Danny there was no sign – still in his bed probably. Both men looked up, and she could see from their approving glances that she had chosen her outfit well.

'Sleep all right?' Pat asked as he rose to pull out a chair for her.

'Yes, thank you very much. That's a beautiful bedroom,' she said, sitting down.

'Kathy is responsible for all the décor. If it was up to me, everything would be painted white and I'd have the same furniture for years,' Pat said. 'She's the one with the artistic eye.'

'Well, your home is truly the most beautiful

I've ever been in,' Harp said honestly, though she had been in very few houses in her life.

'JJ tells us your own house is spectacular too, though?' Kathy asked, clearly interested. 'I've always wanted to go to Ireland, but Pat can never take that much time off. I did extract a promise from him to take me for a *significant* birthday, though, and I'll hold him to that,' she said, mock stern.

'Your seventieth? Sure, we'll go then,' Pat riposted, winking at Harp.

JohnJoe grinned.

'Oh, right,' Kathy said, 'we're going to have a smart mouth today, are we? That should be interesting to see how you manage the luncheon on Saturday without me then?' She raised an eyebrow, and Pat reached over and placed his hand on hers.

'Just kidding, my love. And if you were to abandon me to the great and the good of Boston, you know it would be a social train wreck, so please don't leave me. I'm just a thick old Irish guy, like a bull in a china shop with the genteel people of Boston. You're the finesse of the operation.'

'I'll stick around for another week. After that, we'll see.' She chuckled.

JohnJoe turned to Harp. 'They go on with this all the time, as if they could be apart for five minutes.'

'Clayton,' Kathy asked, 'can you take Danny breakfast in bed and make sure he gets his eggs over easy this morning? He said that the yolks were hard yesterday. Oh, and could you ask one of the yard boys to go to O'Malley's for him? His horse came home second at Monmouth Park, and he needs to collect his winnings.'

'He's lucky he's not on gruel and hard labour in jail,' Pat said. 'Breakfast in bed, my eye. He's got a complete fool made of you.' He shook out the newspaper.

JohnJoe caught Harp's eye and grinned.

'And another thing, he owes me, so, Clayton, send his winnings my way.'

'Ah, Pat, poor Danny's been working flat out all week. Let him have a sleep, please?' Kathy asked, and Pat just sighed. 'I'll even sit beside the Monsignor at lunch next weekend.'

'All right, it's a deal.' Pat grinned, then sipped his coffee.

Breakfast was a delicious meal of pancakes and crispy bacon, over which they poured a sticky sweet substance from a bottle in the shape of a leaf that JohnJoe called maple syrup.

'It comes from Vermont,' he explained, covering her pancakes in the stuff.

'Have you been there?' she asked.

He nodded. 'It's lovely. We went hunting there two years ago. They got all sorts of bears and moose and things – it's real wild country. Beautiful, though.'

'I hope you didn't kill anything,' Harp said, shocked. She couldn't bear the idea of hunting for fun, killing some innocent animal.

'Oh, no, Harp. JJ here just cuddled the big old bears,' Pat said from behind his newspaper. 'Are you against hunting?'

'I agree with Oscar Wilde, that it is the unspeakable in pursuit of the uneatable,' she replied, knowing she should probably be more circumspect.

Pat lowered his newspaper. 'A lady who knows her own mind, JJ. I got myself one of those too. They can be troublesome, but they're worth it.' He winked at Harp to show he was joking. 'All right, enough with the chat – I got work to do. See you all later.'

He rose just as Clayton appeared with a telegram on a silver platter. Pat went to take it, but the butler stopped him. 'It's for Miss Devereaux, sir.'

'Ah, right. Here you go, Harp.' Pat took the telegram and handed it to her.

Harp opened the small envelope and felt her mouth go dry as she read the short lines therein. *Your mother and RD to marry 1 month from now. Cis + Liz*

'Harp? What is it?' JohnJoe asked.

Harp fought the feelings of panic. How could this be? Her mother would never agree to marry Ralph, not in a million years. Rose couldn't bear him, and besides, she loved Matt Quinn. Something terrible had happened. But what? Had the Devlins got it wrong? Doubtful. They would never have sent a telegram without checking the facts.

'I have to go home, right away. I need to go today... I have to...' She could hardly formulate a sentence. How on earth could this be happening? This was not possible.

'Why?' JohnJoe asked. 'What's happened?'

'I don't know, something at home. I'm so sorry, but I need to get back. I have to get back to my mother... She's all right, not ill or anything, but she needs me and I have to go...'

Before JohnJoe had time to resist, Kathy interjected. 'Of course you must go back, my dear, if that's what you need to do. I'll have someone arrange tickets. You can change yours, I'm sure, and we'll add Danny and JJ on as well. Mrs Dennis and I will have to spend the remaining hours sewing, but it can be done. Please, my dear, don't worry. We'll get you home if home is where you need to be.'

'But she can't just go. We were supposed to meet Molly and everything...' JohnJoe looked stricken.

Kathy looked at him kindly. 'I know, darling, it's very disappointing, but Harp says she needs to go, and if she does, she does. You two will be going with her, so we'll just move the dates up a little. Now, take her to the post office to send a telegram to Molly saying you can't make it this time. I'll work on sorting out tickets.'

CHAPTER 21

*H*arp walked down the street to the post office, JohnJoe by her side. Should she telegram her mother? She mulled it over as they walked. *Best not for now.* Rose clearly didn't want Harp to know about the engagement, otherwise she would have contacted her herself. It was best to say nothing for now. She should reply to the Misses Devlin, though.

JohnJoe must have known by the set of her jaw that she was in no mood for chatting. She'd told him the basic contents of the telegram but needed to mull it over herself before discussing it further. This was a catastrophe. How on earth could Ralph have convinced her? He had some hold over her, of that Harp was certain. She had no idea how, but a horrible feeling in the pit of her stomach told her it was something to do with Pennington. But what?

They went into the post office and sent the telegram to Molly, apologising that they couldn't meet up, and another to the Devlins acknowledging receipt of their telegram, nothing more. She longed to know more, but it would have to wait until she was back home. She thought about asking Matt but decided against that too. Anything she wrote would be dictated here and read and transcribed by Miss Hodgkins in the post office in Queenstown and then given to Alfie Cummins, the telegram lad, so the fewer people who knew their business, the better.

As they emerged JohnJoe said, 'We got some time before lunch. I know you're worried about your mom but there's nothing more we can do for now, so how about I treat you to a Greek New England Coffee?'

'A what?' Harp was so distracted she had trouble focusing on what he was saying.

'These two Greek brothers have started up a New England coffeehouse. They deliver coffee beans all over the city already, but now they got a place, just a couple of blocks away, where you can have a cup of coffee or a cake. How about it?'

He looked so crestfallen that she was cutting the trip short and had been so kind that she felt churlish refusing, though she longed just to be alone, to process this new wave of horrible news. It wasn't JohnJoe's fault, and he was right – there was nothing to do but wait now anyway. She might as well try to be enthusiastic at least. 'I've never tasted coffee in my life,' she said.

JohnJoe took her hand once more. 'There's a first time for everything.'

'But won't your aunt be expecting us back?'

'Don't worry about that.' He put two fingers in his mouth and emitted a piercing whistle. Immediately the group of boys who had been loitering on the corner rushed across.

JohnJoe took a small coin from his pocket. 'You're Seamus Collins' kid, right?'

A dirty boy with bare feet nodded.

JohnJoe tossed the coin at him. 'Go to Mr Rafferty's and tell them that me and Miss Devereaux are going out for lunch and that we'll see them later. You got that?'

The boy nodded. 'Yessir.' He scampered away, his tribe of urchins following him.

'Do you know everyone?' Harp asked with a smile.

JohnJoe shrugged. 'Not everyone – this is a big city – but most Irish people know us.'

The coffeehouse was a large glass-fronted building at the junction of Milk and Broad Streets.

A waitress led them to a table, and JohnJoe ordered for them. As they sat down, something hit JohnJoe in the back of the head. He spun around and immediately his tense body relaxed. He picked up a rolled-up copy of the Boston Herald.

'Gotcha! You need to pay more attention,' A young man dressed in cream trousers and an open-necked shirt grinned as a blond girl in a pink dress giggled.

'Yeah, yeah, Georgie. You got me this time, but you ain't no Babe Ruth, y'know?' JohnJoe replied, clearly with no hard feelings.

'Aren't you gonna introduce us to your girlfriend?'

'No, I'm not,' JohnJoe replied, and turned his attention to Harp. 'Sorry about him. He's one of the crew. Georgie Flynn. He's got a big mouth and a bigger ego, but he's OK.'

'What's a crew?' Harp asked.

'Oh, just the guys that work construction for us. I got one crew, Danny's got another, and a guy called Fletch has another one. We all work for Uncle Pat, but it's kinda how things work.'

'And is Babe Ruth one of your crew too?' she asked innocently.

To her surprise JohnJoe burst out laughing. 'Are you kiddin' me? Babe Ruth? You really don't know who that is?'

Harp shook her head.

'Harp Devereaux, you know a lot of stuff about a lot of stuff, but jeez, you sure do got some big old holes in your education. Babe Ruth is the pitcher for the Red Sox, best pitcher the world has ever seen. Ringin' any bells?'

Harp smiled. It was true; she had no idea about any kind of sport and assumed he was re-ferring to one of them. The last thing on earth she wanted to discuss was some bewildering American game, but this situation in the loud busy café didn't lend itself to confidential conver-sations and confidences. 'And the Red Sox are a sports team, I take it?' she tried, managing a grin at his incredulity.

'Yes, they are a *sports team*, as you put it. They're the best baseball team in the world, the Boston Red Sox, and Babe Ruth is our hero.'

'Well, consider me educated,' she said primly.

'Oh, we got a lot more to do, believe me.' He

winked at her as she sipped the frothy drink the waitress delivered.

Initially it was sweet and warm, but there was a bitterness to it that she was unfamiliar with. She grimaced.

'You don't like it?' he asked.

'I don't know. It's more bitter than I expected, but no, I think I do. I just need to get used to it.'

'When I came here first, Aunt Kathy tried so hard to get all these things for me to eat – she even went up to Chinatown to see if they had anything I'd eat – but everything made me sick. I'd been living on gruel and bread for so long, and even though I had lovely food at your house, it was plain and I didn't overdo it. Here everything had so much butter and cream and spices and things like that, my stomach couldn't take it.'

'And now? Do you like the food?' she asked. She knew she was stalling. She would have to tell him something about her sudden departure home but needed some time to formulate it in her mind. If she could keep him talking about inconsequential stuff, it would give her breathing space. 'Not just the things we are used to, but all the foreign things?'

She'd been astounded passing Chinese restaurants, Japanese, Russian, all with their own writing. She knew America was multicultural but hadn't been prepared for just how many nations were represented. Even on the streets, the dress of different nationalities was so obvious. She realised how sheltered her life to date had been.

'Oh, yeah. Me and the guys go to the North End all the time, where the Italians are. They got this thing called pizza. A guy called Lombardi set it up, and it's like a big flat bread but with all sorts of things like meat and cheese and tomatoes on it and baked in an oven... Man, you'd eat your fingers. Aunt Kathy loves it too, but we can't tell Uncle Pat – he doesn't get along with the Italians. As far as he's concerned, nothing good ever came out of Italy. Some wop made a nasty remark about Aunt Kathy's hair or something thirty years ago, and Uncle Pat never forgot it, and if he thought we liked their food, he'd lose it, so we gotta keep it quiet,' he whispered theatrically.

'What's a wop?'

'It's what we call the Italians, wops.'

'And what do they call you?'

'Mr Rafferty.' He grinned. 'If they know what's good for them.'

'Oh, I'm sure they are all in awe of you, all right,' she teased.

JohnJoe looked sheepish. 'Well, not me, but

who I am. It was so strange, Harp, when I came here, to go from being nobody to someone that people...I don't know, not looked up to exactly. Back in Ireland, I was just a kid in the way, someone nobody wanted. But over here I'm Pat Rafferty's nephew, his inner circle, and that means something in Boston.'

'He's not like I imagined,' Harp said. 'I don't know exactly what I was expecting, but he's not it. I like them a lot, though, and they clearly adore you.'

'I love him and Aunt Kathy. He's been more of a father to me than my old man ever was, I can tell you.'

Harp remembered the night JohnJoe admitted his deepest fear to her, back in 1912, when he told her that he thought his father might have sold him. 'It's worked out, and I'm glad for you.' Despite her best efforts, she could feel the tears pooling in her eyes.

Georgie and his girlfriend passed the table on their way out, Georgie cuffing JohnJoe across the head playfully. 'Why don't you two come to the Hibernian Hall Saturday night? There's a band comin' from Atlantic City, playing something called jazz. Goosey Sheehan's old lady heard them before and says they're good.'

JohnJoe caught Harp's eye. 'We'll be heading back to Ireland by Saturday, I think, but maybe next time?'

'Goin' back so soon? But didn't you just get here?' Georgie asked Harp.

'Harp, Harp Devereaux.' She introduced herself. 'Yes, a flying visit, I'm afraid.' Harp sounded as genuinely disappointed as she could. 'But I do plan on coming back, so we'd love to join you next time.' As if sailing across the Atlantic was a commonplace activity, to be done on a whim.

'OK. Safe travels, and it was nice to meet you, Harp.' Georgie departed, his pink-clad sweetheart on his arm.

JohnJoe turned to her, his face all concern. 'Harp, please just tell me. I know you're shocked about your mother and your uncle, but it feels like there's something more. I don't know. I know you don't like him, but if she has chosen him, well, isn't that enough? You said yourself you're going off to university and all of that, so you won't even be living there any more after this year, so...'

'It's not that.' Harp swallowed and the tears spilled down her cheeks.

'What is it then?' he asked gently, taking her hand in his. 'You can tell me anything, Harp.'

'I…' She lowered her voice. 'I think he's black-mailing her into marriage.'

'What? Why? What could he possibly have to blackmail Rose about?' JohnJoe was confused. 'What has she done?'

'Not her. Me.' Harp's words were barely audible.

JohnJoe leaned his head closer to hers. 'You? What about you?'

'You say I'm your best friend and I'm special and all of that, but you won't think that when you know what I am, what I've done,' Harp whispered.

JohnJoe's grip on her hands was so strong, she was sure the imprint of his fingers would remain on her.

'Listen carefully, Harp Devereaux. You are my best friend, and nothing – and I mean nothing – you could say will change that even a tiny bit, so you can tell me anything and I promise you I'll still be here beside you.' His eyes bored into hers as she looked up, the passion and intensity of his words written all over his face.

'I killed a man.' She whispered 'And Matt Quinn and my mother arranged to throw his body in a grave before someone else who was being buried so he'll never be found.'

Slowly the whole sorry tale emerged. JohnJoe never let go of her hands but let her talk. The crowds in the café talked and laughed all around them, and there was a kind of peace in the noise. There was nobody listening; there were just her and JohnJoe in the world.

He waited until she finished and then moved his chair around to sit beside her, putting an arm around her, holding her close and not caring who saw them.

'So now you know what I am, what kind of person I...' she said, pulling back from the comfort of his embrace.

He exhaled through his nose, his jaw set in fury and determination.

'I shouldn't have told you. I'm sorry...' Harp longed to run away, back to the port, back on the ship, back to her mother.

For the first time since her arrival, JohnJoe didn't look like the polished all-American young man he now was. Just for a moment, he was little JohnJoe O'Dwyer, the lad left adrift when his mother died and his father proved useless, an illiterate child.

'Of course you should have told me, and I'm so glad you did, Harp. If I seemed...I don't know, upset, it's the idea of someone hurting you. How dare he? I'll tell you what – he's lucky that blow killed him because if I got my hands on him… And I'm glad you had Matt Quinn to help you.' He shook his head, his face dark. 'You are not to feel one second's regret for him, do you hear me, Harp? Not a second. He's dead and good riddance. Men like him don't deserve to live. So all this talk of his family and it playing on your mind – forget it. His parents reared him that way, to think he could behave like that, so they don't deserve any sympathy. But this Ralph Devereaux is another matter. I know exactly what kind of person you are, Harp. A good, kind one. And if you believe I'd think any less of you for defending yourself against a monster like him, then you have me all wrong. Not only do I not blame you, I'm so proud of you. You're so brave and strong.'

'But now you see why I have to go back and stop this marriage? I'm convinced the two things are connected. Pennington and Ralph were thick as thieves before that night, and he's always been sniffing around the Cliff House. He has to accept the facts of Henry's will and his naming of me as his heir, but he hates it, and he really thinks that the Cliff House should be his. He's after my mother because she's beautiful, of course, but also because in marrying her, he gets to call the Cliff

House his. I don't know how, but that night and this marriage are linked somehow – I've never been surer of anything. And I have to stop it.'

JohnJoe thought for a moment. 'Right. Well, let's get back there as quick as we can and see the lie of the land. Whatever needs doing, Harp, you're not on your own. You'll have me and Danny, and together we'll figure this out.'

'But what will we do? We can't let her marry him! He's so awful. Honestly, he really is.'

'I believe you. But realistically there's not much we can do from here. Let's just go back, the three of us. We'll tell Uncle Pat and Aunt Kathy about the wedding and that we're invited too, so we'll stay for that and take it from there. Trust me, Harp, we'll fix this somehow, I promise. Matt, the Devlins, they'll be able to help, and we'll think of something.'

Harp looked into his face and felt relief. She wasn't alone. He believed her and he didn't hold what she'd done against her. Maybe they could fix this. She knew one thing for sure – there was no choice. She could not allow Ralph Devereaux to marry her mother.

CHAPTER 22

Kathy Rafferty called Harp into her study the following morning. Harp and JohnJoe had walked all over Boston the previous day, talking, being silent, making and instantly dismissing plans and theories as to what might be going on back in Ireland.

The Raffertys had dinner plans that evening, so they had supper with Danny, who was full of excitement at the trip. Over a delicious dish of chicken noodle soup, served with sardines on small triangles of toast, they explained everything to Danny.

Like JohnJoe he was appalled but kind. 'Jeez, Harp, what a rat, that guy. Don't you feel sorry for him, you hear me? He got what he deserved.

But as for your mom, we gotta get back there and see what we can do. I know what I'd like to do…' he added darkly.

Seeing Harp's look of panic, JohnJoe quickly interjected. 'Let's see how things are when we get back. We'll figure it out then, I promise.'

Harp had slept fitfully, dreaming of the leering Ralph at the top of the aisle with poor Rose beside him. In the dream Rose was wearing handcuffs. Harp woke properly at 4 a.m., managing not to wake Celia this time, and watched the pink dawn streak the Massachusetts sky.

The maid came and helped her to get ready. She asked Harp about her day wandering around the city, and Harp found her so easy to talk to. Girls her own age were a bit of a mystery as she had nothing in common with the girls in school, but this Black girl raised in service in Boston was someone she could identify with. She wished they could be friends.

'Would you write to me?' she heard herself ask, immediately regretting it. Perhaps Celia couldn't read or write?

'Why?' Celia seemed genuinely perplexed.

'Y-you don't have to,' Harp said, blushing to the roots of her hair as Celia brushed it.

'No, I'd like to and my mama taught me how, but why would you want to hear from me?'

Harp felt a slight relief. 'I collect letters from people who emigrate, people who stay at our guest house, and I like to hear about people's lives in faraway places. I just would like to hear how you are getting on, I suppose...' Her voice trailed off. She must sound pathetic.

'I would love that, and would you write to me too?' Celia asked, her brown eyes bright.

'If you'd like me to, then yes, of course I would.'

'We could be pen pals!' Celia exclaimed with delight. 'I ain't never got a letter in my life, and my mama would be so happy to think I had a friend far away. She wanted so much for me.'

'Well, perhaps you'll visit Ireland sometime. We have a big house, so you could stay with us, and I could show you around – it's very beautiful.'

'You know, Miss Devereaux, when you said that, I thought you was just being nice, y'know, kind to the servant. But I think you really mean it.'

'I do, of course.'

'Well, maybe someday I'll save up my dimes and quarters and buy myself a ticket on a big old ship and cross the sea and go to visit my friend

Miss Devereaux. Wouldn't that be something? Is there many Black folks where you come from?'

'I've never seen even one,' Harp said, and for some reason that caused both girls to descend into uncontrollable giggles.

As Harp went downstairs for breakfast, Kathy called her into a side room she'd not been in before. It was a smaller sitting room, decorated in shades of lilac and pink, and it looked less austere than the rest of the house. A pair of chintz-covered Queen Anne chairs sat either side of a small marble fireplace. Being summer, the grate was filled with silver cones for decoration. There was a side table with two brass photo frames, each containing beautiful charcoal drawings of JohnJoe and Danny. Judging by the boyish smiles, the drawings were done when they were around fifteen. Dotted here and there were photos of them, some of the two of them together, some with Kathy and Pat, a few done in a studio. On the wall was a certificate JohnJoe had won for his art and a picture of Danny in the uniform of a sports team of some kind. Several others were of Danny in a boxing ring, his arm held aloft by a variety of referees to indicate he had beaten his opponent. Harp knew Kathy saw the boys as her own, but this room was like a shrine to them.

The fur coat was draped across the back of one of the chairs.

Kathy had been so warm and welcoming, as well as so beautiful, but now she was something else too. Harp tried to put her finger on it but couldn't.

'Are you having second thoughts about this?' Kathy asked directly but not unkindly.

Harp thought about her response. The truth was that she was nervous of course, but any danger was overshadowed by fear at what was happening at home. 'I'm not. It will be fine. I don't think anyone would suspect a girl like me of anything. Girls are kind of invisible to the authorities anyway…'

Kathy didn't speak when Harp's voice petered out. The silence hung heavily between them.

'Right, let's try this on you then,' Kathy said, lifting the coat.

Harp was wearing a light summer dress in rust-coloured silk her mother had made, and as the coat slipped over it, she had to admit to luxuriating in the sensation of the smooth lining against her dress, though she still hated the fur. There was no indication whatsoever that the lining also contained lots of $500 notes. It had been shortened along the bottom, and now the hem fell to Harp's mid-calf. It was heavy but not prohibitively so. Immediately she felt warm, however, as she stood in the morning sun that beat in through the window.

'We ran up a coat in cotton and stitched the money to it. That's inside the lining of the fur coat. So even if the lining was torn, all you would see is the cotton – the money is between that and the fur. I don't think it makes it bulky at all, and we checked it for rustling and I think it's fine. This is the most valuable garment you'll ever wear.' Kathy laughed. 'I know it will be hard to wear in this weather, but once you get to the ship, you can hang it up in your cabin. I've arranged a single cabin for you so you'll be alone, and Pat is going to get you a padlock for the wardrobe door just in case. Danny and JJ will be with you too, so you'll be fine.'

Harp nodded. 'Thank you, and thanks for arranging the passage back. I need to get back for my mother's wedding and…' Her voice trailed off. She hated lying, but she couldn't tell these people the truth; she just couldn't.

'My pleasure.' Kathy smiled but it didn't reach her eyes. 'Do you ever think, you know, that what we're doing is bad?' the older woman asked, apropos of nothing.

'With the Irish cause, do you mean?' Harp asked, afraid she had picked up on something else.

'Yes,' Kathy said simply. Obviously the older woman took Harp's changed demeanour to be as a result of trepidation about the money.

'Well, no,' Harp replied. 'Do you?'

Kathy shook her head. 'No, I don't. But you seem, I don't know, distracted, worried. This is a lot of money, Harp, and it's important that it gets where it needs to go. We need to be sure you're comfortable doing this.'

'I am,' Harp replied, praying the woman wouldn't dig further.

'And with that in mind, I wonder what made a girl from a family such as yours want to run a risk like this?'

'What do you mean, a family such as mine?' Harp didn't mean to sound impertinent, but this was clearly a no-holds-barred conversation.

'I don't mean any offence, my dear, just that you're the child of a member of the British aristocracy, at least from your father's side. You live in a big house, the British officers frequent your mother's guest house, your uncle is a loyal British subject, working for the Crown in India, you plan to attend Trinity College... You can surely see how none of that looks like someone who would be on our side?'

'Do you think I'm not trustworthy?' Harp blazed with inner indignation. How dare Kathy cast such aspersions! She knew nothing about Harp or the Devereaux family.

Kathy smiled and placed her hands on Harp's shoulders. 'I'm not suggesting anything of the kind. But JJ is blind where you're concerned, and I just need to be sure.'

Harp swallowed. 'My father might have been one of the British aristocracy by birth, but he felt no loyalty whatsoever to them. He was a patriotic Irishman and proud of it. As for my uncle, well, I hate him and all he stands for. It's true British officers stay at our house, but what would you have us do? Refuse them admittance? You don't understand what it's like there. They don't ask – they demand. And people do as they're told or face the consequences. I hate them, I hate what they've reduced our country to, and I hate the way they treat us, the disdain and the superiority.' She swallowed. 'The way they treat the men, but the women too, like we're nothing, there to be used and abused as they wish with no repercussions.

'There are two women in our town, the Devlin

sisters – I think you and your husband know of them at least – and they are involved in Cumann na mBan, the women's army, you know. They asked me to join and to do this. I feel passionately about the idea of women's suffrage and women's education, and I think independence is inextricably linked with that. So for a myriad of reasons, it's high time the British were made to leave by whatever means necessary. So no. I don't have any moral problem with it. Sometimes just because something is the law doesn't mean it's moral.'

Kathy smiled and nodded. 'All right, Harp, you've convinced me. I agree with you, actually. Especially about us women. And as for the legal element, well, my husband wasn't always what you might call one hundred percent legitimate, Harp. Not for years and years now, but when I first knew him, he was a poor Irish guy, trying to make his way. He was smart and a natural leader, so people were drawn to him. They still are. He makes his money mostly in construction, legitimately, but there may have been a bit of booze and tobacco running in the early days to build up revenue. He only employs Irish guys. He gets contracts with the city because he has a lot of connections, and he can make certain things

happen for people who help him, if you know
what I mean?'

Harp didn't exactly, but she'd seen enough of
the way people reacted to Pat Rafferty to know
he was someone who commanded a lot of respect. 'I suppose I do,' she said uncertainly.

'But we don't do things that run contrary to
our own moral code, ever,' Kathy went on. 'Pat, JJ,
Danny and me, we are a unit. I never had children
of my own, a source of real sadness to me, but
those two boys, well, they mean the world to me.'

Harp felt for this woman. Her loss was palpable. All indignation at her questioning was gone.
Kathy needed to be able to trust Harp, not just
with the money but with JohnJoe too.

'JJ loves you. We love him. Every bit as much
as if Pat and I had conceived him and I'd given
birth to him myself. That said, I know that if JJ
had to choose, us or you, much as he loves us, he
would choose you every time. I'm not so naive as
to think otherwise.' She gave Harp a look that
spoke volumes, and deep down Harp knew this
woman was right.

'I...I'm not trying to take him from you –' she
began.

Kathy raised her hand. 'I know, but it will
happen. It was inevitable. All mothers feel the

same, I'm sure. I was lucky to have had them as long as I did. Danny's mother, my sister, has a load of kids, and she was more than happy to off-load one, so he's been mine since he was little really. And then getting JJ four years ago, well, I felt like their mother. I do feel it. But boys grow to be men and they marry and their mothers lose them – that's how it goes.' She shrugged. 'But it's not just that. Pat thinks I'm fussing unnecessarily, but I'm always worried, for both of them, actually. Danny thinks it's a lark to get into trouble with the cops, but it's not. He's got too much swagger, that boy. But more than that, I'm terrified they'll be drafted. The war is really heating up now, as you know, and Wilson says he's committed to keeping us out of it, but I don't know. And then there's the danger of sailing. The Germans sank the *Lusitania*, and that was a passenger ship, so the idea of you all being out at sea so vulnerable...'

'Well, the Germans have made a commitment not to attack any further passenger vessels, so we'll just have to take them at their word.' Harp tried to reassure her. 'And as for conscription, well, surely the American public won't stand for that? The stories coming back from the front are horrific, truly. We're seeing more and more broken men returning every day. Once word reaches here of the fate that awaits them, American families surely won't give their sons up to such slaughter.'

Kathy shrugged. 'You'd like to think so, but I honestly couldn't be confident...'

'Well, there's no way they'll ever try conscription in Ireland, you can be sure of that. They can barely contain the anti-British sentiment as it is, so to try to force Irish men into the trenches in British uniforms would be a folly that even the British wouldn't risk. If they did, the reluctant recruits would be more likely to turn the guns on their brothers in arms beside them in the trenches than the poor old Germans.'

Kathy gave an involuntary snort of laughter. 'Can you just picture it?' She chuckled as she removed the heavy coat from Harp's shoulders.

The gentle breeze through the window was so welcome after the heat of the coat.

Harp watched Kathy's beautiful face intently as she spoke, her lustrous red hair, her sapphire-blue eyes, her flawless complexion, the slight touch of lipstick.

Kathy arched one perfectly shaped eyebrow. 'I couldn't bear to lose them, Harp. I just couldn't.'

'You won't,' Harp reassured her.

'Well, my boy is so deeply in love with a girl who lives on the other side of the Atlantic, and he wasn't even my boy to begin with, so I fear I might be letting him go in some capacity at any rate.'

Harp coloured. 'He loves you, and nothing anyone could say or do would change that. No matter who JohnJoe married, you wouldn't lose him.'

'Not deliberately, I know. But men go where their hearts take them, sometimes other bits of their anatomy too, of course.' She winked and Harp blushed deeper. 'And as I said, I wouldn't fancy my chances if he had to choose. I hate the thought of him leaving, but if it was for a girl he adored, who loved him too, I could live with it. I know how he feels about you – that's as plain as the nose on your face, as my Irish grandma used to say – but how about you? I know you're young, but still – is it a two-way street?'

'It is,' Harp said, voicing it for the first time, even to herself. 'He was my first and best friend. But I don't feel like I could leave my mother, my hopes and plans for the future, any of that. Also I'm only sixteen, too young to make such decisions. I never envisioned myself settling down with anyone, to be honest, but I do...well, I have feelings for him.'

Kathy's blue eyes locked with hers. Harp felt as if her very soul was being examined. The older woman exuded love and good spirits, but there was something else, a core of loyalty and protection of her family.

'And is a friend all he can be, in your estimation?' Kathy asked.

Harp thought about it. 'I don't know,' she admitted. It was too much to process here and now.

'Is there someone else you feel strongly about?'

Harp guessed JohnJoe had told her that he worried about Brian. 'If you mean Brian Quinn, then I've explained to JohnJoe that we're more like family. Brian and I are close, it's more in a brother and sister way. I've never... Well, I've no experience whatsoever of boys or romance or any of that, and I don't feel ready.' Harp paused, something making her want to confide in this woman. 'And my mother...well, she's very ladylike and wouldn't like the idea of me having that sort of thing going on.'

'Why not?' Kathy asked. 'I'm not suggesting you two shack up together or anything, but he's eighteen and you're sixteen. Would a little ro-mance really scandalise your mama that much?'

'I think it would, to be honest. You see...' Harp felt disloyal but knew this woman would under-stand if she explained it properly. 'My mother was seduced by an older unavailable man when she was my age.' She neglected to mention that she was the result. That was nobody's business but hers, her mother's and Henry Devereaux's. 'She fought so hard against the reputation such a thing carries with it, and she's anxious that I would too. I think she'd be fearful of something like a romance, as you put it. Not that I would do anything wrong, I wouldn't, but she wouldn't like to give people anything to gossip about. That would be really important to her.'

Kathy gave a knowing smile. 'I can see why that's important. A reputation once damaged is close to impossible to repair, especially in a small place, and that is just as true here in America as it is in Ireland. Now, forgive me for contradicting your mother, but that's not the most important consideration when thinking about such matters, my dear. You are on the cusp of womanhood, Harp. Let me give you some advice.' She sat down and gestured that Harp should take the chair op-posite. 'For most girls and women, they plod along, find some nice guy and settle down, have some kids and live, if not happily ever after, at least not miserable. That's enough for most people. But you're not most people. You are unique, Harp Devereaux, uncommonly intelligent, musical talent far in excess of those much older and experienced. You are articulate and wise, so I don't feel in any way that I am conversing with a girl of sixteen. You say you're inexperienced and I believe it, but you are old beyond your years, Harp. You know what you want and how to get it. You are as yet unaware of your allure to men, but it will become increasingly obvious as time goes on. You intrigue people because you are – and I mean this as a compliment – such an oddity.'

'People have always seen me like that. No offence taken.' Harp gave a rueful smile.

'You know who you remind me of?' Kathy asked.

'No, who?'

'Jane Eyre, when she says she has no intention of fitting in, that she is "no bird; and no net ensnares me: I am a free human being with an independent will." That's a rare thing for a woman, but you have it. Do you know how I know that?'

'How?' Harp found herself realising there was much more to Kathy than she'd first imagined.

'Because I have it too,' she revealed with a conspiratorial grin. 'My husband may be the patriarch of this family, but in the words of William Ross Wallace...' She paused and let Harp finish the sentence.

'"That hand that rocks the cradle is the hand that rules the world."'

'Exactly. Women have the power, maybe not on paper, but a clever woman can outmanoeuvre any man without him ever realising what's going on. But that's exhausting, so whoever you choose, make sure he's your equal, someone who sees your intellect as something to be admired and cherished, not curbed or, worse, hidden.'

'Is JohnJoe my equal, do you think?' she asked, interested in this astute woman's opinion.

Kathy laughed. 'Well, that is for you to decide, but I can tell you, finding a guy who is willing to cross the world to keep you safe, who speaks about you and your talents incessantly, a boy who has no shortage of admirers, I might point out, but is oblivious to them all is certainly worth consideration.'

Harp smiled. Maybe Kathy was right.

CHAPTER 23

The huge ship, the *RMS Athenia,* was sailing from Boston first to Halifax and then on to Liverpool. They couldn't get passage direct to Queenstown as so many of the British liners had been commandeered for the movement of troops, so the more circuitous route was all that was available at such short notice. They had reserved a double cabin for the boys and Harp had a single cabin of her own for the voyage, which was going to take seven days because of the detour to Canada. But she didn't mind; she was going home and that was all she cared about.

The railing was crowded with passengers waving frantically to family on the quayside below.

Danny and Harp had embarked together as a couple allegedly, with Kathy dressing Harp and doing her hair and make-up to make her look older, and JohnJoe went aboard alone. He'd objected, but Pat had ruled that Danny pose as her spouse as he was older and therefore would attract less attention. The coat was heavy and stiflingly hot, but she endured it. To her astonishment, as well as their luggage, there was a large box containing one of the carpet cleaning machines she'd mentioned to JohnJoe. They'd had the Cliff House wired for electricity the previous year. It had been brought to the town as street lighting and to benefit the British military base, but anyone who could afford it had it installed in their houses now as well.

She was overwhelmed, especially when she saw how much the machines cost, but the Raffertys insisted it was a gift for Rose to say thank you for taking such good care of Danny and JohnJoe four years ago. Harp knew her mother spent so long sweeping and beating rugs for dust that this would save her a lot of work.

Pat had hugged her in the house before she left, and she knew he was genuine in his affection for her. They'd discussed her future with the Devlin sisters and Cumann na mBan, and he was so encouraging. He was heartfelt in his approval of them and her potential involvement with them. He asked her about the extent of Matt Quinn's role with the Volunteers, and when she didn't know, that seemed to earn his respect as well. The idea that a man could operate under the noses of the enemy and even his nearest and dearest were in the dark as to the true extent of his activities was a trait to be admired, it would seem.

'Dark days are coming, but the darkest hour is just before the dawn, Harp. We will get there, and in our lifetime Ireland will be free. We're so close, we can touch it, and with the help, financial and moral, from the States, it can be achieved. What a day that will be, what a day. And we'll all have played a part, every one of us with Irish blood in our veins. I'll go home then, and boy, will I celebrate. I left West Clare as a lad of seventeen, the son of tenant farmers. So many of my family were lost in the Famine, either to emigration or starvation, as they exported ships full of food from the port outside your front door. They starved us, they subjugated us, they imprisoned us. They took a battering ram to my grandfather's house, putting his family out on the side of the road in February, the depths of winter, because he couldn't pay the rent. They had no choice but go to the workhouse. My grandmother died in there, along with three of her children. And anyone who tried to speak up for us, tried to help us, was executed or transported. Only that an aunt of mine paid my passage out here, God knows what would have become of me. And mine is the typical experience. Every man and woman I meet here in Boston, they have the same story. We might seem like Americans to you – we sound it, we live a different life – but in here' – he placed his hand on his heart – 'in here we're Irish. And we're here because our people had no choice but leave. For the first time, I think I'll live to see Ireland free. I really do.' He was the most animated when he talked about the struggle for Irish independence. He wasn't just willing to pay lip service; he was willing to act.

As they left, he hugged her once more, murmuring in her ear, 'What do you call an English soldier at the bottom of the sea?'

'I don't know?' Harp replied, not realising it was a joke.

'A great start.' Pat guffawed and clapped JohnJoe on the back, drawing him in for a bear hug. 'Mind yourself now, do you hear me? Do what he says.' He nodded at Danny. 'And you,

Dannyboy, no heroics or showing off. Just get the job done and get back in one piece, all right, Son?'

'You got it, Uncle Pat.'

JohnJoe smiled and kissed his aunt, who held him tightly. 'Be careful, and get back soon. I miss you already.' She placed a hand on his cheek, and her blue eyes shone with unshed tears. 'And as for you' – Kathy drew Danny in for a hug – 'watch that smart mouth of yours. The British in Ireland are not like the cops here. They'll shoot you as quick as look at you, so keep that trap shut.'

Danny wore a bowler hat and a long coat and could have been any age from thirty to sixty. He also had wireframe spectacles and a cane, and he walked with a completely manufactured noticeable limp.

'You look like Jack Daniel.' Pat chuckled in the hallway as Kathy hugged them both one last time.

'He does,' JohnJoe agreed, punching Danny on the arm playfully.

'Who is that?' Harp asked.

'The distiller? Jack Daniel's Tennessee Whiskey?' Pat explained, seemingly astounded she'd not heard of him.

'No, afraid not.' She grinned.

Pat put his arm around Danny's shoulder and

whispered something in his ear. Danny just nodded, then they left.

They took a taxi to the port. The embarkation
process was uneventful. Nobody seemed to think
there was anything untoward about Mr and Mrs
Devereaux on their honeymoon. They were escorted to the comfortable double cabin by the
purser and told their bags would follow presently. The plan was to swap cabins once they
were at sea.

They took off the coat and stored it safely,
using the small padlock to secure the wardrobe.
Harp felt relieved to be rid of it. They then went
to find JohnJoe.

All three of them leaned on the railings.

'Remember me takin' you over here?' Danny
nudged JohnJoe. 'And you was all, ooh look at
this, look at that. Feels like a hundred years ago,
don't it?'

'Sure does. I can't believe we're goin' back,'
JohnJoe replied.

Danny lit a cigarette and stood back from the
crowd to smoke it.

'How does it feel? Are you happy to be returning to your homeland?' Harp asked JohnJoe,
still at the railing.

JohnJoe held his arm out to protect her from

an enthusiastic waver beside them. Another one shoved in beside her, pushing her roughly against JohnJoe, so they withdrew to join Danny on a seat on the starboard side overlooking the harbour where there were fewer people.

'I guess,' he answered as they walked. 'I don't know really. It's not like I'm going to see my old man or my grandfather's farm or anything.' He shrugged.

'We could take a side trip up there if you want?' Danny suggested, budging over on the bench to make room for them. 'It might be good to see him?'

Harp felt a wave of affection for Danny. For all his bravado and joking around, Danny had a heart of gold.

JohnJoe shook his head. 'No. I've not heard a word from him since the day I left. He might be dead for all I know.'

Harp remembered JohnJoe's sorrow when he told her about his mother's death, his father's re-jection and the loss of his two sisters. When she first met him, he was hopeful of being reunited with Kitty and Jane, but another aunt had taken them to England. 'Did you ever manage to track down your sisters?' she asked.

Danny had said back in 1912 that Pat would

make contact with the sister who was raising the girls. She had often thought about asking in her letters, but she remembered the pain in his eyes when he spoke of them and didn't like to raise it. She caught an unspoken conversation in the glance between Danny and JohnJoe.

'No. Well, I know where they are. But Uncle Pat tried, Aunt Kathy too, but my aunt, Mammy's sister, is married to a vicar, a Reverend Hugh Atlee, and they said we were not the type of people they associated with and it wouldn't be good for Kitty and Jane to be in contact with me or any one of the Raffertys of Boston. I wrote lots of letters, but they got returned unopened.'

Harp saw the hurt in his eyes and longed to do something to help. 'What was that supposed to mean?' Harp was indignant on their behalf.

'I think in the early days' – JohnJoe sighed – 'Uncle Pat might have had some small brushes with the law. Nothing major and it was years ago, but apparently his sister was not willing to overlook it.'

'Where do they live?' she asked.

He shrugged. 'Merseyside is the address, but I don't know what part of England that is.'

Harp thought for a moment but didn't say

anything. She had an idea but didn't want to get his hopes up.

* * *

THE VOYAGE WAS A ROWDY AFFAIR, with a group of young men and women singing and drinking and then paying for the debauchery by throwing their guts up over the side of the ship on the high seas. Harp, Danny and JohnJoe stayed much more low-key. The two-bedded cabin was quite spacious, with a little table in the middle and two port-holes, so they spent a lot of time there. Harp's cabin was tiny, barely enough room for her and her trunk.

They took their meals together in the dining room and played cards. Harp would have rather read, but Danny and JohnJoe insisted on teaching her how to play poker. To their astonishment, within a few hands she was beating them both easily.

'How are you doin' that?' Danny demanded on the third day of the voyage.

Harp caught JohnJoe's eye and smiled, then spoke slowly. "'An Ace of Hearts steps forth: The King unseen lurk'd in her hand, and mourn'd his captive Queen. He springs to vengeance with an eager pace, and falls like thunder on the prostrate Ace.'"

'What you talkin' about, Harp?' Danny was agitated; he liked his reputation as a card shark, and being beaten by a novice girl over and over wounded his pride.

'It's from 'The Rape of the Lock' by Alexander Pope?' she said, assuming it would ring some bells. Seeing his blank face, she was about to explain when JohnJoe interrupted.

'It's a poem. You sent me a book of poems last year, and it was in it. Belinda is a kind of flirty girl, and she's playing cards with two guys. In the poem you follow the game, card by card, until the last trick, on which it all turns, and Belinda wins.'

Harp laughed. 'Exactly.' She revealed a full house and scooped up all the matchsticks they were using as chips.

'I'm glad you liked the poetry,' she said quietly as Danny stood up and lit a cigarette in frustration, staring moodily out of the porthole.

JohnJoe coloured. 'I didn't understand a lot of it, but I liked that one.'

'Who's your favourite poet?' she asked.

'That's easy – Robert Burns. I can understand him, and I love the way he expresses himself.'

'Ah, the ploughman poet.' She smiled. 'And what's your favourite poem?'

JohnJoe shrugged.

Danny turned back to them then, good humour restored. 'Tell her,' he teased.

'Tell me what?' Harp asked.

'He's got a favourite poem and it's a song too, right, JJ? The guys found his diary, and he'd written the words out, and on the top –'

Before Danny could go any further, JohnJoe had launched himself on him and was pummelling him. Danny laughed hysterically, tears rolling down his cheeks as he fended off the blows of the now puce-red JohnJoe. Within seconds Danny was on his back with JohnJoe sitting on his chest.

'OK, OK… Nothing, Harp. He never wrote nothin' about no one in no poem.' Danny gasped; JohnJoe had him by the throat. JohnJoe released him and Danny staggered up, theatrically rubbing his neck.

'I'm going for a beer. After that, I need it.' He winked and cuffed JohnJoe across the head affectionately; he clearly had no hard feelings from the recent attack. 'Be good, you two. Don't get up to nothin' now,' he called as he left the cabin.

'Sing it for me,' Harp said quietly when they were alone.

'What?' JohnJoe pretended not to know what she meant.

'Your favourite poem is "A Red, Red Rose", am I right?'

He coloured, the tips of his ears even turning pink.

'Please, you have such a lovely voice. And I've played for you,' she said with a smile.

He looked at her and she could see the conflict in his mind. Then he sighed resignedly, paused and closed his eyes.

'My Love is like a red, red rose
That's newly sprung in June;
O my Love is like the melody
That's sweetly played in tune.
So fair art thou, my bonnie lass,
So deep in love am I;
And I will love thee still, my dear,
Till all the seas gang dry.
Till all the seas gang dry, my dear,
And the rocks melt with the sun;
I will love thee still, my dear,
While the sands of life shall run.
And fare thee well, my only love!
And fare thee well awhile!

And I will come again, my love,

Though it were ten thousand mile.'

When he'd finished, she just sat and gazed at him. He was an unusual mixture of strength and vulnerability, pride and humility, simplicity and complexity. He slowly opened his eyes and looked straight at her, no hiding his feelings. Kathy's words rang in her ears: *He's fallen in love with you.* And for the first time in her life, she couldn't define or put words on what she felt. It was a feeling as much physical as cerebral. Her stomach lurched, and she just knew she wanted to be close to him. She opened her mouth but no words came out.

'It's all right, Harp. It's nothing I'm sure you hadn't realised already,' he said, and his eyes were so sad, so resigned. 'I've loved you since I was fourteen, and I know you probably don't think of me like that, and you're right not to, I'm sure. I don't want or expect anything from you – having you as my friend all these years has been enough – but I suppose I had to tell you how I really felt sometime. But of course you'll be looking for someone smarter, a professor or something like that... I'm sorry for putting you in an awkward position. I...I'll just go find Danny.' Before she had a chance to object, he was gone out the cabin door, face flaming red.

Harp tried to process what just happened. On the two occasions in her life when a boy had said he liked her, it ended in him bolting off and her feeling bewildered. This time was different to last, though. While she genuinely had no romantic interest in Brian, the same was not true of JohnJoe. Why was this all so hard? In the novels, it all happened so seamlessly, but she seemed to make a dog's dinner of it. She found her mind wandering back to Queenstown, to Mr Devereaux. In so many ways, the person she was now was because of his nurturing care, his sharing of his love of learning, of books, of music. But maybe she had inherited his awful human interaction skills too? He hated mixing with people, and on the few occasions she saw him in company, it was excruciating. He just wanted to be with her and her mother.

Despite his oddness, she'd adored him but never said it; nor did he, apart from giving her an engraved pen on the day he died and telling her he knew she was a Devereaux. A year or so ago, her mother had confided that the letter Mr Devereaux wrote to her, the letter Mr Algernon Smythe delivered posthumously, told her of his feelings for her, how he'd loved her and Harp too but could never tell them. Harp had asked her mother at the time how she would have reacted had she realised his feelings before he died, and Harp would never forget her mother's reply.

'I honestly don't know, Harp. To me, Henry was the owner of the house, and while we didn't have an employer and employee relationship, I did work for him. I liked him and felt great affection for him and his quirky ways, and maybe I could have felt something else, but it was never anything I thought about. So to be honest, I'm glad he never declared himself, because if he had done, perhaps I would have rejected him. I was a different person then.'

'And when you read how he really felt about you, what do you feel now?' she'd asked.

'I've thought a lot about that, knowing what he'd done, leaving the house to you, acknowledging you as his child though you weren't, thinking back on the love and attention he lavished on you in his own way, and the way he treated me, so respectfully, with such kindness. I realised after he died that he was a very special man, and I would have been honoured to have had him as my husband.'

Harp struggled to understand. 'So you are

glad he never proposed to you when he was alive because you would have said no, but now that he's dead you feel like you would have liked to have married him?'

Rose had sighed and nodded sadly. 'That's it exactly. Life is complicated, isn't it?'

It had all seemed so unsatisfactory to her at the time, but as she grew older and began to understand the subtleties of the relationship between men and women, it made more sense.

She was pulled back to the present and to JohnJoe. The space he'd occupied was now so empty, the little table between the two beds, their suitcases stowed underneath.

What was stopping her telling him she felt the same way? Her mother and what she would think? Fear that she'd have to give up on her dreams? Fear that he'd want more than she was willing to give?

She thought about it and dismissed each reason effortlessly. Her mother would expect her to behave like a well-brought-up young lady; she could tell JohnJoe she had feelings for him and still behave properly. As for her future, JohnJoe admired and celebrated her academic dreams; he wouldn't stand in her way. And as for him pressing her to do anything she wasn't ready for, well, there was no boy on earth less likely to press his advantage.

The girls at school were forever going on about boys, this local lad or that one, and already some were even engaged. She never thought that was a life for her. When she imagined the future, it was always her alone, coming home to Queenstown to visit her mother, perhaps having a few friends, like-minded people who found the same things in life interesting as she did. But the idea of being involved romantically held no attraction whatsoever. She even skipped over the romantic parts of books. She loved Jane Eyre when she was being herself, but when she got all soppy about Mr Rochester, Harp lost interest. Increasingly she read nonfiction. But now, sitting here in the cabin in the middle of the ocean with this boy – no, this man that JohnJoe had become – she felt not like a girl any more but a woman. While her mother had prepared her for such matters as her monthly menstruation, and the horrible business with Pennington was clearly sexually violent, they had never really discussed matters of the heart. Even the relationship between her mother and Matt had come as a surprise. She couldn't imagine either of them courting or being flirtatious.

Did she really not want a relationship? If not, why did the prospect of JohnJoe returning to Boston without her fill her with such dread? Why, if she wasn't interested in boys, did she long to be physically close to JohnJoe? Why did she dream of him kissing her?

The thought of JohnJoe pouring his broken heart out to Danny made her want to rush to find him. She locked the cabin door, making sure the coat was secure before she left, and went searching for him. There was a bar in the aft on the top deck; it was likely that's where he was.

She hurried along the corridor and decided she would make better progress if she went outside and climbed the stairs on deck. As she wrestled the heavy door to the promenade deck, she spotted him, sitting on one of the benches, his arms resting on his knees, the gentle breeze ruffling his hair. His face was downcast, and he was staring at his hands.

'JohnJoe,' she said, and he looked up, shielding his eyes from the sun with his hand.

His pale skin never coloured despite the Boston sun, and she could see the freckles across the bridge of his nose were still there. His eyelashes were long and thick, naturally curling upwards, and a lighter colour than his blond-red hair. His body had filled out, and his shoulders were broad now, not those of the skinny boy who'd left Queenstown in the autumn of 1912. He shaved every day, but she could see the beginnings of auburn stubble on his cheeks and chin. He was handsome, and she knew Kathy was telling the truth when she said a lot of girls found him attractive.

'I've never been in this situation before,' she began. 'Well, that's not true, actually. Before he left, Brian said that he had feelings for me, but that conversation went badly as I never really thought of him that way. I'm really fond of him, of course, but I couldn't ever feel, well, you know, romantically interested in him. As for the idea that I'd end up with a professor, well, that's hilarious. What on earth would a professor of anything want with a small, skinny oddity of a girl from Cork, would you mind telling me that?'

He looked down once more. 'You're not an oddity. You're special, unique,' he said, his voice husky.

'Well, I think you're rather special too, and not just as a friend...' Harp could hardly believe the words coming out of her mouth and tried to imagine what her mother would say at such forwardness.

He glanced up, and she saw the hope in his eyes. 'What are you saying, Harp?' he asked.

She flushed. 'I…I'm saying that I feel differently about you than I do about Brian, or about anyone else. I love you as a friend, of course – I always have. But now there's something else, something different. I'm not sure what to call it, but I know I hate the thought of ever being parted from you.'

'But are you saying you could think of me… romantically?' he asked so tentatively it almost broke her heart.

'I could,' she replied softly. 'I do.'

JohnJoe stood, and his face lit up with incredulous delight. 'Really? For real? Not just because you feel sorry for me?'

Despite the seriousness of the situation, Harp laughed. 'Why on earth would I feel sorry for you?'

'Because you can see I'm in love with you and you don't want to hurt my feelings?' he said honestly.

'I don't want to hurt your feelings, but also I… I love you too. Not just in a friend way, but in like…' She exhaled impatiently; for someone so verbose, words were failing her.

'Like this?' he asked gently, his hands now on

her hips. She saw the gold St Christopher medal glinting around his neck and recalled Molly giving it to him back in Ireland. She said St Christopher was the patron saint of travellers and that JohnJoe would need it more than she would. He never took it off.

Harp moved slightly forward and found her arms snaking around his neck. She felt him draw her closer. JohnJoe dipped his head and tentatively kissed her lips. She wished this moment could last forever. As his lips pressed softly against hers, she opened her mouth slightly, and this time he kissed her deeply and passionately. She was glad of his arms around her as she felt her legs might give way beneath her. On and on they kissed, and she longed to remain there, on the ship with him, forever, to never again have to leave or see another living soul.

CHAPTER 24

*T*he ship docked in Liverpool, England, at 6 a.m., and the sailing to Ireland was not till the following day. Kathy had booked them into the Adelphi Hotel in the city. Harp slept remarkably soundly considering it was the first time in her life she'd slept alone in a hotel room that wasn't the Cliff House. It was refreshing to be in a room that wasn't moving after the long journey, though she missed the closeness of the boys. Hanging in the voluminous wardrobe was the fur coat. Nobody had remarked upon it or looked at them in any way askance during the voyage from Boston, but she was all too aware that that was not going to be the difficult part of the journey. Getting from England to Ireland and from Dublin to Cork under the watchful eye of the British was the tricky bit, but she felt confident. She could play the aristocratic young lady easily, and her accent could cut glass if necessary.

As she lay there in the early morning, thinking about everything that had happened since she was last at home, she felt like she'd grown up more in the last two months than in the last two years. That fateful night with Pennington had changed everything, but she felt better able to cope with whatever came next now for some reason. Perhaps it was travelling to Boston alone, or having JohnJoe and Danny by her side, or the prospect of getting involved with the Devlins, but she felt optimistic that the Ralph Devereaux situation would be dealt with satisfactorily, though how she had yet to figure out.

Not only had she Danny and JohnJoe, but while Matt Quinn might not have been in a position to openly declare his love for her mother, the fact that he adored Rose was without doubt. He wouldn't stand by and allow this abomination of a marriage to go ahead; he couldn't, surely? Between her, Matt and the Boston boys, not to mention the Devlins and Matt's Volunteer connections, they could deal with her despicable uncle.

She threw back the covers of her small but comfortable bed and felt a pang for Celia. Though their acquaintance was short, Harp had forged a real connection with the other girl. Before leaving, she gave Celia a present, a little gold chain with an angel on it. Her mother had seen it in a shop in Cork and thought Harp might like it. Rose wouldn't mind if Harp parted with it, though; it was just a trinket. Celia had been so happy. She in turn gave Harp a gorgeous handkerchief with her initials, HD, embroidered beautifully on the corner. The girls had parted with promises to write and someday see each other once again.

Harp rose and dressed, choosing a lovely wine blouse today, with a cream lace trim around the neck and cuffs, and an ivory silk skirt with a lace overlay. It was an old one of her mother's, altered and spruced up for the trip, and Harp felt very grown up in it. Celia had shown her how to do her hair, and Kathy had insisted that she take the curling iron with her, claiming she could easily replace it.

She giggled at her reflection as she brushed her hair, the sunlight streaming in the windows highlighting the coppers and blond. She wondered what her mother would make of this new sophisticated Harp. She curled and pinned her hair and added a touch of powder to her cheeks.

She knew her mother saw her as a child, but she wasn't that any more; too much had happened. Her innocence was gone, but she had no sadness for it. She'd never felt like a normal child anyway. Perhaps a well-read, intelligent, thoughtful adult would be a person the world could accept better than those traits in a child.

As she pinned her cream hat with the burgundy flower on her head, she wondered if her mother would know about her and JohnJoe. Was it written all over her face? She would tell her, of course; not to do so would be impossible. But she knew how her mother felt about young ladies and their reputations.

Her mother's viewpoint was forever coloured by the fact that she fell afoul of Ralph's seduction when she was just seventeen herself, and were it not for the fear of scandal on the part of old Mrs Devereaux and the inherent kindness of her son Henry, both Rose and Harp could have faced a much harsher fate. The world was not kind to unmarried young women who sinned like that. She could just hear the Redemptorist priests going on about it at the mission Mass held once a year. The visiting priests would come, and each night a different topic was driven home forcefully to the people of the parish. The one about purity and sins of the flesh was particularly vehement, and there was no softness or compassion or understanding there. Sinning indeed. Why was the woman branded the sinner? Marked as the harlot? What about the men? It took two people to conceive a child, but the mothers were damned while the fathers got off scot-free. It was just one more in the bewildering number of inequalities endured by women every day.

Up to this time in her life, she couldn't understand why women and girls risked sex outside of marriage. There were of course those misfortunate women who were raped, but she'd heard of many who chose to have sex with men of their own volition. The consequences seemed so dire if things went wrong that she'd never understood why they did it, but when JohnJoe kissed her, she felt something she had never experienced before. For the first time, she understood the desire people had to be together completely, and realised how hard it was to resist. She would resist, of course. Besides, JohnJoe would never do anything that would jeopardise her or her reputation. But she knew for the first time what that sacrifice meant. It surprised her, the primal nature of it. Human beings were just like the beasts of the field, compelled by some powerful and ancient longing of life for itself to unite.

She put her fitted powder-blue jacket on before going downstairs. She'd never felt pretty before; she always thought she was too slight and odd to be attractive. The boys in school seemed to prefer the bigger girls with visible busts and curls in their hair. She always felt like a little bird beside them. But wearing the lovely clothes Mammy made, doing her own hair and make-up and having JohnJoe love her had made her feel like a different person.

She walked down the large sweeping carpeted staircase, the lobby below milling with people, and made her way to the dining room. The room was beautiful, thickly carpeted in gold and blue with heavy navy-blue damask drapes falling from the floor-to-ceiling windows. There was a huge buffet table laden with pastries, fruit, yoghurt and breads of all kinds, and the liveried staff circulated, offering hot breakfasts. The food on the ship was nice, but Harp was queasy a lot, so this was the first time she felt actually hungry in over a week. Like the big hotels in Boston, anyone could be discussing anything and nobody would take the slightest interest; it was refreshing compared to the stuffy nosiness of Queenstown.

Harp noticed how they curled the butter into little balls, setting it on a bed of ice to stop it melting. She observed everything to tell her mother; perhaps they could use some of the ideas at the Cliff House.

JohnJoe was scouring the entrance for her and waved enthusiastically when she appeared. A broad grin split his open, kind face as she sat down.

Danny made a low wolf whistle. 'Well, look who's all grown up?' He winked. 'You're a beauty, little Harp, like that girl in the paintin' Aunt Kathy has over the fireplace in her study – you know the one?'

Harp did know and was flattered, but the idea that the *Woman in White* by Raimundo de Madrazo y Garreta looked anything like her was a load of poppycock. It was just Danny being his usually flirty self.

'Ah, stop it, will you.' She brushed off his compliment with a friendly cuff on the arm.

'He's right for once,' JohnJoe said sincerely. 'You always look lovely, but something about you today – you look so beautiful, honestly, like a painting.'

'Well, you're a right pair of flatterers, that's for sure.' She grinned as a waitress appeared and took their order. She ordered bacon and eggs, and the boys got kippers and kedgeree. They talked easily as they enjoyed the delicious breakfast.

'OK, lovebirds,' Danny announced after finishing his food and placing his napkin on the empty plate. He stood up, shrugging his jacket on. He always dressed to the nines, and today was no exception. His charcoal-grey three-piece suit, complete with gold pocket watch and scarlet-red silk tie and pocket square, fit him like a glove. He still had the beard, but now it was neatly trimmed and made him look, Harp thought, like a dashing pirate. On the boat several young ladies and their eager mamas engineered it to take their stroll about the deck when Danny was around, and Harp spotted them often giggling or whispering in corners only to stop and pose when he arrived. He was free with his charm, smiles and winks, and the girls blushed under his attention. Even the waitress made it her business to come and clear the table immediately, glancing coquettishly from under her lashes at Danny, though the table beside them had been vacant for a good twenty minutes and nobody had cleared it yet.

He was good-looking in a way that was undeniable, but she didn't find him so. It was strange. JohnJoe wasn't as exotic as Danny, with his dark hair, swarthy skin and flashing eyes, but to her he was infinitely more attractive.

'You two gotta tear yourselves away from each other today. Me and JJ got some business to attend to. Uncle Pat has some contacts here that he wants us to meet, some business opportunities in the future, so you can go shoppin' or whatever it is girls do and we'll meet you back here for dinner, all right?'

She'd heard Pat mention a need to supply building products and even crews in Britain in the event of enemy bombardment, and he had a contact that might be able to put him in line to do that. It seemed an enormous undertaking to be involved in construction on both sides of the Atlantic, but Pat Rafferty didn't seem to think it was an issue. She would miss JohnJoe – they'd spent almost every moment of the last week together – but she was happy to let him go. Besides, she had plans that day.

'I'm going to go to the library, actually,' Harp announced. 'There are several Carnegie libraries here in Liverpool, but I'd particularly like to see the Kensington Library because there's a quotation over the lintel by Sir Francis Bacon that reads, "Reading maketh a full man, conference a ready man, and writing an exact man.""

Danny failed to hide his smirk. 'Of course you would. I mean, in a city of bars and clubs and shops selling pretty fancy stuff for girls, who wouldn't want to go see some old guy's quotation on a stone?'

Harp was used to his good-natured teasing. Danny was a philistine and proud of it.

'He's not just some old guy.' JohnJoe rushed to her defence. 'It's Sir Francis Bacon, the Member of Parliament for Liverpool in 1588, but in many ways, he is the father of libraries because he designed the first cataloguing system.'

Danny outright guffawed. 'Oh, great, now I got two book experts to deal with. Hey, Harp, don't be fooled – he ain't no intellectual, let me tell ya that. He's just showin' off to impress ya.'

'Ignore him, JohnJoe. Just because there's more culture in yoghurt than there is in Mr Coveney here.' She sighed and JohnJoe relaxed.

'All right, lover boy, time to do some real work.' Danny swallowed the last of his coffee and gave Harp a peck on the cheek. 'So we'll see you back here later. You take care now, Miss Devereaux, though how much trouble you could get into in a library, I dunno, but knowing you...' He grinned.

'I'll be fine, don't worry.'

JohnJoe looked reluctant to let her out of his sight. Since that night they'd kissed, they'd been together constantly. Nothing else had happened apart from lots of kissing, but after a man-to-man talk to which Harp was not a party, Danny had discreetly moved to Harp's cabin and Harp and JohnJoe stayed together in the twin one. Obviously if anyone knew about that, they would be in deep trouble – nice young ladies did not do such things – but Harp just wanted to be beside him all the time. They lay in their separate beds, just feet apart each night, talking, and it was heaven. He turned his back while she got into bed, and she did the same. The beds were close enough together that they could hold hands, though.

'Go on. I'll be careful, I promise.' She smiled at him.

'Are you sure? Would it be better if you just stayed here for the day? I hate the idea of you wandering around Liverpool alone.' JohnJoe was clearly torn.

'JohnJoe, I'm sixteen, not six. I'll be fine. Please do whatever you need to do, and I'll see you later.'

Harp stood, and Danny almost dragged JohnJoe away.

She had never been alone anywhere before, it was true. But while it was frightening, it was also exhilarating.

She telegrammed her mother from the telegraph office conveniently located for guests' use in the corner of the lobby, letting her know of their arrival. They would take the train down to Cork from Dublin and then catch another to Queenstown.

All well. See you on 29th. Harp.

She left the telegram office and crossed the lobby to the main reception desk. A young lady dressed beautifully in a chocolate-brown skirt and coffee-coloured blouse smiled as she approached. 'How may I help, madam?' she asked pleasantly. Harp wasn't used to being addressed as an adult.

'I was looking for a way to find an address for a Reverend Hugh Atlee of Merseyside.' She tried not to blush. 'Is there a directory I could consult or something like that?'

'Well, I think we can do better than a directory – I'm not sure one even exists, actually.' She smiled at Harp, who loved listening to the melodic Liverpudlian accent. 'But there's a vicarage at the end of this street, and I'm sure Reverend Hawkins will know him. Or if he doesn't, he could direct you to someone that would? I expect all vicars know each other.' She grinned.

'Thank you, that would be most helpful.'

'So it's out the door, turn left and keep walking. At the corner you'll see St Barnabas' Church, and the vicarage is behind it, a red-bricked house. Just knock there, and I'm sure someone will help you.'

'Thank you very much.' Harp turned.

The porter at the large glass hotel doors, dressed impeccably in the plum and gold colours of the hotel staff, opened it for her with a nod.

The instructions were easy to follow, and she found herself enjoying the walk. Such freedom was a new phenomenon in her life, and she felt very grown up. Liverpool was resplendent in the morning sunshine. Everywhere she looked there were men in uniform, some injured, others home on leave from the front, she assumed. The streets were busy with trams and horse-drawn carts delivering supplies to the huge array of shops and businesses. As she walked she glanced left and right through ornate windows into shops and cafés. Canopies covered the strollers from the sun or a passing shower, and Harp wondered if the people who went about their business in this English city had any real understanding of the fate of the Irish under their rule. She had no issue with any of these people, but why on earth, if one lived in such a lovely city, would they feel the need to subjugate another people across the Irish Sea? Colonialism was something she could never understand, particularly the colonisation of a place so similar to one's original country.

She didn't agree with the British rule of India or Australia, for example, but she could see what was in it for them: access to products that could not be produced in England, willing assistance in the event of a war. But Ireland and England were so similar, and goodness knows the occupation of Ireland could only be seen from the British perspective as a giant pain in the neck.

The Devlin sisters had told her about the Liverpool Volunteers, a group of men and women who'd come over to Dublin last Easter to assist in the Rising. Liverpool had always been the most Irish of British cities. Cissy and Liz were particularly enamoured of Rose Ann Morgan, a Liverpudlian woman who joined Cumann na mBan and ran as a courier during the Rising at great personal risk.

Liverpool was a major port, and so the level of

military presence was greater than elsewhere, she suspected, but it didn't intimidate her in any way. For some reason the British soldiers here seemed harmless, unlike the menacing presence of Crown forces at home.

A group of young men in uniform walked towards her, one of them lanky with red hair, and for a second, she thought it might be Brian. Of course it wasn't, but he came to mind, and with the memory occurred a feeling of dread. She wished he'd make contact. Perhaps he had while she was gone; that would be such wonderful news. But the fleeting joy at the prospect was quickly quashed. She'd asked her mother to telegram if he did, so the fact that Rose hadn't must mean there was still no word. If he even sent a one-word telegram saying he was all right, it would be enough. Though what would he think when he realised she had become involved with JohnJoe?

The reality of their situation hit her like an icy wave. Out on the sea, with nobody to disturb them, she and JohnJoe were perfect. He loved her and she loved him. But how would it work on dry land? He lived in America, and she was tied to Ireland. She shook the thought off; there was

enough to contend with for now without worrying about that.

She came to the church and did as she was instructed, easily finding the vicarage behind. The
house was immaculately kept. The small lawn
was as green as a billiard table, and each win-
dowsill had a flower box spewing lilac-coloured
petunias. The door brasses were polished and the
windows gleamed. The front door was wide and
solid wood with stained-glass panels.

She had prepared a speech and hoped she
could deliver it properly. Talking to strangers was
still her least favourite activity on earth, but she
needed to do this for him after all he was doing
for her. She took a deep breath and with a gloved
hand gave three hard knocks on the door.

A woman emerged and Harp instantly relaxed. She was like a granny in a story book, all
round. She had grey curly hair and round glasses,
and her figure seemed solid and rotund, though
she was less than five feet tall. She wore a long
dark-green dress buttoned up to the neck; even
on someone as elderly as this woman, it looked
old-fashioned.

'Good morning, dear, can I help?' she asked
kindly.

'I...em...I hope so...' Harp stumbled, and

willed herself not to blush. 'I was looking for an address for a vicar in Merseyside, and the lady at my hotel thought you might be able to help me?'

'I will if I can.' The woman smiled. 'What's his name, dear?'

'Reverend Hugh Atlee.'

The woman's brow furrowed slightly and her lips pursed in thought. 'I think I do know them. They are out Birkenhead direction, if I'm not mistaken? My husband and I met them at a charity function, if I have the right people. I think they have a niece who works in Elegant Lady Hats on Bridge Street. What is her name now?' The woman gazed up and tried to remember. 'I got a hat there for my son's wedding, and she recognised the name when I asked her to send the bill. She was very friendly, actually. Lovely looking girl, copper-coloured hair. Ooh, I can't think...'

'Kitty?' Harp suggested. Jane would be still too young to have a job in a hat shop.

'Kitty...no, I don't think it was... Katherine!' she announced, delighted at her memory. 'Yes, Katherine was her name. As I say, she remarked upon it when I said my name, and she told me her uncle was Reverend Atlee and that he and his wife had taken her and her sister in when they were little girls. If you look for the vicarage on Argyle Street, that's them, I'm almost sure.'

Harp thought quickly. It was undoubtedly JohnJoe's sister. She'd gone by Kitty as a child, but it sounded like the reverend and his wife were quite snobbish, judging by the way they rejected the Raffertys, so changing her name from Kitty to Katherine would be in keeping with that. 'Thank you so much. I really appreciate your help.' Harp smiled and went to leave.

'You're Irish, I assume, from your accent?' the lady asked, not unkindly.

Harp paused. She'd never experienced any anti-Irish sentiment personally, but JohnJoe had told her enough about how some people in Boston looked down on the Irish and she'd seen enough of the superiority of the British officers to know that for a portion of the British population at least, they saw Irish people as very much beneath them.

'Yes,' she said proudly. 'From Queenstown in County Cork.'

'And have you met the Reverend Atlee and his wife?' she asked, and Harp could sense a hesitancy there.

'No. We have a mutual acquaintance who

asked me to pass on their regards.' It was a lie but one she felt necessary.

'Well, as I say, I've only met them once or twice at the most. But...well, on one occasion, that charity event it was, Mrs Atlee was speaking about a recent public controversy regarding a cartoon in *Punch* magazine depicting an Irishman as a dim-witted drunkard. She was defending the stereo-type, saying all sorts of nasty things about the Irish – you know the sort of thing, I'm sure. Well, my husband's mother was a Maureen O'Doherty from County Donegal, so he took issue with her and, well, it got a little heated. My mother-in-law was a lady to her fingertips and very proud of her Irish heritage. So to say Mrs Atlee dislikes your fellow countrymen would be to understate the case somewhat. Forgive me, my dear, if I've spoken out of turn, but I just felt I should warn you.'

Harp warmed to the woman even more. She had a kind heart. 'Thank you. I've never met her, and by the sounds of it, that's a good thing. Per-haps I won't seek her out after all. But here's a little information that you may not have known.' Harp leaned closer and whispered, 'Mrs Eileen Atlee is in fact a Rafferty from County Clare, so she's a born-and-bred Irish woman.'

The older woman looked at first shocked and then descended into a laugh that convulsed her whole body. 'Wait till I tell my Rodney this evening when he comes home for his tea. He will enjoy that.'

Harp strolled back to the hotel in the sunshine, composing the letter in her head. Once back she took some hotel notepaper and began.

Dear Kitty,

My name is Harp Devereaux, and I am a friend of your brother, JohnJoe. He has been trying to get in touch with you for years but was unable to do so. I know he is really most anxious to be back in contact with you and Jane, and he speaks of you both with great fondness. He lives in Boston, USA, now, but he will be staying with my mother and me at the Cliff House, Queenstown, County Cork, Ireland, for the next few weeks. So if you would like to write to him there, I know he would be very happy to hear from you.

Kindest regards,

Harp Devereaux

She addressed the letter to Katherine Atlee, assuming she now went by her aunt and uncle's name, Elegant Lady Hats, Bridge Street, Liverpool, and went downstairs to post it.

She set out again once she'd done the job,

hoping she was doing the right thing and that Kitty would get the letter and would write. She could just imagine JohnJoe's delight to be back in touch with his sisters. The aunt, Pat Rafferty's sister, sounded awful. She hoped Kitty and Jane had not had a terrible time at her hands.

She spent the rest of the day happily poking around the Francis Bacon library, and it was sheer bliss.

CHAPTER 25

*R*ose sat opposite Ralph in the dining room of the Cliff House, where he insisted they breakfast together, and tried not to wince as he clicked his fingers at the new waitress. The young woman was serving breakfast to a full dining room, and it was her first day. Ralph refused to allow Rose to help her, and the whole thing was a shambles. Rose had tried reasoning with him, saying that they didn't need all the extra staff he'd hired, but he snapped that it was unbecoming to have his wife skivvying like a common maid and so insisted she act the lady of the manor. Standards were slipping and she hated to see it, but if she tried to do anything, he went mad. The money that was going out in wages now was cutting so deeply into the profits, but he didn't seem to care. All over the town he was running up bills, splashing the cash about as if it were confetti.

His thick, wavy, dark hair was perfectly coiffed and oiled, and the dark shadow of beard was barely visible on his smoothly shaved face. He'd grown a moustache, a thick bushy one as was popular now, and it too was oiled to perfection. Below the dark hair on his lip, his full lips curled cruelly.

He was dressed in yet another new suit, the bill for which would no doubt arrive to the Cliff House from the tailor in Cork, and it was well cut. The waistcoat fastened over the beginnings of a paunch, and the sharp white shirt collar hid what was becoming a jowly jaw. Ralph was so vain. He thought himself quite the ladies' man and spent a huge amount of time and an extortionate amount of money, her money, on his appearance.

He'd even employed the lazy, bad-tempered Katie Lucey for the position of housemaid. She already came to help her mother with the laundry, and Rose knew Harp would hate the idea that Emmet Kelly's girlfriend was now in the house full time.

She cringed and fought the urge to assist the young waitress, who had just sent an entire tray of china crashing to the floor. The last time she went against Ralph, things ended badly. She'd covered the bruise on her face as best she could with make-up but feared it was still evident.

'Coffee,' he barked impatiently at the girl without looking up from the newspaper.

He was punishing Rose; she knew it. He'd come up from the hotel a few days earlier, full of whiskey paid for by the British officers no doubt, and came straight to the kitchen. She'd never heard him come in. He was furious when he found her sitting at the table with Matt, having a cup of tea. Once Matt left, reluctantly it must be said, Ralph decreed yet another thing that was unbecoming of his wife – to associate socially with the working classes – and forbade Matt inside the house again.

Henry's brother made her flesh crawl. Once he'd issued his instruction on the subject of Matt, he'd moved closer to her. The reek of whiskey and cologne was nauseating, and she ducked away, saying something about needing to hang the tea cloths up to be dry for the morning.

'We'll have to have more people to run this.' He'd waved his hand dismissively around the kitchen. 'In fact I think we'll move out of here, let this run as an income source. It's not right that we should have to live beside the sort of riffraff that come here. I've my man in Cork looking for a suitable property, one that accurately reflects our status.'

He had notions that he was now the lord of the manor; the reality was that he was in fact poor as a church mouse, which he conveniently forgot. He was deluded and convinced he could just walk away from the Cliff House, dragging her with him, and they would do no work, spend money like water and live in the lap of luxury.

'I don't want to leave here, and I do want to stay running the business,' she'd said calmly, de-spite seething with resentment that he would have the audacity to order her about. 'I enjoy it, and besides, we can't afford to employ people to do everything. We are still a young business and need to reinvest the profits to bring the whole house up to standard. There is still a lot to be done.'

She hoped she could get it through to him that there weren't unlimited funds. Sure, she'd saved assiduously since the house opened, investing frugally in the property each year while squir-relling away some money for Harp's future a little at a time. 'We've yet to convert the stables,' she explained, 'and the lawn needs reseeding. I was thinking of building a pergola in the garden and serving afternoon tea, not just for overnight guests but as a supplementary business. I know they do it in the hotel, but the dining room there is dark and not very welcoming, and I thought people, ladies mainly, would enjoy the garden while they had a cup of tea.'

'No.' He stood with his back to her, looking out into the dark night.

Indignation bubbled within her. How dare he? He was entitled to nothing, and yet here he was, behaving as if he were the owner of the whole operation. This was her business, hers and Harp's, and the audacity of the man left her almost breathless. 'What do you mean, no?' she managed.

'I mean no. Negative, contrary, refusal, rejection. No. We will not be doing any of that. In fact, I'll need access to the accounts – there are some things I need to sort out.'

'That won't be possible,' Rose said through gritted teeth.

He turned, his lips curled in a cruel smile. 'You will do as you're told unless you want to finish your days at the end of a rope, with that sly undertaker on one side of you and your daughter on the other.'

The words slid over her like cold silk. How she despised this man. Something inside her snapped. 'Is this how it is going to be? You threatening me at every hand's turn? I won't have that, Ralph, I just won't. I agreed to marry you, you're getting what you want, but I won't have this held over me every minute of the day for the rest of my life.' She fought the urge to scratch his face.

She wasn't expecting the blow, and it sent her reeling. The back of his hand connected painfully with her cheekbone, his heavy signet ring doing the damage. She staggered backwards and banged her hip hard on the dresser. She barely righted herself and stood, her hand to her injured face, incredulous.

'You will not speak to me in that tone of voice, am I clear? Nor do you issue instructions on what you will and won't do. You will do exactly as you are told, what I say, when I say it.' His voice was artificially mild and detached, but she could see he was seething. 'You will give me the details of the accounts, you will not allow that Quinn back into this house, and you will not do any more skivvying.' He turned and in his most dismissive, bored tones went on. 'Please do not be dull about this, Rose. You are getting a good deal, if only your dim-witted brain would allow you to process it. Marriage to one of the Devereaux brothers, ownership of the finest house in Queenstown, a position in society that would have been hitherto unavailable to you. Try to see the good side.'

She fought back the tears. How could this be happening? *Henry*, she silently whispered, *protect us now, please, protect us from him, this devil incarnate.*

He cited ownership of the house as a perk of the deal in her marriage to him. She and Harp already owned the house; he was the one gaining the Cliff House. Her whole head throbbed with the pain of the blow as he went on.

'Now, on the matter of conjugal rights, bear in mind I will be taking mine. You and I are not strangers in that regard, and as I recall, you were most eager the last time, so if you could summon some of that girlish enthusiasm, it would be more pleasant for you. But know this – it will happen either way.' He'd turned on his heel and left the kitchen.

She'd been awake most of the night, tossing and turning, unable to sleep. Her face hurt, a throbbing pain that seemed to envelop her entire head. And as the pale morning light painted the Queenstown sky, she knew she had no choice. He held all the cards. He'd waited until Harp was gone to America to show his hand, and she knew then that she was trapped.

The one bright spot in this whole mess seemed to be the departure of Major Grant. He'd never visited the Cliff House again, and according to Matt, he'd asked a few questions round and about but seemed satisfied that the disappearance of Captain Robert Pennington was just that, a man who'd had enough and went AWOL instead of returning to his regiment. It was a common enough occurrence, and the fact that Joe Cummins, the stationmaster, thought he did see a man matching the description of Captain Pennington board a train for Cork on the day he vanished seemed to seal the deal. Joe Cummins was an IRA volunteer and so his recollections were most likely fabricated as a favour to Matt, but it seemed to have worked.

She could not see Matt any more, much as she longed to. He wasn't going to be happy about it, but she sent a message to him to stay away. His presence antagonised Ralph, and if Matt saw the bruise on her face, he'd go mad. It was best to keep them apart.

How she loathed Ralph and was dreading the wedding. She wondered if Harp had somehow heard about it. It would explain why she was coming home early. Rose had hoped to have it done before Harp returned from America, knowing her daughter would refuse to accept her decision, but now Harp was going to be here before the wedding so she'd need to convince her not to make a fuss. Marrying Ralph, no matter how repugnant a prospect, was the only way. Harp would have to understand that.

The waitress poured his coffee with a shaking hand, spilling some. 'Can I get you anything else?' she asked as he glanced up from the paper.

He put the paper down and smiled. 'What's your name?' he asked.

'Pearl, Mr Devereaux, sir,' she said, her face puce and her eyes like a dazzled hare's.

Rose knew she was one of the Walsh family. The father had been killed in a fishing accident, and the mother had seven children to raise. Pearl was the eldest at fourteen.

'You are dismissed,' Ralph said, and returned to his paper.

Pearl glanced at Rose, uncertain. Did he mean from his presence or from the job or what, her look asked.

Rose gave a slight nod in the direction of the kitchen. She knew she would have to handle this. The girl departed.

'Ralph, dear,' she said. The effort of smiling hurt her face, but she needed to be on good terms with him.

He folded the paper and placed it on the table, his face a mask. He was so transparent in so many ways, so snobbish, so vain, so downright arrogant, but when he chose to, he could be a study in guarded reticence.

'Shall we go for a stroll in the garden? It's a beautiful day. We can let the girls clear up in here?'

He glanced in distaste at the dirty dishes on the tables. 'Very well. We have some matters to discuss anyway.'

'Fine.' She smiled again. 'I'll just pop in the kitchen to make sure all is well and meet you outside.'

She retreated to the kitchen where Mrs Lucey was just leaving with that day's bedsheets and towels. Rose turned her face but it was too late; the all-seeing piggy eyes of the older woman spotted her bruise. Mrs Lucey was stout and short, with a lined, weather-beaten face. Her hands were like leather from years of taking in laundry, and the hardship of her life had rendered her entirely without empathy for anyone. She was a widow with six children and was shameless in their promotion. She'd got both her sons, bad-tempered, unkempt fellows, apprenticeships with a local builder, and her eldest daughter had fallen pregnant to the only boy of a large farm outside of town. The farmers were none too pleased with the match, but propriety dictated that he marry her with all haste. Rumour had it that Mrs Lucey was behind the entire thing, especially as the girl tragically miscarried two weeks after the wedding. Katie was next.

'What happened to you at all?' Mrs Lucey asked suspiciously.

'Oh, em...' Rose thought quickly. 'Nothing. I was carrying a bundle of books upstairs and couldn't see where I was going and bumped into the door. Lazy man's load.' She grinned self-deprecatingly.

'Bumped into the door?' Mrs Lucey wasn't going to let it go. 'But sure if you were carrying the books, how could you have done that?'

Rose's brow furrowed. 'Well, I dropped the books, and bending down to pick them up, I bumped my face. Now, is that all for today, Mrs Lucey? You took the linens from the gable room, did you? And the extra towels from the bathroom on the landing?'

'I did.' She nodded. 'But are you sure you don't need to see Dr Lane about that? It looks nasty.'

'Honestly, it's nothing. Probably looks more dramatic than it is. See you tomorrow, Mrs Lucey.' Rose tried to usher her out.

'I'm so glad Mr Devereaux hired my Katie.' The woman refused to be shooed out. 'She is mad looking for work. Herself and Emmet are setting the date this Christmas, and she could use the money. He's after being stationed in Midleton, which is great, and he's getting on well. He has real prospects, that lad, but it will be great for them to get a few bob behind them, y'know, before the wedding like, before the babies come – you know yourself.'

Rose could just picture the awful Emmet Kelly rising up through the ranks of the Royal Irish Constabulary, exacting terror on his former neighbours and enjoying every second. Once a bully, always a bully, acting the big man, with a badge and a uniform now to legitimise his behaviour.

Matt always said the first line of attack in achieving independence would be eliminating paid spies and informers, and the RIC would be the first targets of any campaign. As far as the rebels were concerned, the RIC were the eyes and ears of the Crown and therefore the enemy, even if most of them were born and bred in Ireland. They would be told to resign their positions, and failure to do so would result in the inevitable consequences that any spy would face. If things went as Matt and the Volunteers expected, Emmet's future might not be as bright as his prospective mother-in-law imagined.

Rose had resisted the none-too-subtle pressure of Mrs Lucey for years. She was fine for doing the laundry – she just collected it and dropped it off – but Rose neither liked nor trusted her. And as for the sour daughter Katie, she would have been the very last person Rose would have offered employment to. But Ralph had undermined her on that front too.

'And sure she knows the place inside out, coming in and out with me these last four years, and you know she's a good worker.' Mrs Lucey was really warming to her theme now.

The kitchen door opened to reveal Ralph, so Rose was spared answering.

'I got tired of waiting for you.' He addressed Rose impatiently, totally ignoring Mrs Lucey and the now-miserable Pearl who was washing up, her hair hanging over her face.

'Ah, 'tis yourself, Mr Ralph.' Mrs Lucey went into full-scale charm offensive. 'And can I say how nice it is to see you back in the Cliff House. I remember your mother and father, God rest them, and they were wonderful employers. I'm sure you and Mrs Delaney here will continue with that great tradition. I was only saying to Mrs Delaney what a fantastic girl my Katie is and how she's really looking forward to being a maid for ye here. And thank you for giving her the chance, sir. 'Twas very good of you. And sure between us all we'll have this place running like a mouse's heart, so we will, all of us together working here. And my Katie is getting married soon, but don't you worry about a thing, Mr Ralph, as I have two more girls. They're still at the school below, but they'll follow neatly in her footsteps when she has her babies, please God. So between us all, it will be a great little hotel altogether.'

Ralph looked at the rotund Mrs Lucey as if she were something unpleasant he found on the bottom of his shoe. 'No. Once Rose and I marry, which will be shortly, we will most likely move out, this will be run as a hotel, and we'll use the new house for private entertaining.'

Mrs Lucey looked astonished and puffed up in indignation. 'Mrs Delaney is to leave the Cliff House? You're surely not serious...'

Ralph opened the back door and stood there expectantly. 'I am. Deadly. Now if you'll excuse us, Mrs...ah...'

'Lucey,' Rose volunteered.

'Indeed. Mrs Lucey. Goodbye.' He stood, one arm outstretched, into the open doorway.

For once, Rose was glad of his imperious nature.

'But if ye are moving out, ye might need a manager like Mr Bridges below in the hotel, and I am well able to run a house like this, so you might...' She saw her chance and leapt in.

'Good lord, no.' Ralph looked so appalled, it would have been funny if it wasn't so rude. 'We'll need someone much, ah...much better.' He made no effort to soften his insult.

Mrs Lucey left in high dudgeon, no doubt ready to tell her tale at every shop counter in the town, her righteous indignation fuelling her wrath.

'Dreadful woman.' Ralph dismissed her as he closed the door. 'I hate that we must fill the house with such people. At least in my parents' time, people like her knew their place, seen and not heard. But honestly nowadays, to hear her, you would think she was my equal.' He gave a snort at his own joke, and Rose cringed. It seemed to have slipped his mind that she and Mrs Lucey were precisely the same class.

Rose arranged her face into a smile, hoping it would hide the turmoil inside her. Every time she was alone with him, her mouth went dry and her stomach did somersaults. Not with the excitement it had when she was a young impressionable girl and he the son of the house, but with a nauseating sense of foreboding. Could she bear it if he pressed his advantage physically? Could she go to bed with him? Surely he wouldn't actually force her before they married?

He saw little Pearl at the sink and walked over, sighing heavily. 'What are you doing here?' He spoke slowly as if the girl were mentally impaired.

'I...I work here, sir, M-Mr Devereaux, sir,' she managed.

'No you don't. Get out.' He opened the door once more, ushering her in the wake of Mrs Lucey.

Pearl left, choking her tears. Her family needed her wages so badly, and Rose felt awful for the poor girl. It wasn't her fault, thrown in the deep end on her first morning. She was younger than Harp. Rose wished there was something she could do. Perhaps she could reinstate her at a later date, but for now she had bigger problems.

In the now-empty kitchen, Ralph turned to her, his lips curling into a self-satisfied smile. 'I'm glad to see your little temper tantrum of last week is over and you are feeling a bit' – he took an apple from the fruit bowl and bit viciously into it, his even white teeth crunching – 'more accommodating.'

She swallowed. He was ruthless, and Harp was coming home; she badly needed to get him on her side. Harp antagonised him. Her daughter wasn't able to hide her abhorrence, and it goaded Ralph. One cutting remark from Harp is all it would take to send him running to his friends at the barracks.

'Yes, and I'm sorry, Ralph. I shouldn't have spoken to you like that.'

'No, you should not, but I trust you've learned your lesson and we won't need a repeat of that. Now, the first thing is, I'll be going to Cork today, so I will need the bank book or whatever you use.' He took another bite. 'I need to make some wedding arrangements, order my clothes, book a honeymoon. I was hoping we could go to the

French Riviera, but the blasted war is ruining everything. There's even a champagne shortage, would you believe, so I thought we might go to Tuscany instead.'

She clearly wasn't going to be consulted on any of it. She could feel her savings being frittered away on Ralph's expensive tastes.

Rose had spent most of the previous night figuring things out. She'd managed so far to avoid giving him complete free rein over her finances, and he'd not pressed the issue, instead just running up bills. But since the night he hit her, he was being less velvet glove and more iron fist. Placating him was the only option for now, but she was trying to come up with a way of siphoning off her money before he saw it.

'Of course. But I actually lodge the money into the post office, and that is closed this week. Poor Miss Egan has broken her ankle and has gone to stay with her sister in Waterford. I believe the GPO are sending someone to keep it running in her absence, but it will take time.'

A dark shadow crossed Ralph's face; he found such small-town talk beneath him.

'But I do have some cash because I've not been able to lodge that, so I could give you that? In the meantime?'

'How much?'

'I think there's around four pounds in the tin?' She went to the kitchen pantry and took the money tin from behind a bag of oatmeal. She handed the tin to him.

'It will only suffice in the short term. I have some other business that will require more than that. Let me see the post office book.'

Rose fumbled in the drawer of the dresser and pulled out the cherry-red embossed book, with the gold oval badge that read Post Office Savings Bank. It was one of two she had; this was for running expenses of the house, and she had another separate account for Harp. If she handed it over without a quibble, surely he would lower his guard.

He could go to Cork and withdraw the contents from that account; it was a possibility. But she knew there was a cricket match planned for that afternoon and he would rather stay in Queenstown and drink all day at the cricket club. She hoped against hope that the four pounds would be enough to make him delay his plan.

He opened the book, and despite his best efforts to look disdainful, she could see the greed gleam in his eyes. In four years she and Harp had managed to save a considerable sum. It was to pay to refurbish the outbuildings and to make more accommodation options for the ever-increasing guest numbers. They'd lived frugally, happily squirrelling it all away year after year, and the thought of Ralph tearing through their hard-earned money like wildfire made her ill.

'Yes, well, it will do for now, I suppose,' he said dismissively, placing the book in the inside pocket of his jacket. 'Now as you know, I was speaking with the vicar, and though you are not Church of Ireland, he was willing to overlook that provided you'd convert. I assured him that it would not be an issue. I know I said we'd get married within the month, but the vicar can do it this weekend, so I told him to make it so for Saturday.'

Rose inhaled. The sheer impudence of the man was infuriating. He was rushing the marriage through to get his hands on her money and this house as soon as possible. She knew he was deep in debt – the letters arrived daily – despite his best efforts to hide it from her.

'I've just had word,' she began, hoping her tone was wheedling enough to dissuade him, to buy a little time. 'Harp is coming home early. I'm sure she'd love to be a part of the wedding, so perhaps we should hold off just a little while, you know, to give her time to catch her breath.' Though she knew it was pointless, even if he did agree to wait. There was no option but marry him, and stalling wouldn't change the inevitable.

'When is she coming back?' He looked very put out.

'The day after tomorrow, I think, so Friday, and if we have the wedding on Saturday, it will be too soon after she arrives home. She might be tired.'

'So she stays here and doesn't go to the church if she's too tired.' He was dismissive.

'But now that she is coming, I would dearly love to have her beside me.'

Ralph sighed impatiently. 'You've mollycoddled that girl far too long. She's an adult now and will not be living with us. It's high time she made her own way in the world anyway. What we do is not her business.'

'Well, she is my daughter,' Rose replied, tired of pandering to him. 'But yes, you're right that she may not be here forever. After all, she will go to university once she has matriculated next year. That's her plan at any rate, and her teachers all think she is very bright, so I don't see any obstacles to her –'

'I do.' Ralph cut across her. 'I'm not funding

her foolish pretentions. Who on earth needs an educated woman? It will work against her in finding a husband. No man wants a know-it-all as a wife.'

Rose felt her face flush. 'Well, Ralph, Harp is too young to consider marriage, and she's had her heart set on going to university since she was a little girl. Henry encouraged her.'

'I'm sure he did.' The derisive note in Ralph's voice grated on her. 'But that's off the cards now. She'll have to marry and get out from under our feet. We can get some chap to take her on. I'll convince one of the officers or something. She's not awful looking. A bit too tiny and not curvaceous enough, but attractive, I suppose, in a quirky way. She'll have to tone down all that nonsense she spouts, though.'

Rose smarted. How could he discuss her darling daughter in such a way? Harp was so special and remarkable, and she was nowhere near ready for marriage.

He is trying to rile you, trying to get you to react. Don't rise to the bait. If he hit her again and Harp or Matt saw the results, there would be all hell to pay, and a cornered Ralph was like a cornered rat – extremely dangerous.

'Well, it is 1916, not 1816. Women do have

choices now, Ralph. But we can certainly discuss it with her. She and Henry talked endlessly of what she would study, though, so you might have a job to steer her from that course.' Rose gave a smile as if they were discussing something of the most trivial nature.

'Typical of one of my brother's foolish notions.' Ralph dismissed any mention of Henry. Rose suspected that deep down he was jealous of him. 'He wasn't right in the head – we always knew it. Mama lived in terror of guests running into him when they visited, never knowing what utter tosh he was going to come out with next. Though he got that from her side. All of my mother's family were feebleminded. He looked like Mama's family too. Papa and I got the Devereaux good looks.' His arrogance meant he saw no absurdity in such a statement.

'He was a very kind man, Ralph, and very good to Harp and me.' Rose had to defend him.

'Well, I think we all know what he was to you.' He raised an eyebrow suggestively. 'To be honest, I was astonished that he'd fathered a child, even if it was a bastard. I never thought he had it in him.' He shrugged. 'Anyway, I'll tell the vicar we'll go ahead next Saturday.'

He turned to go and then thought again. He

crossed the room and grabbed Rose, pressing his lips to hers, his arms vicelike around her waist. He forced her lips open and kissed her hungrily. She didn't respond.

He released her just as abruptly. His mouth curled into a sneer, like a cat watching a mouse. 'Ah,' he murmured, almost to himself, 'you're a fine filly that I'll surely enjoy breaking. You were too eager last time, as I recall, no challenge. That was boring. But now you're a different person, and I like a bit of resistance.'

He left, leaving Rose reeling and sick.

CHAPTER 26

The train pulled into Queenstown station, and Harp, JohnJoe and Danny rose to gather their belongings, including the carpet cleaning machine.

Nobody had any idea she'd brought the boys back with her, and so they decided it might be best to walk separately to the Devlins' house. Harp was once again wearing the heavy fur coat and was sweltering. Matt could well be outside the station waiting to collect guests, so Harp suggested that she take the back entrance onto the quayside while the boys took the more usual passenger exit. Rose may have told Matt she was coming, but she needed to offload the coat first,

and the fewer questions about why she had to answer, the better.

She could skirt along the quay – and she'd go
straight to the Devlins to hand over the coat.
They would all regroup there. Kathy had sent a
coded telegram to the sisters telling them to expect delivery of the goods today.

Matt would not recognise JohnJoe after all
these years, and Danny as well looked different
with his beard and glasses, so they hoped they
could all get to the grocery shop in the centre of
town undetected.

Luckily a large ship had docked en route to
Halifax from Cherbourg, and the town was busy.
Locals were outnumbered by travellers and holi-
daymakers at this time of year, so an elegantly
dressed young woman would not raise any eyebrows. Harp was one of many.

She made her way quickly and unimpeded to
the Devlins, but instead of going in through the
shop, she tapped on the back door of the sisters'
house. The bells of the angelus rang out over the
harbour from the carillon of St Colman's Cathedral, and Harp felt a surge of something – home-
sickness, nostalgia? She wasn't sure. It had been
the background music to her childhood, the bells

of that beautiful cathedral standing guard over Cork Harbour, and though it was fanciful, she knew, they gave her a sense of peace and hope. She was home. This was her place; these were her people. Everything would be all right – it had to be.

The door opened and she was pulled inside quickly. Cissy hugged her in the large coat and whispered, 'Liz is just closing up for lunch. Come in, come in, before you combust with the heat of that coat. Here, let me help you. I can't believe you managed it, Harp. Honestly, 'tis only smashing. You're a brave girl and no mistake – I knew it. Since you were only knee-high to a duck, there was something about you, but by God, you've proved it now.' Cissy gushed her praise and admiration as Harp gratefully divested herself of the fur.

'Are JohnJoe and –' Harp began.

'Inside, having tea, the two of them. Sure we wouldn't recognise small JohnJoe now, the fine strapping lad he is. They must have great grub over there in Boston altogether, because when he left here, a gust of wind would have knocked him over.'

She propelled Harp out of the small back hallway into the kitchen. Sure enough, there were the two boys, tucking into tea and fruitcake.

Liz appeared with an unaccustomed beam on her face. 'Welcome home, Harp, and well done, very well done.'

'We'll have a job to unpick that fine stitching on that beautiful coat and get it back to Mrs Rafferty,' Cissy said, 'but we'll manage it. Normally we'd ask your mother – she's a fine hand with a needle, so she is – but she has enough to deal with at the moment, the poor woman...' She and her sister exchanged a look.

'You telegrammed. Please tell me...' Harp refused tea.

'Sit down, love,' Liz instructed, and Harp sat beside JohnJoe, all eyes on the sisters now.

'We hope we did the right thing, sending you the telegram. She begged us not to say a word, but we felt it was the right thing to do...' Cissy said.

'You did,' Harp answered. 'But I don't understand... She hates him...'

Liz was the one to explain. 'Your mother was in here one day, not long after you left, and I just mentioned that the Cliff House bill was quite big that week and would she like us to split it over two weeks to make it easier.' Liz poured Harp a cup of tea though she'd said she didn't want any.

Cissy took up the story. 'She didn't know why

the bill was so much bigger than normal, so we showed her the account. There was whiskey and tobacco and fancy chocolate he'd ordered from London, and tonic water, a special kind, and loads of other things that Ralph Devereaux had put on the account. She said she'd settle it, but I could see there were tears in her eyes. She has a bruise on her face too, and I suspect he gave it to her. So Liz put the kettle on, and we brought her in here.'

'He hit her?' Harp could barely get the words out.

'She said she fell but...' Liz's face told Harp what she didn't say.

'The poor woman was distraught.' Cissy leaned against the range and continued. 'Apparently your man is after running up huge bills all over town and she was having to pay them. Well, we told her that he had no right to do that and that she should tell each shop not to offer Cliff House credit to him and that she wouldn't be honouring his debts, but she broke down in earnest then. She couldn't talk to anyone else, but she ended up telling us the story of the night with your man Pennington.'

Though Harp was blameless, she felt her

cheeks burn at the recounting of that night. 'Please go on,' she managed in a strangled voice.

'Well, it seems that he heard something in your room that night' – Liz took up the story again – 'and put two and two together. He knows Matt Quinn was somehow involved – he watched him arrive in the dead of night with your mother – and he threatened Mrs Delaney that if she didn't marry him, then he'd go straight to the British and all three of you would hang. She felt she had no choice but give in. She knew if she said a word to Matt, he'd surely challenge Devereaux, and that would result in Matt being led away in chains too, so she's marrying him to save you all. She made us promise not to say a word to Matt Quinn and we didn't, but we knew Mr Rafferty was sending Danny, and now JohnJoe, back with you and the coat, and we thought we'd telegram you and you might be able to do something...'

'Like what?' Harp asked, struggling to take it all in. Her gut feeling was right; Ralph was blackmailing her mother. She couldn't stand for it. There was no way she could allow Rose to marry that slimy toad to save her. She heard the note of hysteria in her own voice. 'I'll have to confess –

there's no other way… I'll have to tell them and hope…'

'Harp.' JohnJoe took her hand, calming her. 'Listen to me. Nobody is going to the cops here, not you, not Devereaux, nobody. You can't. They'll hang you for murder, and they'll know you couldn't have acted alone so your mother and Matt will go down too. So we can't do that.'

Harp realised he was right. It wasn't just herself she would be sacrificing. 'What can I do?' Her eyes raked each face, first Liz, then Danny, then JohnJoe and finally Cissy.

'He has to be eliminated, Harp. There's no other way,' Cissy said quietly, her normally jolly demeanour suddenly deadly serious.

'Eliminated, as in…' The enormity of Cissy's suggestion sank in. 'But no…we can't… I mean, it's impossible! I couldn't do it…to k-kill him…in cold blood.' Harp shook her head, her heart racing.

Danny and JohnJoe exchanged a glance, Danny giving his younger cousin an almost imperceptible nod.

'But we could,' JohnJoe said quietly.

'No…no, absolutely not. He's my biological father and it's a sin and it's wrong. No, we can't do that, we just can't…' Tears were now flowing down her cheeks. She'd blurted out the secret she'd never told anyone. If it came as a shock to any of the gathering, they gave no indication of it.

Danny moved to go on his hunkers in front of her; JohnJoe held her hand.

'It's the only way you and your mother can live peacefully, Harp,' Danny said. 'This lowlife ain't got no right to do what he does. You say he's your old man... Well, I dunno what that's all about, but whatever went on in the past, it don't matter. He's no good, Harp, and he's threatening you and your mother and this Matt guy, and it's either you or him, simple as that. I'm no killer, Harp, but I can do this. Me and JJ here, let us do this for you...'

'But that will make murderers of you both. I couldn't... Please don't. Can't you just talk to him, maybe scare him a bit, make him leave us alone? I can't let you kill him! There's been enough killing...enough...' Her body racked with sobs, and she felt JohnJoe's arm tighten around her shoulder.

'It's all right. We won't do it if you don't want us to, Harp,' he soothed.

'Yes, the lads here can hopefully give him a bit of a hiding and send him away with threats of worse if he was ever to return,' Cissy said.

Harp buried her face in JohnJoe's chest and never saw the look that passed between him, the Devlin sisters and Danny.

Once she'd recovered, Cissy gave her a handkerchief to wipe her eyes and poured her a fresh cup of tea. 'Now then, you go up to see your mammy. I'm sure seeing your face will lift her spirits no end. And she'll be delighted altogether with that thing for cleaning the floors. I can't believe you dragged it all the way back with you. I'll send young Bertie O'Shaughnessy up with you to carry it – we have him doing a bit of clearing of boxes and the like in the yard today. Now on with you, and we'll put these boys up here, out of the way, and I'm sure they'll find an opportunity to have a word with Mr. Ralph Devereaux in the near future.'

Harp reluctantly left JohnJoe and walked up the Smuggler's Stairs to her childhood home, ten-year-old Bertie almost lost under the big box behind her. It wasn't heavy so much as unwieldly. She felt bad for the lad and offered to help carry it, but he seemed determined to manage.

She longed to see her mother as she missed her so much, but she dreaded seeing her uncle in equal measure. She should never have blurted out her secret like that. But, she reasoned, the four people she told were trustworthy. Still, her mother would hate for anyone to know the secret.

If Ralph ever got wind of the truth, that Henry had lied about her paternity, they would face all manner of dire repercussions, not least that Ralph was, in fact, the heir to the Cliff House.

Ralph posed such a threat to her and her mother, it almost took her breath away, but the idea that he should be killed was deeply shocking to her and she was relieved that the Devlins accepted her refusal. That repugnant man was her father. It was a fact she tried not to dwell on. In her mind and in her heart, Henry Devereaux had that title, and to all intents and purposes, he was. He'd loved her, nurtured her, made time for her, all the things a good father should do. What had Ralph ever done? Nothing but draw misery on her and her mother. But she couldn't countenance his premeditated murder; it flew in the face of morality.

Even agreeing to having him roughed up didn't sit well with her, but she could bear it if it meant he left for good. And she wasn't worried that Ralph would get the better of them; he was unfit and wouldn't be expecting it. She would have feared for JohnJoe on his own – she couldn't imagine him in a fight – but though it was never said outright, Danny probably could handle himself in the kind of situation they proposed. He had several boxing medals, and she remembered the fight back in 1912, when Molly's father and fiancée turned up. Danny got stabbed in that incident, but he'd seemed well able to fight. Danny was agile and strong and JohnJoe was well built, so together they would surely be more than a match for Ralph.

She opened the gate into the garden, and though she'd not been gone that long, it felt like years since she'd been home. The beech hedge Matt had planted three years ago along the southern boundary of the garden was turning russet and gold and looked lovely. The horse chestnut too was heavy with the weight of the spiky green chestnuts just waiting to be knocked down by little boys who used the brown shiny conkers inside as toys. Mammy let the local boys in to knock them down each September, which made her popular. The same lads often dropped up some fresh fish if they caught any as a thank you.

'You can leave the box there. Thanks, Bertie,' Harp said, giving the boy a farthing for his trouble. He beamed and sprinted back down the steps.

The lawn was cut perfectly, and the fuchsia and montbretia were fighting for supremacy; the deep-red and purple flowers of the fuchsia filled the corners of the garden, while the flame-orange montbretia filled the beds along the garden wall. Everything looked the same, the white wrought iron table and chairs, the wooden bench, the azure blue of Cork Harbour laid out like a painting, with the sailboats and fishing trawlers bobbing happily. To anyone else this was a scene of tranquillity and peace, but the reality was anything but.

She must say nothing to alert Ralph, or her mother for that matter. The Devlins were adamant on that subject. Rose was determined to marry Ralph, regardless of the personal consequences, to save Harp and Matt. If Harp rebelled against that, it might scupper the plan, so she would have to look like she was going along with it. The thought felt like acid in her mouth, but she would have to play along.

The Devlins were not what anyone thought they were, sweet old ladies who ran a shop. No, they were politically astute and, she was realising, ruthless in their cause to gain Ireland's freedom. They hated the very class Ralph Devereaux represented, so his removal held no qualms for them. He was a member of the Anglo-Irish ascendancy, whose wealth and privilege was stolen from the rightful owners of the country, and now they, along with the whole republican movement, were taking back what was theirs. The cost in terms of human life was inevitable and necessary; they had only one goal. Harp knew that they would kill in the blink of an eye and not hesitate for one second.

CHAPTER 27

*R*alph was in the sitting room, reading the newspaper on the sofa, with a cut-class tumbler of whiskey beside him. Harp crossed the gravel towards the front door but then went around the back, letting herself into the kitchen.

To her surprise there were three girls she didn't recognise there, and one that she did, unfortunately.

'Ah, 'tis yourself, Harp, back from your travels.' Katie Lucey smiled obsequiously, her eyes taking in Harp's clothing, hat and gloves.

Harp would not give Katie the satisfaction of knowing she had no idea what the other girl was doing there. Summoning up her newfound confidence, she decided to act as the daughter of such a fine house would when speaking to a servant.

'Ah, Katie, yes. Where is my mother?'

'Sure how would I know?' Katie replied, belligerent now at being spoken to in such a manner.

As she did, Rose appeared. 'Katie, please get on with your work. Those potatoes should have been peeled by now, and in the future, you will address my daughter as Miss Devereaux.'

Katie opened her mouth as if to say something, but Rose's arched eyebrow made her close it abruptly again and return to the sink of vegetables.

Harp hugged her mother and allowed herself to be led upstairs on the pretext of showing her the dresses for the wedding, away from prying eyes and ears.

'So you're marrying Ralph?' Harp asked as Rose shut the bedroom door.

Rose smiled. Harp saw the pain in her eyes and the falsely bright smile on her face.

'It's for the best, but let's not talk about that for now. Plenty of time for that later.' The bruise on her cheekbone was turning a mixture of yellow and purple.

'What happened to you?' Harp asked.

'Oh, nothing, I just bumped into the door.

Now, tell me all about America…' She patted the bed and Harp sat beside her.

Harp was sure that her mother had never lied to her before, but for now, Harp would go along with it and pray Danny and JohnJoe could do enough to get rid of that demon for good.

She told her mother all about Boston and the Raffertys, and about meeting Chief O'Neill and transcribing his tunes for him. She explained about the carpet cleaning machine, and Rose was intrigued and touched at the Raffertys' generosity.

They chatted and never mentioned the wedding again. Harp longed to be honest with her mother, but too much was at stake. They kept the conversation light, discussing the new staff and the comings and goings in Queenstown since Harp left. Harp longed to stop her mother mid-sentence and beg her to reconsider. But she knew her mother wouldn't, and even if Harp could convince her to reject Ralph, what then? There was only one way, and it was to go along with the plan.

'Now, we'd better get ready. We are due to dine at the hotel tonight, and now that you're back, you must join us. The table is booked for six thirty. Ralph is meeting Major Graves for an aperitif first, so he'll meet us there. We'd better get a move on.'

* * *

THEY'D DECIDED the garden gate of the convent was ideal. It was set into the wall of the Smuggler's Stairs twenty feet below the gate of the Cliff House. The Devlins suggested it and assured them that nobody ventured down that far in the nuns' garden. The gate was rarely used, considering the hefty shove JohnJoe had to give it to get it to open.

He and Danny stood inside the garden, the door slightly ajar, waiting for their target. They'd gone over the plan in their minds, several times, and were sure it would work. The Devlins gave a few details of his comings and goings. The sisters checked with a contact working in the hotel and knew that Ralph and Rose had a table booked, and they knew he always arrived at the hotel an hour before dinner for a drink with the officers. Rose, and presumably Harp now that she was back, would join him later.

Danny nodded as they heard gentle whistling. As Ralph trotted down the steps, Danny moved out in front of him and JohnJoe behind him, effectively corralling him between them.

'I say, let me past,' Ralph demanded irritably.

'We wanted a little word, Mr Devereaux,' Danny drawled, nudging Ralph towards the door of the convent garden.

'What? Get away from me! Who are you? How dare you...' Ralph spluttered but stopped abruptly as he felt the barrel of JohnJoe's pistol in the small of his back.

JohnJoe and Danny had both been astonished when the little old ladies produced the Luger. They had been further amazed when Liz gave them a demonstration on how to use it. JohnJoe could not imagine any other occasion when he would be reconciled to shooting someone, but this man had hurt Rose and was threatening her and Harp, and JohnJoe felt no compunction whatsoever.

They dragged him through the gate and shoved him into the overgrown corner of the stepped garden, behind a stand of trees and bushes. There was no way anyone from the convent could see them, and they were far enough away that they were out of earshot as well.

'Who are you? Let go of me this instant!' Ralph demanded.

Danny shoved him roughly against the wall, sending him staggering backwards. Ralph kept his eyes warily on JohnJoe, who had the pistol trained on him.

'It's time you left, Mr Devereaux,' Danny said conversationally, pausing to light a cigarette.

'Left? Left where? What are you talking about? I demand to know –'

The blow to his jaw sent Ralph reeling, and he cracked his head against a protruding rock in the garden wall. As he recovered, Danny caught him with another savage punch to the belly. Ralph grunted and doubled over, winded, but Danny allowed him no recovery time, grabbing a fistful of Ralph's lustrous hair and pinning him to the wall.

'Listen carefully. You are gonna announce tonight when you're havin' dinner that you need to go back to India right away, some business there or somethin' – I don't care. Make sure your British officer friends hear about it too. Then tomorrow morning you'll go to the railroad station and buy a ticket to Dublin. From there you'll catch a boat to England and from there... Well, to be truthful, Mr Devereaux, from there we don't care where you go so long as you don't show your sorry ass around here ever again.'

'Why on earth would I do that?' Ralph spluttered, trying to wriggle free. 'I'm getting married...'

Danny shook his head. 'Nope. Not happenin'.'

'I...I don't understand. Who are you people? I think you have the wrong person...'

'No. You're definitely the guy. Look, Ralph, it's like this. Nobody around here wants you. You owe a lot of money to some guy over there in England, Benjy someone? No matter. Now, I don't work for him, but the guy I *do* work for is a good friend of his, and he happened to hear about you and then saw that you decided to hurt Mrs Delaney, also a friend of my boss, and so you've kinda blotted your copybook, you know? Add to that the local boys here, you know, the guys who are fightin' for a free Ireland? They don't like men like you, cuddlin' up to the enemy. So basically, you're in trouble on a lot of fronts, but my boss is a nice guy, believes in givin' a man a chance. We all make mistakes, right?'

Ralph's prominent Adam's apple moved as he swallowed nervously. 'And who do you work for?' he asked.

Danny shrugged. 'That don't matter. All that matters is that you get out of town tomorrow. Now I know you might be thinkin' that you could spill the beans with your buddy the major over dinner, that he might protect you, but I wouldn't advise that. We got guys inside there too. You got a lotta enemies, my friend, *a lot*. And we're not the only ones watchin' you. And the Volunteers are not as likely to be so compassionate as me and my friend here. They take a very dim view of informers, as you probably know. Every move you make is diggin' you deeper into this hole. This is a lifeline – take it.'

'I don't believe you,' Ralph said mutinously.

Danny tightened his grip on Ralph's hair and cracked his head off the wall once more. Ralph groaned and Danny shrugged again. 'That's up to you. My boss would be happy for my friend here to put a bullet in you right now. And believe me, that is still an option. But as I say, those ladies, Mrs Delaney and Harp, they didn't want that. They are good people, y'see?'

'Rose knows about this?' Ralph was incredulous.

'She does. We saw what you did to her. As I said, people look out for her and Harp – that's why we're here – and they don't want you around, Ralphieboy, they just don't. Now as I say, if it was up to us, we'd be ending this right now, but they asked us to be more lenient so we promised them we would – if you play ball, that is.'

'I will not be bullied like this. Harp and Rose have secrets, and they know that I –' He made to pull away from Danny's grip, but JohnJoe cocked the pistol, the ominous click stopping Ralph in his tracks.

'You have no cards here.' Danny spoke quietly into Ralph's ear. 'Major Charles Grant has made his investigation into the disappearance of Captain Robert Pennington, and concluded... What did he say now? Can you remember, buddy?' Danny asked JohnJoe.

'AWOL, last seen gettin' on a train to Cork, the day after he was last seen. It seems Captain Pennington had no intention of returnin' to his post. He was on leave and had it all worked out to jump ship stateside and leave the mud and the trenches to the rest of them. He was just a little chicken, Ralph. All that talk about working for the government and going to the USA for meetings was a cock-and-bull story. He was AWOL, and Major Grant's job was to track him down. A body was pulled out of a river near his home in England three weeks later. Case closed.'

Danny jerked his head, and JohnJoe stepped

forward, placing the barrel of the Luger on Ralph's temple.

'But that's not true…' Ralph protested. 'P-Pennington was mur –'

'Nobody cares, Ralph, nobody.' Danny straightened Ralph's tie and smoothed the lapels of his jacket. 'Your buddy Pennington was a piece of trash, and nobody cares that he's gone, same as nobody will care if we put a bullet in you right now, except two nice ladies who want us to give you a chance. Somethin' you don't deserve, by the way.' Danny brushed imaginary dust from Ralph's shoulders and smiled. 'Now, we're all gonna have a nice dinner in the hotel, and you're gonna announce that you need to go away for a while – you don't know how long for. Tell as many people as you can, and me and my buddy here will be sitting close by. But remember that we're not alone. Everyone in that dining room is watching you. So one wrong move – and I mean a toe out of line – and then things go a very different way. Are we clear?'

CHAPTER 28

*J*ohnJoe saw Ralph's eyes dart frantically around the room. Two men sat at a table in the corner, neither man taking his eyes off Ralph. They were associates of the Devlins undoubtedly. At the window seat sat Major Graves and his wife; to the left of them were the Devlin sisters, also watching him. Harp focused on her plate, not daring to make eye contact.

Dotted around the room were groups, mostly of men. Ralph would have no way of knowing if they too were in on the plan, but it was clearly enough to rattle him. He was quiet and seemed pale. He ordered something to eat but barely touched it.

It was hard to hear what he was saying, but he seemed to be delivering the news, and as he did, Mr Bridges appeared. Rose looked incredulous, and Harp just continued cutting her meat, not saying anything.

The hotel manager's voice was louder, 'I understand congratulations are in order?'

Ralph looked up, startled.

'I hear you're to be married, and we are delighted for you both.'

'Yes, well...' Ralph muttered, focusing on his meal.

'Marvellous, marvellous,' Mr Bridges said.

But Harp detected the note of insincerity there. Mr Bridges had been very supportive of them ever since they first started the guest house at the Cliff House, and she knew the man held her mother in the highest esteem. Did he realise how far beneath herself in terms of character she was allegedly settling by marrying Ralph Devereaux? Harp suspected that he did.

'Mrs Delaney has done such a smashing job with the Cliff House. The luxury is a rival to any accommodation in the country, including here at the Queen's, I might add, and it is all by the sheer hard work and determination of this lady. You're a lucky man, Ralph, a very lucky man indeed.' Mr

Bridges smiled at Harp as he spoke, and she knew he meant every word.

'Indeed,' Ralph replied silkily. 'We are both lucky. However the wedding shall have to be postponed indefinitely as I have some urgent business matters to attend to overseas. The timing is unfortunate, but there are certain issues that have to be dealt with personally and I'm left with no option but leave presently.'

Rose stopped chewing and gazed in astonishment.

'I know you must be very disappointed, my dear,' Ralph went on, 'and I do apologise, but it can't be helped.'

'And how long will you be gone?' Rose asked, her voice sounding nothing like normal.

Ralph exhaled and sighed, his eyes darting nervously to the table where JohnJoe and Danny ate, seemingly oblivious. 'Oh, it's hard to say. By the time I get back to India, take care of things there, I couldn't be sure...' He swallowed, and Harp noticed the bead of perspiration on his brow. 'I'm sure you'll be fine here, cooking and cleaning and such, as you've always done. Perhaps the life of a lady wasn't one at which you'd excel anyway. Best you continue keeping house.'

Harp was seething. Even now he couldn't resist trying to undermine her, dumping her in public like this. Even though Harp hated him, she felt deep sadness at her mother being humiliated. Rose had nothing to be ashamed of, and she was from the working class and never sought to pretend otherwise. Harp fought to keep the fury from her face. She had to let Ralph have his little gloat. It was pathetic, but to challenge him would scupper the entire plan.

Mr Bridges assessed the situation and sought to spare Rose's blushes. 'Well, Ralph, I wish you a pleasant journey in that case, and please, don't worry about Mrs Delaney – we'll take good care of her.'

'Oh, she won't need taking care of. She's well able to fend for herself.' His eyes blazed with sheer hatred, and it frightened Harp. 'She's no damsel in distress, I assure you. She'll manage to turn any situation to her advantage.'

'Mrs Delaney certainly is an enterprising lady,' Mr Bridges said, deliberately misunderstanding him. 'And there's nothing wrong with working for a living, Ralph. We all do it.' He chuckled, and though the tone was jocular, Harp heard the edge there. Mr Bridges was of the same frame of mind as she was when it came to her uncle, she was sure of it.

Ralph smiled but his eyes were wary, and as Bridges moved to another table, he caught John-Joe's eye. JohnJoe and Danny met his gaze.

They finished dinner, and Major Graves and his wife stopped by the table before retiring upstairs. They lived full time in the hotel, as the barracks quarters were a little rough and ready for the major's wife. Ralph told his tale again.

'Oh, that is rather a bother, and can you get passage?' the major asked. 'What with everything, passenger travel is very restricted, I know.'

'I expect I'll manage something,' Ralph replied, through almost gritted teeth.

'Very well, old chap,' the major boomed. 'Bon voyage! Give my regards to Shimla!' He guffawed, clapping Ralph on the back, and departed.

Ralph paid the bill, and within moments they were outside, Rose, Harp and Ralph beginning the short stroll home.

Rose looked perplexed at the turn events had taken and was just about to question Ralph once more when Harp took her arm and led her on. They were just yards from the hotel entrance when JohnJoe and Danny caught up to them. They clearly didn't want to leave the women alone with Ralph for a second.

'Ah, Miss Devereaux, thank you for recommending that place. The food was delicious,' Danny announced, falling into step beside them.

Rose was shocked to see Danny and JohnJoe but managed to recover quickly. She glanced at Harp, her eyes questioning.

'Oh, I'm so glad you enjoyed it,' Harp replied. 'I met these gentlemen on the ship. They were asking about dining in Queenstown,' she explained to Ralph and her mother.

'We sure ate well, didn't we, buddy?' Danny carried on.

'Absolutely. I had the salmon – it was the best I've ever had.' JohnJoe joined in with the camaraderie.

Ralph looked decidedly uncomfortable, and Harp urged her mother onward, walking a few steps ahead of Ralph, now flanked by Danny and JohnJoe, both making friendly conversation. To anyone looking on, they were just a group returning from a nice meal.

Ralph remained silent as they climbed the Smuggler's Stairs.

'How about a nightcap, Ralph?' Danny asked, leading him and JohnJoe upstairs.

'What's happening?' Rose asked, panicked. 'Harp, what's going on?'

'Just keep walking, Mammy,' Harp said quietly,

firmly gripping her mother's arm and leading her down to the kitchen.

'But, Harp, I...' Rose craned to see what was happening.

'Mammy, trust me. Just come to the kitchen.'

* * *

DANNY AND JOHNJOE escorted Ralph to a back bedroom on the third floor, directly above the drawing room. It was never used for guests, but even if he did shout out, nobody would hear him all the way up there. Placing him face down on the bed, they bound him hand and foot.

'Now, Ralph, you catch some shut-eye there. We need you seen getting on the mail train in the morning. Don't worry, we'll pack your suitcase.'

JohnJoe positioned himself on a chair, the pistol in his hand cocked and aimed at Ralph.

'Why are you doing this?' Ralph pleaded. 'I will pay my debts. Very soon I'll be in a position to –'

'With your hands in Mrs Delaney's money-box? I don't think so,' JohnJoe replied.

'Rose and I are going to be married. You have completely the wrong end of the stick. She loves me...'

'Ha!' JohnJoe snorted. 'Loves you? She hates you. So does Harp. Now why don't you do us all a favour and shut up?'

Ralph began protesting, but JohnJoe took his handkerchief from his pocket and stuffed it in Ralph's mouth unceremoniously. 'That's better.'

Slowly, the late summer twilight became dark for just a few hours, then the morning sun streaked across the sky. They roused Ralph a little after 5 a.m. He incredibly had fallen asleep. They untied him and instructed him to walk to the railway. They explained how they would walk behind him, looking like they too were taking the early train, and that they would have the pistol trained on him at all times, as would several IRA members located in various positions en route. One move out of place and he would be shot on sight. The part about the snipers was completely untrue, but Ralph didn't need to know that.

Ralph did as he was instructed. Carrying his suitcase, he walked down the steps and turned for the railway station. He looked terrified.

'I want to be the one to do it,' JohnJoe said quietly as they walked a few yards behind Ralph.

Danny looked sceptical. 'No way.'

'Danny, please, I want to.'

'No, JJ. You ain't never fired a gun in your life

before, and all of a sudden you're Humpty Jackson?' Danny murmured as Ralph strode on. The agreement with the Devlins was that Danny was to be the one to pull the trigger when the time came.

'I know, but I want to do him. He hurt Rose and he hurt Harp, and I just want to do it. Please, Danny, I won't screw it up. I promise.'

Danny thought for a moment and then relented. 'OK. But no dramatics?'

JohnJoe nodded. He was determined. The Devlins were right. Harp could never countenance ordering the execution of her uncle, or her father or whatever he was to her, but there was no other way. If he was allowed to live, there would be nothing to stop him making mischief at any time in the future. JohnJoe fervently wished his future would be with Harp, and he wanted more than anything to make her happy and keep her safe. He could only ensure that if Ralph Devereaux were no more. He'd weighed it all up, predicating his relationship with Harp on a lie or saving her and Rose from a lifetime of threat that might end up with their own deaths. He had no choice, and his mind was made up.

Ralph was surprisingly docile as he approached the station, though his eyes did betray him as they darted left and right as he looked for snipers.

JohnJoe and Danny were only feet behind him. Two men appeared out from another set of steps in the town wall – the entire town was crisscrossed with steps – and Ralph visibly started. They were men on their way to work on the docks, clearly, but to Ralph they were surely Volunteers ensuring his departure.

They made for the platform and the early morning train. It was a wet, cool morning, and the sky was a gunmetal grey, bathing the entire town in an eerie opaque light. They greeted the stationmaster.

''Tis early ye're out, gentlemen,' the stationmaster remarked, punching their tickets.

'Gotta collect some things for Mrs Delaney in Cork this morning and make the afternoon train back,' Danny explained.

'And yourself, Mr Devereaux? Are you up to the city for the day too?' he asked pleasantly.

'Ah, no, I'm going ultimately to India, via London. I...' – he glanced at Danny – 'I've some business to attend there.'

'India? Janey mac, but that's a fair trek, right enough. Sure that'll take months, won't it, to get there? But were yourself and Mrs Delaney not to be wed?'

'There's been a change of plan,' Ralph replied tightly.

'Fair enough. Sure you know women.' He rolled his eyes and chuckled.

The three men took one of the few seating compartments on the mail train. No other passenger boarded. The rain that began as drizzle was heavy now, and it trickled down the windows, making visibility poor.

The Devlins had said they should dispatch him over the water. The railway line ran over the harbour halfway between Queenstown at Cork city. Some research on the tides told them that it was full tide right now, so the body should sink to the bottom – especially as they had a lead belt to place around him at the last minute – and be carried out into the Atlantic on the tide. Liz Devlin had told him that it was a rare thing that a body was washed up in Queenstown, the pull of the tide being what it was in the harbour.

The locomotive blew its whistle as smoke filled the station, and soon they were underway. Ralph gazed out the window. There was nothing to see but a mixture of smoke and rain, and he refused to even acknowledge his captors.

Thirty minutes into the journey, as the track left land and the train puffed its way across the bridge spanning the harbour, Danny nodded. 'Right, Ralph, let's go.'

Ralph Devereaux looked stricken. 'What, where?'

Danny didn't answer him but dragged him to his feet.

'What are you doing? You said if I went quietly...' Panic made his voice high-pitched.

Danny twisted Ralph's arm behind his back, causing him to yelp in pain. The train driver and the mail sorters were in the carriages to the front, so it didn't matter how loud he was; there was nobody to hear.

'Yeah, well...' Danny shrugged, then shoved him out into the corridor.

There was an exit door across from their compartment, the reason Danny chose it. JohnJoe drew the pistol once more, the silencer screwed firmly to the barrel. Ralph was corralled between the men, the movement of the train making it hard to stay upright. Ralph looked terrified but knew escape was by this stage impossible. Danny took the lead weight from his bag and tied it around Ralph roughly, then he opened the door. In the murky light, the water glittered darkly below. The wind and rain whistled through the open door, soaking them as Ralph tried to grip the walls either side of the door.

'Please, I'm begging... I have money! I can pay you, please...'

'Now!' Danny yelled.

JohnJoe pulled the trigger as Danny shoved, and Ralph Devereaux fell forward, tumbling and crashing into the swirling waters below.

Danny shut the door and both men resumed their seats.

CHAPTER 29

*H*arp entered the hallway at the sound of the knocking. It was almost 6 p.m., an unusual time for guests but perhaps some had arrived late.

Standing at the door were two people, a young woman a little older than Harp and a girl much younger, perhaps only nine or ten. The young woman had gorgeous copper hair and was tall and willowy. Harp's face broke into a beam; it could only be one person. Kitty O'Dwyer wore a lilac dress topped with a beautiful gold brocade coat and a plum-coloured hat with wine trim and a small green feather. Harp thought she looked like an exotic bird of paradise.

Holding her hand was surely Jane, small for

her age and slight, her face hidden behind a curtain of dark-brown hair. She wore a pinafore and coat of ivory cream, and she had black patent shoes with buckles on her feet. Beside them were two brown leather suitcases.

The young girl didn't raise her head; she just stared at the step beneath her feet.

'Are you Kitty O'Dwyer?' Harp asked with a smile.

'Well, nobody's called me that for years. I'm Katherine Atlee now.' She had JohnJoe's blue eyes and her hair was pinned up, cascading in curls under her hat. She had the same freckles over the bridge of her nose, and her eyes crinkled when she smiled just as his did. 'So are you Harp?'

Harp nodded and warmed to her; she was direct but friendly.

'I couldn't believe it when I read your letter. Thank you for sending it. I hope you don't mind Jane and me just turning up out of the blue like this, but we had to come.'

'No, I'm delighted to see you, and JohnJoe will be as well, I can assure you.' She addressed the younger girl. 'And you must be Jane.'

Harp was gratified to see the child raise her face slightly, her hazel eyes making momentary contact with Harp's. She was not like her older brother or sister; her build and colouring were different. 'Come in. He's not here at the moment, but he should be back soon. He's gone down to the town for art supplies. He's in the middle of some top-secret project that he refuses to tell me about.'

Harp led the two girls into the sitting room, which was thankfully devoid of guests for now. Rose was up at Matt Quinn's house, and Danny had gone for a drink in the hotel. He was becoming very friendly with some of Matt's younger associates and seemed to be getting more and more enamoured with the republican cause all the time.

Ralph was only gone a week, but there was an atmosphere of light airiness since he'd departed. JohnJoe had assured her that everything had gone according to plan. The stationmaster had commiserated with Rose at her fiancée's hurried departure when he met her the next day down the town, and Rose had accepted his condolences gracefully.

Harp had asked JohnJoe specifically, 'Did you see him go?'

'I did,' he'd replied.

'And he won't come back?'

'Definitely not.'

That was good enough for her; she didn't need the details. They mustn't have roughed him up too much as the stationmaster never mentioned anything. Perhaps the threat of a hiding was enough. Ralph was a coward at heart. If JohnJoe said he was gone, then he was.

Rose could hardly believe it and had cried tears of relief and gratitude when they filled her in on what had happened.

Kitty and Jane turning up now was just the icing on the cake. Kitty did all the talking; Jane sat close by and said nothing.

'We were told that our brother died, that he was killed in a farming accident.'

Harp sought to reassure her. 'Please have a seat. No, he's very much alive. He was taken to America by your Uncle Pat, your mother's brother, when he was fourteen and has lived there since.'

'But...why were we not told?' Kitty's brow furrowed. 'I don't understand.'

'He wrote to you,' Harp explained. 'Well, he tried to, and your uncle wrote to your Aunt Eileen on a few occasions too, but your aunt replied once saying that she had no interest in further contact and that she did not want you or Jane having anything to do with them.'

'They told us that JohnJoe was dead. They had a service for him and everything.' Kitty sounded so hurt and confused.

Harp wished she could comfort her but had no idea how. 'Well, I don't know why they said that, but he's not.' Harp tried to reassure her. 'He grew up in Boston. Well, he was in Ireland until he was fourteen, and that's when I met him. He stayed with my mother and me here during the summer of 1912, and we've stayed in touch.'

'I can't believe this. You swear this isn't some kind of a prank or something?' Kitty's blue eyes bored into Harp's.

'No, I promise you. I don't know why your aunt lied, but JohnJoe is alive and he's fine. I never told him that I was going to try to find you as I didn't want to get his hopes up, but you and Jane mean so much to him and it was his dearest wish that you would be reunited.'

The girl's eyes were bright with tears. Her little sister silently gave her a handkerchief. 'I'm sorry. This is all rather a lot to take in.' Her accent was cultured and British, no trace of her West Clare origins at all, though she'd only been eleven or twelve when she left and Jane just a newborn. The young woman sitting beside her on the sofa was now twenty-one and Jane must be nine.

'I can't believe Aunt Eileen and Uncle Hugh lied to us. I just can't believe it, but they did. And a part of me knows it's true.' It was as if the young woman was talking to herself. She turned to face Harp. 'What's he like?' she asked. 'Our brother? He used to be lovely, gentle, with a great singing voice.'

Harp tried not to show the love she had for JohnJoe as she began. 'He's still lovely. He sounds American, of course, and he's tall. And, well, he was skinny when I first knew him, but he's filled out now. He looks just like you, actually, and he's kind and funny and he likes to read and he's an amazing artist and he...'

The look on Kitty's face stopped her.

'Books? JohnJoe?' The first hint that things were perhaps not as they seemed showed in the disbelief that crept across her face.

'I know.' Harp rushed to explain. 'He couldn't read at first. The teachers at his first school couldn't teach him, and then in the borstal, well, he never learned, but he did that summer with us and now reads all the time.'

'What else did he tell you about our family?' Kitty asked, and Harp knew she was being investigated.

'He told me that your mother died,' Harp said

honestly, 'and that you all lived on your grandfather's farm, and that he's named for both his grandfathers, John and Joseph, and that your grandfather on your mother's side was a great farmer and your mother was a wonderful gardener. You had a huge kitchen garden at the side of the house, and JohnJoe loved to help her there. He told me that you and Jane were taken by your aunt but he was put into borstal when your mother died. Your father wasn't able to cope, it seems.'

Kitty snorted. 'Couldn't be bothered to, more like.'

Harp tactfully didn't comment on that. 'He told me your mammy's favourite song was "I Dreamt I Dwelt in Marble Halls".'

Kitty smiled sadly. 'It was, and she had a lovely voice. I remember her singing that.'

'He'll be so thrilled to see you both, I can't even tell you. It makes him so sad that you've lost touch. Now, while we wait, can I get you a cup of tea, or a cordial maybe?' Harp addressed John-Joe's youngest sister, who had yet to make eye contact.

The girl moved even closer to Kitty, and the older girl explained. 'Janie, she... Janie hardly speaks, Harp. She only says a few words and only to me, not anyone else, and she doesn't like strangers. She very rarely leaves the house, so this is a big ordeal for her.' Kitty sounded sad. 'Our aunt and uncle have taken her to lots of different doctors. They can find nothing wrong. They say she's choosing not to speak.'

'Did she ever?' Harp asked, feeling awkward discussing the child while she sat beside them.

'She was never chatty, if that's what you mean. My aunt is not an affectionate person. I'd known a mother's love by the time we went there, but Janie never had, and the lack of love, of a maternal bond, has had an effect on her, I think. Then when she was three, I was sent away to boarding school and she pined. I begged to be allowed to stay at home, to attend as a day girl, but my aunt and uncle refused, and Janie hasn't spoken properly to anyone but me since. She doesn't go to school or have any friends or anything like that.'

'Oh dear, the poor girl.' Harp knew what it was to feel alone in the world, to be seen as odd.

'But' – Kitty placed her arm around her little sister, speaking to both her and Harp – 'she knows about JohnJoe. I tell her stories about the mischief we used to get up to as children.' Kitty exhaled. 'I won't ever forgive her for this. Uncle

Hugh either. They gave us a home and saved us from a worse fate, as she often points out, but this is such a betrayal. I swore I would never forgive her for sending me away from Janie, but I did. But this...no. There's no coming back from this.'

Though Harp didn't know her, she believed her. 'Well, my mother and I run this guest house, and I know she'd be happy for you both to stay here until you decide what to do next.'

'Thank you. We'll pay of course,' Kitty answered quickly.

'So do your aunt and uncle know you're here? Are they expecting you back?'

Kitty shook her head. 'No, we left without saying anything. They don't deserve an explanation after the lies they told us. But it's not just that. I'm engaged to be married since Christmas. They don't approve. Seamus isn't from good enough stock, they think, but I don't care. The only thing stopping me eloping last Christmas was Janie, but Seamus loves Janie and accepts that we come as a package.'

Harp tried to hide her shock and admiration at the older girl's confidence. She also noted that she wore no engagement ring.

'But eloping isn't an option now anyway. He was in Dublin, you know, last Easter.' The pride in Kitty's voice was unmistakable. 'He was one of the Liverpool Volunteers. He was born in Liverpool, but his parents are from Wicklow. Aunt Eileen would like to forget that she's Irish at all, and so associating with an Irish rebel was a source of horror to her. I told her I broke it off, but I didn't really. He's in Wormwood Scrubs prison now – he was arrested after the Rising – but is sure he's going to get out. He wants us to wait, not get married yet, because he has every intention of staying here once the fighting really starts and didn't want me caught up in all of that. But this changes everything. Aunt Eileen lied to me and to Janie – she made us believe our brother was dead. What kind of evil monster does that?'

Harp had no answer.

'No, that's it. Enough. She's gone too far this time. She's made Janie and I feel beholden to her all these years, and Uncle Hugh is so caught up with his prayer book and the next life that he never bothers to look at this one.' Fury flashed in her blue eyes.

'Well, as I say, you are both welcome here. Let me get you some tea before JohnJoe gets back.'

CHAPTER 30

'Who is Danny?' Kitty asked, and Harp explained how he was a cousin of JohnJoe's, though only through marriage, and went on to explain more about JohnJoe and the Rafferty family.

'Aunt Eileen always said her brother Patrick was a bad egg, someone best avoided. She was never very specific, but the more I think about it, the more I'm not surprised at what she did. She's a terrible snob.' Kitty had a kind of knowing about her; clearly she was someone not to be trifled with.

Harp shook her head. 'Well, the Raffertys are very wealthy and live in a beautiful house in a very fancy part of Boston, so I'm sure whatever image she has of her brother is quite wrong. Pat Rafferty is a builder, and a very successful one. He's a leading figure in the Irish American Association and is outspoken on the subject of Irish independence. I think years ago there may have been some minor shady business deals, dealing in whiskey and tobacco and that sort of thing, but as I say, it was years ago. Pat and Kathy Rafferty are as nice a couple as you'll meet, and they adore JohnJoe and Danny more than if they were even their own sons.'

'I'm glad our brother landed somewhere he was loved,' Kitty said quietly. 'He always was a soft soul. So are they all involved with the cause? JohnJoe and this Danny as well?'

'I think so,' Harp said, and Kitty nodded approvingly.

Kitty told Harp all about life with the vicar and his wife, how they were all right, she supposed, but they found the Irish to be an uncouth bunch and hated any suggestion of an association with them. She and Jane had been encouraged to reject any elements of their Irish heritage and were raised as young British ladies. Kitty had attended a girls' boarding school in Lincolnshire and had even gone to Switzerland to a finishing school for a year. Her aunt was sure she could make her a good match that would elevate not just Katherine but the Reverend Atlee and his wife into the upper echelons of society. But the day Kitty ran into Seamus O'Grady, everything changed.

'How did you meet?' Harp asked.

Kitty grinned. 'He sells fish. Well, he and his brothers are fishermen, and they have a stall at the market in Great Charlotte Street. I always tease him that it takes a certain kind of constitution for a woman to fall for a lad that stinks of fish, but I did. He's special.'

'But a fisherman wasn't good enough for your aunt?' Harp guessed.

Jane was happily eating a scone and listening to the conversation but said nothing.

Kitty pealed with laughter, and it was one of the most infectious, happy sounds Harp had ever heard. 'She nearly had a stroke. Seamus and his brothers Donal and Tadhg are working class, and Irish, and left school at twelve. His mother is a cook at a home for old people, and his father works on the docks. The idea of breathing the same air as them made Aunt Eileen shudder.'

Harp noticed a shy smile on Jane's face. 'So what happened?' She was intrigued.

'Well, we started seeing each other. I had to

sneak out, of course, but the more time I spent with him…I don't know. I felt like all the years I'd spent over here were fading away and I was reclaiming my country, my roots or something. He made me feel Irish again. It probably sounds silly, but everyone over there goes on about the war, the glory of the Empire, king and country and all of that, but Seamus and his brothers are different. They refuse to join up. They even got white feathers in the post.' A dark shadow crossed her pretty face at the memory of the symbols of cowardice that were sent to anyone not in uniform. 'They are far from cowards, but they won't fight in a uniform of a country that is oppressing their homeland, even if they're born and raised in England. The Germans are painted so badly, but we've no gripe with them. They didn't undermine Irish men and women, deny them basic human rights, stand by while their people starved to death. It was the British who did that. And so when the O'Grady boys got the call to join up, to go to Dublin and follow Pearse and McBride, they went. It broke my heart to see them go, but I was so proud as well. I wanted to go too, to join Cumann na mBan, but I couldn't leave Janie. So I let him go. He was wounded, but he's all right – the prison doctors patched him up some kind of way. I've not seen him since last March. He writes to me at the shop, but he's not allowed to write often.'

Harp instinctively knew Kitty was trustworthy, so she told her about the Devlin sisters, how impressive they were.

'And what about you, Harp?' Kitty asked. 'Would you join the cause?'

'I already have. My father, Henry Devereaux, was an Anglo-Irish Protestant, but he felt so passionately about the Irish cause. He taught me the writings of Wolfe Tone and Robert Emmet, and he believed in it so much. He would want me to fight against injustice, to stand up, to make him proud.'

Kitty's eyes blazed as she spoke. 'This fight, this struggle for independence isn't just about Ireland. It's about the class war too, and the gender war. It's about fighting inequality. Jim Larkin got the Dublin workers to strike for better conditions and pay back in 1913, and though they had so much to lose, he convinced them, and it showed the English landlords and factory owners that their employees are people, not expendable units, easily replaceable. And then James Connolly. He was so right, saying that it was the working classes who needed to rise up, that a worker in Dublin had more in common with a worker in Moscow than a wealthy man that lived up the road. And look at what this movement is doing for women. It's advancing the cause of women's suffrage, and it's giving women a voice.'

'I love that idea.' Harp found herself agreeing.

Before they had time to carry on the conversation, they heard men's voices and saw Danny and JohnJoe cross the window en route to the front door.

The sisters exchanged a glance. Kitty reached over, and Jane slipped her hand into hers.

Harp got up and went to the hall, opening the door. She led JohnJoe and Danny to the drawing room, and they stood there, looking perplexed. 'JohnJoe,' she said, 'come in. There are two people here who'd like to meet you.'

He stepped into the room as Kitty rose and walked towards the door, Jane beside her.

'Kitty?' he asked, unsure at what he was seeing.

'Hello, JohnJoe.' She smiled as the tears spilled down her cheeks.

Harp and Danny stood by as JohnJoe incredulously opened his arms and his two sisters walked into his embrace.

CHAPTER 31

*N*obody in the dining room of the Cliff House could have guessed at the relationship between the five young people sitting together and chatting animatedly over a meal of bread, cheese, tomatoes and ham that Harp had liberated from the kitchen. Cooking never was and never would be her strong point.

'That was some stroke you pulled, kid,' Danny whispered out of the corner of his mouth as JohnJoe and Kitty reminisced over a funny story about their grandfather and a goat who ate the seat of his good trousers. Jane sat between them, munching a sandwich, perfectly content. 'How about we bail out and let them to it, eh?' he suggested.

Harp smiled and nodded, delighted it had all worked out so well. Danny went up to his room, and she went to the kitchen, where her mother was just letting herself in. The lines of worry and distress caused by Ralph Devereaux were gone, and Rose radiated happiness. She'd dismissed all but Pearl of the new staff Ralph had hired, taking particular pleasure in giving Katie Lucey her marching orders.

'How was Matt?' Harp asked with a smile.

'Oh, he's fine. He made dinner so I ate with him. How are you? You look excited.' Rose's intuitive eyes rested on her daughter's. 'What are you up to now?'

Even since Ralph's departure and Harp's assurance that he was never going to return, Rose had begun to see Harp in a new light. No longer did she seek to protect her quite so much, realising that she was a young woman of some experience now.

Harp had yet to tell Rose about her romance with JohnJoe, though. Something was stopping her, and she knew it was the fear that Rose would disapprove, thinking she was too young or that she'd get a reputation.

Harp quickly explained what was going on in the drawing room and that the O'Dwyer girls were staying. Danny had taken their cases upstairs earlier.

'Will we have a cup of cocoa?' Rose asked.

'Just like old times.' Harp smiled and sat at the table.

Rose made the drinks, creamy and sweet, and they sat together happily. The kitchen was spotless and ready for the next day's work, the guests were all in bed, and life felt good for the first time in ages.

'I'm so pleased for JohnJoe,' Rose said. 'You really are something else, Harp, do you know that? Henry always said there was something special about you, and I agreed of course – being your mother, I always thought you were marvellous.' She smiled. 'But you are proving yourself to be quite the capable young woman and I'm so proud of you.'

'Well, I had a wonderful role model, you know.'

'Yes, but you're braver than I could ever be. I still don't really know how, and I think I'm better off that way, but you got rid of Ralph, and that in itself is an achievement.'

'Good riddance.' Harp clinked her cup off Rose's with a grin. 'And what about Matt? Is everything back to normal with you two now?'

Rose sighed. 'Yes, inasmuch as it can ever be. Whatever is coming, it will be hard, and Matt will be right in the thick of it. I worry for him, but he assures me he's careful. But he's adamant he doesn't want my name up with his for my own safety, and yours. I believe him, though sometimes I wonder if it suits him too.' She smiled.

'Matt loves you, Mammy. Anyone with eyes can see that. Now we've a full house for breakfast, so we'd better get to bed.'

Harp gave her mother a hug and went upstairs. It had been a long but very productive day.

She washed and brushed out her hair, going over the events that led to that day. The story that Henry was her father, that Ralph had business in India, that JohnJoe was dead... So many lies, and yet here they were, everything having worked out. She thought of Napoleon Bonaparte's remark that history was the version of past events that people had decided to agree upon and realised he was absolutely right. It didn't have to bear any resemblance to the truth.

She was looking forward to picking up *The Three Musketeers* by Alexandre Dumas. Henry Devereaux had read it to her as a little girl, and she'd loved it so much, she reread it every few years as it made him feel closer. She would lend her copy to JohnJoe when she finished. She'd already given him *The Count of Monte Cristo*, which he'd loved, and she was sure he'd be enthralled in the adventures of d'Artagnan too.

She had always slept with her curtains open, allowing the night sky to twinkle its silver stars into her room. The harvest moon hung low in the sky that night, shining a golden orange. This was the room where Pennington died. Although her mother had suggested she move to another room, she refused. This was her space, up under the roof of the Cliff House, her sanctuary. This was where she gathered her letters from the many hundreds of people who wrote from their new lives, having stayed in the Cliff House; it was where she decorated the walls with the drawings JohnJoe had sent over the years. It was where she kept her most special books, the ones that were never shared with guests but stored lovingly in the bookcase under the window. This was her room, her space, and the memories of Pennington would not drive her out of it.

She was just about to get into bed when there was a knock on the door. If it was her mother, she would open it after knocking, but it remained closed. Her heart thumped. What if it was another man intending her harm? She dismissed the thought immediately – *what nonsense.* She wrapped her dressing gown around her and opened the door a crack to find JohnJoe standing there. She stood back and let him in. He was glowing with happiness, and she was relieved.

'I can never thank you enough, Harp. If I didn't already love you so much, I…' The emotion of it all overwhelmed him.

'I'm glad I was able to do it,' she said. She felt his arms go around her waist and rested her head on his chest as he held her close.

'I thought I'd never see them again. I never imagined for a moment…' he whispered into her hair.

He led her to the bed and she sat down. He pulled a chair over so he sat opposite her, facing her. 'I know they've left our aunt's place and all of that, and her fiancée is in the slammer. I feel responsible for them. I know Uncle Pat wouldn't mind if I brought them home – at least I don't think he would – but I doubt they'd go. Kitty is so caught up in the Irish thing. What to do now is the next thing. Your mother is being so kind having us all here, but we can't fill all of her rooms, and I'm worried about Kitty and Jane.'

'Don't worry, JohnJoe. We'll sort something out. Why not just enjoy the little holiday here with your sisters, and we'll deal with the future when it happens.'

He kissed her, leaving her breathless.

'My mother sent you to me. I really believe that, Harp. You're like my guardian angel or something.'

She smiled. He knew she was agnostic, and she'd never heard him mention faith or religion before.

'Honestly,' he went on sincerely, 'I know we're not big on any of that, but I truly believe she sent you to help me and now my sisters. I owe you so much, Harp. And I know we're young and I don't have much to offer you, and you'd probably be better suited to some really smart guy with great prospects, but I want to tell you that even if you and I don't end up together, I owe you so much that I will always be there for you. For the rest of your life.'

'Thank you, JohnJoe. But this isn't a one-way thing, you know. You keep saying I could do better, but I don't think you realise how odd I am. I have so few friends, and not one girl my own age. In fact, the conversation with Celia in your house in Boston was the first one in my whole life with a girl my own age, and you were the first person apart from my mother or Mr Devereaux to love me. To like me even. Most people don't see me the way you do. They either think I'm strange, or too knowledgeable, or a show-off or something. And I sometimes say the wrong thing or I'm too direct and I end up offending people – I don't know. I tried to fit in for so long and nothing worked, so in the end I gave up. Brian was my friend, but it wasn't like us. And so there was just you and me. And now, seeing you reunited with your sisters, I feel so happy for you. I wish I had a sibling, someone to love like that. I dread you going back to America, but I understand your life is there, your future, everything. But I love you.'

He released her hands and placed his on either side of her face, cupping it gently. He kissed her softly. 'I love you too,' he whispered. 'And if you do want me, then I'm willing to give it all up over there, stay here. I'd work. And I know we're young and it's probably too early to even mention it, but I'd do anything for you, Harp.'

She could feel his breath on her face.

'When my Mammy died, I was nine and my old man just wanted rid of us. From that day on I never knew a moment's love or softness. And then Danny appeared and we went to stay at your house and I met you, and it was all so much to take in. I thank God every day that Danny managed to land himself in the hospital that time and I got to spend most of the summer with you. It was the best time of my life, learning to read, hearing you play the harp, drawing. Remember your mother bought me that set of pencils and a sketchpad? I still have them. And whenever you mentioned in a letter a book you were reading, I'd go to the library and check it out. Most of them were very hard for me. I'm so much better at reading now, but I'll never be like you, devouring books. But even poring over the lines made me feel closer to you.'

'I have a scrapbook of all of your drawings, every single one you sent. I even framed some...' Harp pointed to the pictures all over the wall above her bed.

'I...I know we're young,' JohnJoe insisted, 'and I won't ever pressure you, Harp, but I really think we're meant to be together. I know you have plans, and I won't stand in your way – of course I won't. But just to be there, with you, seeing you every day, would be so wonderful.'

'But your life now, with your family in Boston, it's so glamorous and luxurious compared to Ireland –' she began, but he cut across her.

'I love them. They've given me everything, but all I want is a future with you. I'd hate to leave them, or Boston for that matter – I do love it there. But I love you more.'

Time ticked by as the yellow moonlight shone through the window.

'If you ask me to, I'll stay,' he said softly.

'Will you stay?' Harp whispered.

His answer was a kiss, deep and passionate, and Harp felt the familiar longing as she held him close. Eventually JohnJoe pulled away with a groan; clearly he felt it too.

'I'd better get out of here, because if your mother catches me in here, she'll have my guts for garters.'

Harp giggled and shoved him out the door.

CHAPTER 32

The people of Queenstown seemed to accept the departure of Ralph Devereaux relatively easily. Rose believed people were embarrassed on her behalf because she'd been publicly abandoned by her fiancée before the wedding, and the family were happy to perpetuate that myth.

The dress that had been ordered was returned, and the wedding breakfast that had been booked in the hotel was discreetly cancelled. Mr Bridges had very thoughtfully delivered a tray of cakes on the day the wedding should have happened. He'd looked awkward, but Rose was touched that he made the effort.

'I just wanted to say that you and your daughter are most welcome any day to the hotel, and that the behaviour of Mr Devereaux… Well, I'm sure he had his reasons, but I just wanted to say that I consider you a fellow business owner in this town and that I have always held you, and continue to do so, in the highest of esteem, Mrs Delaney.'

'Thank you, Mr Bridges.' Rose took the tray of cakes graciously, and her house full of young people soon polished them off.

It was hard to believe, but life just went on.

Kitty offered to help serve breakfast in the dining room on the first morning and did it with a friendly word for everyone. In just a few days, she was proving to be such an asset and was enthusiastic about all aspects of the guest house. Rose had tried to resist, wanting her to feel like a guest, but the girl insisted. JohnJoe too had been up with the lark every morning tending the vegetable garden he'd planted during the summer of 1912 and was so gratified to see how well cared for it was and how bountifully it supplied the house.

Harp brought him out a cold drink and found him poring over a letter from Kathy.

'See this here.' He called Harp over, handing

her the letter. His broad beam told her it didn't contain anything bad.

Dearest JJ and Danny,

I hope you two are having a wonderful time in Ireland, and I can't wait to have you home to hear all about it. Your Uncle Pat and I have been talking things through, and it's looking more and more like we are entering this dumb war every day. I'm terrified you two will be drafted if you come home, so we thought it might be best for you both to stay on in Ireland for a while.

I know they say there won't be any more attacks on passenger ships either, but I'm awake at night imagining a German bomb blowing you two to bits halfway across the Atlantic, and it's making me crazy. So though it breaks my heart to be away from my boys for longer than necessary, I'd feel better if you stayed where you are.

Pat says there's no way they'll try to draft Irish men, that they wouldn't stand for it and things are crazy enough over there without giving the Irish even more cause to rebel, so he thinks Ireland is the safest place for you too. I couldn't bear anyone to hurt a hair on your precious heads, my darlings.

So obviously we'll take care of you financially. Pat will wire you enough to keep you going. Write back soon.

All my love,
A.K.

Harp was hardly able to believe what she'd read. She knew JohnJoe was determined to stay but dreaded breaking the news to his aunt and uncle in Boston.

'They want you to stay?'

JohnJoe smiled. 'Looks like it.' He put his arms around her and twirled her, making her laugh.

Together they went in and roused Danny from his bed. He had been out with the local boys until late again the previous night and was having a lie in. He too was happy to remain. Then they showed Rose the letter.

Once breakfast was cleared away and the rooms done, the few guests all gone from the house for a day's sightseeing, Rose made a cup of tea in the kitchen. She asked Harp to gather everyone.

The electric carpet cleaner had proved to be a huge advantage and cut the cleaning time considerably. Rose had written an effusive letter of thanks to the Raffertys, and several local people had come to see it in action.

Jane had been glued to Kitty's side from the moment they arrived, but this morning she'd opted to stay in the kitchen with Rose. JohnJoe had taken her out earlier to collect the eggs from the chicken coop, and she was happy to go with him. Harp was glad to see the little girl unwind a little.

Kitty began the wash-up as soon as she entered the kitchen, but Rose stopped her.

Danny appeared, looking dishevelled but ever cheerful. 'Morning, all!' he said, grabbing a piece of toast from the rack on one of the used breakfast trays Kitty was delivering to the kitchen. 'I love it here.'

'Everyone, please sit. Let's have a chat.'

For once Kitty O'Dwyer looked apprehensive, and she sat beside Jane, the little girl's hand snaking into her sister's once more. 'Thank you so much for your hospitality, Mrs Delaney. I know we're imposing, and of course we'll pay for our bed and board...' Kitty began.

Rose placed her hand on Kitty's. 'You are welcome here, my dear, both of you.' She smiled. 'All of you, in fact. And you have all more than paid your way with all the help you've given me. I don't know myself now that I can cook in here and have someone else wait on tables.' Rose looked at Harp and an unspoken conversation passed between them.

'So I understand from her letter, Mrs Rafferty

has expressed concern about the boys returning to America and has suggested they stay here in Ireland. Now I could definitely do with some help around here. The garden is badly in need of some work, and the conversion of the outhouses is something we've been putting off, so if Danny and JohnJoe wanted to take that on – I understand you are both good builders – then I'd be happy to put you up and pay you to do the work.'

'Sounds good to me. What do you think, JJ?' Danny asked.

'I'd love it,' he replied instantly, taking Harp's hand under the table.

'So that just leaves Kitty and Jane.' Rose turned to the girls.

Kitty sighed. 'Well, I sent my aunt and uncle a telegram, just telling them that we were all right but that we would be making our own way in the world from now on. I can't forgive them for telling us JohnJoe was dead – that was so cruel and unnecessary. So we definitely won't be going back there. My fiancée is in prison in England, so I'll wait for him. But any further than that, we've not thought really. I suppose I'll get a job. I have typing and shorthand, and I've saved up a bit of money so –'

'How would you like to work here too?' Rose

interrupted. 'Harp is planning to matriculate this year, so she will need to study, and to be honest, housework isn't her forte.' She winked at Harp, who nodded with a smile. 'You clearly have a flair for the business, and I need the help. We'll be quieter over the winter months, but there's a lot to be done in the house, so if you don't mind rolling up your sleeves, then I'd be happy to take you on. Bed and board would be part of the package, same as the boys, and Jane here could go to school if she'd like that?'

Kitty looked from Rose to Harp and back again. 'Are you serious?' she asked.

'Quite serious.' Rose smiled.

'Oh, Mrs Delaney, that would be just...well, that would be smashing, wouldn't it, Janie?'

The little girl looked up and gave one of her rare slow smiles.

'And we'd work hard, I promise. Janie is a great little baker. She can do bread and scones and buns and take care of the hens...'

'Well, that would be a charity,' Harp said wryly. 'Horrid things – I can't bear them. The way they rush the door of the coop when I go in... So if you'd take that over, I'd be eternally in your debt, Jane. They are such noisy proud creatures. You know, Mark Twain was right when he said, "Often a hen who has merely laid an egg cackles as if she laid an asteroid."' Harp wondered if she imagined it, but did the girl giggle slightly?

'Well, that's settled then. How does fifteen shillings a week plus bed and board sound?'

'That sounds wonderful.' Kitty beamed. 'And I'll be here when Seamus gets out, and we can get married, and I'll have a nice nest egg to get us started. Oh, Mrs Delaney, thank you so much. You're a lifesaver, isn't she, Janie?'

Jane nodded. It was a small gesture, but it was definite progress.

'Right. Let's start as we mean to go on. Shall we start stripping the beds of the guests that are leaving today?' Kitty drained her tea and stood up, Jane beside her.

'Well, if you insist.' Rose laughed.

'And we'll take a look at the outbuildings and see what can be done.' Danny stood as well. 'Come on, JJ.' He seemed to sense that Rose and Harp needed a moment alone.

'So that worked out well, didn't it?' Rose asked when they were gone.

Harp nodded. She was so relieved JohnJoe was staying but didn't want her mother to know just how much.

'Especially considering what's going on between JohnJoe and you?' Rose asked astutely.

'What about us?' Harp coloured.

'Ah, do you think I came down in the last
shower, Harp? Anyone with eyes can see you two
are in love.'

'Nothing has happened, Mammy,' Harp was
quick to say. She knew her mother would think
her far too young and inexperienced for courting.

'But it will, my love, it will.' Rose took Harp's
hand.

'Mammy, I –' Harp wanted to reassure her
mother that she was not the kind of girl who was
seen flirting with boys.

Rose cut across her protests. 'We've been
through so much together, you and I, and to me
you'll always be a little girl. But I have to accept
you're not. Ever since coming back from this trip
– during which I was terrified every second of
every day you were gone, I might as well tell you
– you seem different, more adult, more wise or
something.'

Harp laughed. 'Well, I feel wiser, so I know
what you mean. I was very sheltered here, and
going away and seeing a bit of the world has
changed me.'

'So what now for my girl?' Rose asked. 'Is it

still the plan to study and go to university? Or
have you something else in mind?'

Harp thought for a moment. 'My home is
here, with you. I will travel and study, and I will
leave Queenstown, I know that, but not yet. I
don't feel ready. And besides, this whole
business...'

Rose let out a ragged breath. Though Ralph
was no more and the issue of Pennington had
been seemingly dealt with, she was still a little on
edge.

'It's made me realise we need to stick together,' Harp said. 'Listening to the Irish Americans in
Boston, the Rising was just the beginning.
They're not willing to come so close to freedom
only to let it go, so there will be another strike for
freedom, and I want to be here. I want to participate. I know you might think I'm just an idealis-
tic, foolish girl, but the Devlins and the Raffertys,
they are not foolish. They are patriots, and I think
I want to join them.'

She waited for her mother to dismiss the idea
outright. Rose knew nothing of the fur coat, relieved of its fortune and stitched back together
inexpertly by Liz Devlin. Danny had been going
to take it back with him, but Harp assumed now
they would have to post it. She was prepared for

Rose to tell her off for having foolish notions, or to beg her to stay out of it for everyone's sake, but none of that happened.

Rose just nodded a little sadly. 'Matt says the same, that a war is coming, and soon, while the British are still fighting in Europe. The Volunteers want to strike while they're vulnerable. Something told me you'd want to be involved.'

'I do.'

Rose sighed. 'Do you know, a year ago I would have said that you're being ridiculous, but the events that we've witnessed, that a girl sleeping peacefully can be assaulted in her bed by one of them and that absolutely nothing would be done because he was a British officer and you were an Irish girl, that's just not acceptable. None of it is. While you were in America, the Cooper boys out towards Cuskinny were taken in for questioning for no reason whatsoever and were really roughed up. Last week, outside the Queen's, a gang of soldiers forced poor old Mr Deasy off the pavement, causing him to fall, and they just laughed at him, an old man knocked over on the ground. Again, no way of even complaining. The execution of the revolutionaries, the dismissive way they treat us – someone will have to stand up.' Rose sounded more resigned than passionate, but Harp recognised her determination all the same. She would not do it for glory, or for some abstract notion of sovereignty, but so that people like her and Harp and Matt and the Devlins and the Cooper boys could live in peace.

"'If I am not for myself, who will be for me? And being only for myself, what am I? And if not now, when?'"

Rose smiled. 'I've no idea. Shakespeare?'

Harp shook her head. 'Hillel the Elder, a Jewish scholar from Babylon around the time of Christ.'

'Well, I never even heard of him.'

'It's obscure, I know, but his line, "if not now, when", has resonance for me. There is never going to be a good time, a time that won't cause hurt and pain. But we should take advantage of the war. The enemy are weak now and may never again be so.'

Harp watched her mother deliberate; she was weighing something up in her mind.

'I had a dream the other night. Henry came to me and told me that you were going to do extraordinary things. In the dream I cried, begged him to protect you, but he just smiled. Then it was over.'

Harp chuckled. 'You know he'd say that was a

load of old nonsense, visitations from the dead in dreams.'

'He would, I know, but it happened anyway.'

'Do you dream of him often?'

Rose nodded. 'Sometimes. More of late. Things have been so tense, with everything...' She seemingly dared not mention his name.

'It's over, Mammy. Ralph is gone,' Harp whispered. 'Pennington is buried and nobody will ever look for him again. A body was washed up near where he lived in England, and he was gone AWOL anyway, so all that rubbish about meetings in America was a lie – he was running away. So it *is* over.'

'Is it really?' Rose asked. 'Can it ever be?'

'It is. They were bad people who meant us harm. I know that Ralph gave you that.' Harp nodded at her mother's cheekbone, the bruise almost gone now. 'If he did that when he was still unsure of his place, what would he have done once he was married to you and controlled everything? It doesn't do to let your enemies get too strong. We must fight, not just for the Irish Republic, but for women. Never again should a woman be subjugated by her husband, forced to endure horrible conditions, all because he is a man. Along with independence will surely come rights for women, rights for the working classes. This will change the world we live in forever, and I want to be a part of it. I met a girl in America. She was dark-skinned and worked for JohnJoe's aunt and uncle. I had a nightmare one night, and she came in and told me a story of how she'd been abused so grievously in the house she worked in before Pat Rafferty rescued her. It was as if she didn't matter, that she had no say because she was a girl and a Black girl at that. This thing that's happening here is bigger than us, bigger than Ireland. This is a worldwide movement – my travels showed me that. There is a rising tide of indignation against injustice, against people thinking they are better than others, and I want to be part of it. I want to play my part to make it happen.'

Rose smiled and tucked a stray hair behind Harp's ear. 'I do too,' she whispered. 'I've been in touch with the Devlins. They have a network of women going, and Matt has the men so...'

Harp nodded. A tacit agreement had been made without any formal discussion. They were in, whatever the future held.

'So we got rid of Katie Lucey, thank goodness,' Harp said, changing the subject. 'I think Kitty is going to be marvellous.'

'I do too,' Rose agreed. 'Besides, I knew there was no way we could have Emmet Kelly's fiancée under this roof.'

Harp shuddered at the mention of the name of the boy who had made her childhood a misery. 'They'll be the first to get their comeuppance,' she said darkly.

'Who? Emmet?'

Harp nodded. 'Yes, Emmet and all like him in the Royal Irish Constabulary. Irish men doing the bidding of the British.'

The tap on the back door caused Harp to look up; it was the post. She took the small bundle of letters and cards. There was one from Celia; she recognised the Boston stamp. She'd read it later. She ripped another open and scanned the contents. 'Oh, Mammy, remember that couple who were here a while back? They had to hide from their son and daughter and were planning to emigrate to his brother in Philadelphia?'

Rose's brow furrowed. 'I do, vaguely. Didn't they end up abandoning their plans?'

'They did at the time, but listen to this! "Dear Harp. I don't know if you recall our visit to your charming guest house. We are Michael and Joan McGrath. We had intended on sailing to America, but our son and daughter arrived and we decided

412

to return home. Well, within a few weeks of returning, we reflected on what you said and realised you were right. Our children's displeasure with our relationship was very selfish on their part. Joan and I have both been widowed and are therefore free, and we were doing no harm whatsoever. So we made a decision one day as we went for a secret walk in the woods to marry regardless of their reaction. We booked the priest and the local hotel and sent them each an invitation. We didn't ask their opinion or permission. Maura came with a face that would turn milk sour, but her husband, Gerry, was delighted for us, and her sister, Ann, and my Sean came too. Benny refused and Patrick – he's the priest – did make an appearance, initially sitting at the back. But in the middle of the Mass, our parish priest invited him up to concelebrate the Mass, so he did that and he blessed our marriage. The others warmed to the idea over time, though Benny is still not speaking to us. I think having them see that our friends and neighbours were pleased for us and not remotely scandalised is helping."

"'Anyway, we sold both our houses and bought a lovely house in Kerry overlooking the sea. Near enough for the children and grandchildren to visit but far enough away to be able to live our lives without people sticking their noses into our business."

"'Anyway, we just wanted to let you know that everything worked out in the end and we're very happy."

"'Thank you for your kindness, and your forthright advice. We'll never forget you. Mr and Mrs McGrath".'

CHAPTER 33

The Christmas tree twinkled merrily in the corner of the drawing room as Janie strung the last of the paper garlands she'd made from the central ceiling rose to the corners. She laughed as she balanced on her brother's shoulders to be tall enough to reach.

'Careful, JohnJoe. Don't let her fall, for goodness' sake,' Kitty reprimanded as she carried the trifle to the sideboard.

Danny was clean-shaven these days and looked like a Greek god stretched out sleeping on the fireside chair. He was out at night a lot of the time now, and everyone knew better than to ask what he was doing. JohnJoe too had taken to joining him.

The Devlins were due to arrive shortly, along with Matt Quinn, for Christmas lunch, and it was promising to be a very jolly affair. The turkey had been donated by the Devlins – they kept them and hens in their small yard beside the shop – and Matt had been given a side of smoked bacon in lieu of undertaker fees from a poor family on Spike Island, which he donated to the feast. The vegetables had all been grown and stored by JohnJoe, and the Christmas pudding had been maturing in the larder since September. To everyone's delight, a large hamper of chocolates, brandy, wine and cookies had arrived from the Raffertys, along with gifts for everyone, beautifully wrapped in silver paper and ribbons, which were placed under the tree.

JohnJoe and Danny wrote each week, and though Kathy and Pat missed them, they were relieved that the boys were relatively safe in Ireland. Though undoubtedly Pat at least knew of their Volunteer activities and was, Harp was sure, very proud of them.

There were definite rumblings of German U-boat activity in the Atlantic, so passenger traffic had slowed to a mere trickle.

Harp left the decorating and preparations to retreat to her room. It was warm in the house, and though she loved everyone gathered beneath the Cliff House roof, she sometimes needed some time alone. JohnJoe understood that about her, as did her mother. She was primarily a solitary creature, and constant companionship, no matter how convivial, weighed on her.

She sat at her harp and played a slow air, 'Cill Cais', and sang the words of the haunting melody in Irish. She'd taught JohnJoe the words and he loved it. As she played the closing bars, she heard the Devlin sisters come through the gate off the Smuggler's Stairs and knew that from the moment they came in, the conversation immediately would go to matters political. Everyone gathered was of a like mind, so there was no risk of the conversation falling on the wrong ears.

She allowed herself a few more minutes. The solitude of her room was solace to her soul. Ralph was gone, JohnJoe was staying for the foreseeable future, Danny and he were doing a wonderful job on the renovations, and Kitty was a natural in the guest house. Jane had started school, and while she still only spoke to Kitty, she seemed to be happy there. She adored her big brother and was like his shadow. Matt and Rose were still close, though their relationship was not public knowledge.

Her desk under the window was laden with books and pens and notes, as she was preparing for her exams. She'd promised JohnJoe and her mother she would take three days' break from her studies, but it was hard. There was so much to do.

She opened the drawer by her bed and took out her special pen. She raised it to her lips. 'Happy Christmas, Mr Devereaux, wherever you are. I miss you still,' she whispered.

Christmas was such a cheerful time, but also it was bittersweet because it made the absence of loved ones all the more acute. Every Christmas of her childhood, it had been just her, Henry and her mother, but it was always happy. Santa Claus came and brought her books, all she ever wanted, and they would have a lovely dinner and cake and sit by the fire, reading. She missed those days.

Matt would find today hard too, missing Brian. He'd written to his father once or twice since he left, but the censor had removed most of the text, making it impossible to read. And there had been nothing for months. She and her mother tried to reassure Matt that the army would surely have been in touch if it was bad news, but those words of encouragement were sounding increasingly hollow as word of unimaginable losses filtered slowly back from the front.

She wished Brian had not declared his feelings that night, and she wished she'd reacted better. Having had time to mull it all over, she realised that maybe if she'd explained things better to him, he would not have gone off like he did. She'd written several times, but nothing. Surely if he was dead, she would sense it, or Matt would, but she had no idea.

Things were heating up in the republican movement. Tales of drills and plans being made in British prisons were recounted by the Easter Rising Volunteers, who were being gradually released. They would come back and then regroup and finish what Pearse and Connolly started. And she would be there, on the front line. If Brian did survive, how would he feel about his father, her, her mother and all he knew taking a position against the uniform he wore? She had no idea. Brian joined up to help people; she was sure of that. He wasn't a British toady, but he wanted to go where his skills could be useful. But he was on the wrong side. She was never more sure of anything. It was all so complicated, though. Anyone who saluted the Union Jack, who sang 'God Save the King' was the enemy, but did that make Brian the enemy when he was just trying to help the wounded?

'Harp!' She heard her mother calling. 'Dinner's ready.'

She sighed and dragged herself downstairs. Henry would feel exactly the same way. One to one, she happily interacted, but large groups, even of her nearest and dearest, made her anxious.

As she entered the dining room, she saw that everyone had taken their seats but Rose and Kitty, who were ferrying dishes to the table amid sighs and exclamations of appreciation. The aromas were mouthwatering.

The conversation was, as she suspected it would be, about the current situation. Liz Devlin was at great pains to explain how the executions of the rebels of Easter week was a personal tragedy and loss for the families of the men, and for all who followed them, but that from a political point of view, it had turned the tide of public opinion. She told them how Cork had felt so disappointed to have been excluded from the Rising but that the non-involvement of the rebel county meant the men of the south were armed and ready to go. 'Britain is reeling from the losses in France and Belgium. The news coming in from the battles all along the river Somme is horrendous,' she said.

Harp couldn't think about the war without remembering Brian. Where was he now? Alive? Dead? She saw her mother cast a glance at the man she loved. He was obviously thinking the same. She knew Matt was conflicted too. He adored his only child but couldn't bear the idea of him in the uniform of the country that was going to such lengths to destroy his own.

'Let's just hope they don't push the conscription issue here,' Rose said.

'They can try,' Cissy answered indignantly.

'Aunt Kathy reckons the draft is comin' for us in the USA too. All the rumblings stateside are that they'll be draggin' us in sooner rather than later,' Danny said, then tucked into the buttered carrots.

'Well, they can whistle if they think America will stand for that, with so many Irish there,' JohnJoe said vehemently. 'If there's any American fighting to be done, it will be against the British, not alongside them.'

'They might have no choice if the government conscript them,' Matt pointed out.

'That's why Aunt Kathy is allowing us to stay here. She'd rather we were here and safe, but maybe Ireland can't hold out forever. The pressure to send bodies to the front is growing every day.' Danny shrugged.

Matt shook his head. 'No, Cissy is right. It would be a stupid move on their part, and they need things to stay at least calm here. Forcing conscription would only stir up a hornet's nest. Even the Home Rulers here are backing down now, realising they were sold a lie. Redmond was wrong, thinking that if we could do our bit in the little skirmish, all that over-by-Christmas rubbish, the British would give us Home Rule in return.' He helped himself to another roast potato. 'No, things are different now and there's no going back. People want a republic, nothing less will do, and the men of this country, and the mothers and fathers too, will resist. Just you watch. People aren't stupid. They see the boys coming back, armless, legless, blind, depressed. The numbers are dwindling already. Not even the separation money they use to lure the women to send their men is working any more. If they start muttering about conscription, that's when the republican movement will really come into its own. I'm looking forward to it because the minute they start going on about forcing us into their

trenches, that will be the best recruitment campaign Sinn Féin will ever get.'

'Absolutely,' Cissy Devlin agreed. 'And this time it won't just be the IRA – it will be every last man, woman and child on this island. The time has come. We have to fight and stand strong together. And we are not alone, as Danny and JohnJoe know. We have America on our side too, don't forget.'

Harp looked all around the table. The passion was palpable. JohnJoe reached under the table and took her hand.

'There's a lot of Irish stateside, that's true, but Newton Baker has the ear of Woodrow Wilson,' Danny explained, 'and he's tellin' him that somethin' will have to be done about the low numbers of Volunteers. Wilson is stuck between a rock and a hard place. He's promisin' Europe help, and the sinkin' of the *Lusitania* last year, that really got everyone riled up, so I wouldn't be surprised if we were all in very soon.'

'That won't happen,' Liz said quietly, as if the force of her words would make it so. 'America is built with Irish hands. They won't go to Britain's rescue.'

Seeing things could get heated, Kitty changed the subject. She was hoping Seamus would be released soon, but there was no word yet. 'This turkey was so delicious, and the sprouts with the bacon and cream. Mrs D, you are a marvel.'

Rose smiled. She would have been happy for Kitty to call her Rose, but the girl insisted that 'Mrs Delaney' was more proper, as she was the owner and her employer. They'd settled on 'Mrs D'.

Jane whispered something to her sister.

'Let's get JohnJoe to do it. I don't want you to burn yourself,' Kitty answered.

'Do what?' JohnJoe asked.

'She wants to light the pudding,' Kitty explained. 'Let's all three O'Dwyers go to the kitchen, and we'll try not to burn the house down.'

'We've had enough dramatics in this place for a while, so I'd be grateful if you didn't,' Rose said with a smile; Matt caught her eye and smiled back.

Harp wished they would just tell everyone they were together, but Matt remained adamant it was too dangerous and her mother was mortified that people would think she was so fickle as to go from one man to the next so quickly. Already they thought she had a child by one Devereaux brother and was going to marry the other, when the reality was Rose had not had one whisper of romance in the intervening years since Harp's conception.

Amid cheering and compliments to the cooks, the O'Dwyers arrived, with Janie carrying the flaming plum pudding, beaming from ear to ear. It was delicious. It had been lovingly fed with a capful of whiskey once a week since it was steamed last autumn.

'Good job we live down the hill when we have to roll home later, Liz.' The normally teetotal Cissy laughed.

JohnJoe and Rose pulled a cracker and donated the small pencil inside to a delighted Jane. Harp and Matt did the same, then Danny and Kitty, and soon Jane had a nice stash of trinkets.

'Presents!' Danny announced once the delicious Christmas pudding served with cold thick cream was cleared away and the adults were sipping a seasonal brandy.

Seamus had managed to send Kitty a lovely wood carving with her name on it that he'd made in prison. Her eyes shone as she opened it, and Harp gave her hand a squeeze.

'I miss him.' Kitty whispered. Everyone else was engrossed in opening gifts, so they had a bit of privacy in the mayhem.

'I know,' Harp sympathised. 'But the rumours are rife that the republican prisoners were taking up valuable time and resources that the British don't wish to expend on Irish nuisances, so they were going to be released. The Devlins' nephew from Tipperary was released last week, and the Cotters have a cousin who was lifted in the GPO and he's out too, so I'm sure it won't be long more to wait.'

'Thanks, Harp. You'll be my maid of honour, won't you, when we marry?'

Harp was overwhelmed. Having JohnJoe was wonderful, but to have a friend who was near her own age and a girl was tremendous and something she could never have envisaged. Kitty didn't seem to find Harp at all odd, and their easy friendship was a source of delight and amazement to Harp.

'Will you?' Kitty asked again. 'Unless you'd hate it… I understand…'

'I would love it,' Harp said, her voice choking on the emotion of it all. 'I would really love it.'

Kitty smiled and her face lit up. She had a smile that Harp always thought radiated joy like a lighthouse. Seamus was lucky to have her, as were they.

'"Those friends thou hast, and their adoption

tried, grapple them unto thy soul with hoops of steel."'

'What?' Kitty asked with a grin, and Harp flushed, not realising she'd spoken her thought aloud.

'Oh, it's from *Hamlet*. Sorry, I thought I was thinking it...' she said, further increasing her embarrassment.

'No. I love it. I studied *King Lear* at school, a dreadful long thing about some idiotic king that everyone hates or something. I couldn't stay awake. But that one sounds better, the one about friends. Tell me about it. Was Hamlet really wise or had he great friends or something?'

Harp was trying not to hide her literary life any more. It was part of her, and her people seemed to love her for it. The days of being teased for being clever were behind her, she knew, but old habits died hard.

'Well, actually that was said by Polonius to his son Laertes, but he was a dreadful old bore, so perhaps we should take his advice with a pinch of salt.' Harp laughed.

'That William Shakespeare seemed to specialise in fellows droning on and on for hours about things normal people have no idea about, but I like the thought of finding good friends and sticking with them through thick and thin. I feel like no matter what life throws at us now, we'll be all right because we'll stick together.'

Their conversation was interrupted by Jane's excitement at her gift. Santa Claus had left a lovely doll's house, made lovingly by JohnJoe and stored in the sheds until today, and the Raffertys had sent a whole box of little pieces of furniture and some little dolls. They also sent Kitty a silk robe and cologne, and books and clothes for the boys. Rose got ten yards of 22-momme silk in a beautiful rose colour, as they knew she was an expert seamstress. They sent Harp a beautiful jewellery box in which a ballerina danced when it was opened. It was exquisite.

Danny received lots of gifts from local girls, as well as a number from Boston. He had quite the reputation as a ladies' man now on both sides of the Atlantic, resolutely resisting urges from Rose and the Devlins to settle to just one.

JohnJoe's gift to Harp was an incredible portrait of Rose, Harp and Henry Devereaux, using the one of Henry and Ralph that had been consigned to the attic. He'd been working on it for months, and it was a masterpiece.

It had saddened both Rose and Harp to hide the portrait of the brothers away, but they couldn't bear to look at Ralph's face every day. Unbeknownst to Harp but with Rose's help, JohnJoe faithfully reproduced the portrait of Henry and added her and Rose. She absolutely loved it.

They were almost to the end of the pile, everyone having had at least one or two gifts, when Danny pulled out a slim one. 'This one is for Harp, but it doesn't say from who?'

Harp took it and removed the wrapping. It was O'Neill's new collection of tunes. He'd mentioned it was at publication stage when they met. Harp remembered the delight that Henry would experience when he got a new O'Neill collection in the post, and she felt that same thrill now. Henry had given her so much, not just a home and a future but a love of literature, learning and music. How she wished he could see them now.

Inscribed on the inside was a personal note.

To Miss Harp Devereaux,

Thank you for all your help and for allowing me to hear you play. Please keep it up – you have a rare gift. I wish you well and hope our paths cross again someday,

Best wishes,

Francis O'Neill

She turned the page and read the index of

tunes. Rose looked over her shoulder, following Harp's finger down the list.

There it was. 'Harp Devereaux', page forty-five. Harp turned to the page, and there in her annotation was the tune, forever immortalised.

'This was for you, Henry,' she whispered softly.

EPILOGUE

The fan spun lazily, barely moving the sultry heat in the bar of the Orchid Hotel high in the Himalayas. The Indian air was heavy with the sickly scent of the overblown blooms in man-sized glass vases dotted around the room. Some idiot had placed a Christmas tree in the corner and had decorated the surrounding area with tinsel and paper garlands, and the whole gaudy mess looked utterly ridiculous.

The bar was normally the central hub of British India, rife with gossip, broken dreams and catty remarks, but was quiet today, everyone preparing for the fancy-dress yuletide ball that evening in the Viceregal Lodge. He was glad of the relative peace and solitude. At least he was spared having to stop and charm the ladies playing bridge games. Their simpering giggles usually made him want to slap one of them.

He sighed and shifted his weight in the rattan seat. *Dreadfully uncomfortable things.* He wondered why they bothered with them. The place looked like a jungle outside; why on earth were they trying to re-create it inside too? Glass-topped tables with cane legs, huge carved elephants either side of the door – it was all so hideous.

A properly upholstered Queen Anne would have been so much better. Some Axminster carpet and some hunting scene oils on the walls. Make people feel for at least an evening that they were in a proper country, a civilised place. Not this armpit.

In one corner, in the booth, Bunty Fitzwilliam was deep in conversation with Delia Suchard, the wife of the Dutch East India Envoy, Edgar Suchard. They'd sneak upstairs later, thinking nobody knew of their affair when in fact it was common knowledge. Secrets were a luxury not afforded to most in this place. You had to be very clever to remain aloof while seeming friendly. Luckily, he was.

Out on the veranda, being fanned by one of the young boys the hotel employed for a pittance, was Mrs Finkleton, boring two newly arrived wives half to death with the gospel of life in the British Raj, according to herself. Mildred Finkleton had let herself go. She was passably attractive when he'd first bedded her a decade ago, but he wouldn't dream of going back to that well. She probably felt the same way about him, to be fair. Why wouldn't she?

The younger one, the blond, might have been worth a crack if he could be bothered. She looked like one who might give in out of sympathy. But he probably wouldn't waste his time. He could go to Shimla to Madame LeCompte's and pay for whatever he wanted in his bed without having to get involved in the boring nonsense of a summer romp that inevitably ended in some silly housewife's tears and a disgruntled husband threatening all sorts. He could get his pleasure without having to endure the pity in their eyes. The women who worked for the madame had enough problems of their own without worrying about his.

A fly buzzed on his arm, and he slapped it.

Such tedium. The same people, having the same conversations. All pretending that this was something else, that they were the crème de la crème of British society, chosen to represent the

Empire here in the jewel in Britain's crown. They stood patriotically for 'God Save the King', drank gallons of tea, played cricket and told themselves and each other the lie that they mattered.

They looked down on the Indians, but the caste system played out in the Viceregal Lodge just as obviously as it did with the natives in the streets of Calcutta; the only difference was they covered it up in a veneer of respectability. At least the natives were honest about who went where.

The crinoline-dressed ladies, the wives of clergymen or civil servants, wouldn't normally dare engage the vicereine or her ilk in conversation. But that night, for the yule ball, as they'd done forever, they'd dance the boring dance of polite society. Vicar dancing with vicereine, typist with tycoon. He couldn't bear it. He'd make some excuse.

They'd dance and tinkle false laughs and sip gin and tonics. They'd discuss the war as if it were all a jolly game, not the mindless slaughter of a generation, and the mothers would boast of their sons' eagerness to shed their blood for king and country. He could endure it sometimes – the free food and drink made it worth it – but that night he just couldn't. The façade, the forced charm, the social patter were becoming too difficult.

The head bartender, Daksh, an obsequious native born and raised in Shimla, eyed him carefully from under beetle-black brows as he clicked his fingers. Daksh nodded and immediately the young waiter appeared. He was dressed in dazzling white, and his brown face split into a gap-toothed smile. 'Please, sahib?'

'Gin and tonic.' He handed the waiter the empty glass. 'Lots of ice.'

'Very good, sahib.' The boy nodded and backed away.

The waiter returned moments later, the tumbler full with ice and boozy tonic, a wedge of lime adding a delicious bitterness. He accepted it, and the boy nodded and smiled again. The waiter probably didn't earn the cost of one of those drinks in a month – what the hell had he to smile about?

He drained the glass, resisting ordering another as he reluctantly recalled the outstanding bill that would have to be paid at the end of the month. He pushed the unwelcome reality to the back of his mind. Something would turn up. It always did. Even if it didn't, Sarita would pay. He'd have to charm her again, get back in her good books after last week's bust up, but the lure of this life, the life of the consort of a well-connected White man would be too much. Of course he'd have to promise to take her here and there, to be her gateway into this world, and she was deluded enough to believe that he would actually do it.

She was a fool, but at least she wasn't duplicitous. And for some reason she was a fool for him. Her father was a swarthy Bengali who'd warned his daughter off gold-digging Englishmen before he died. Sarita's father made a fortune in some grubby little trading business – he shuddered to think – but it meant she was solvent, and for that reason alone, he'd keep her around. She was too brown to be White, and not brown enough to blend in with her own. Her mother was a French missionary or something. She'd told him but he hadn't been listening.

He pushed himself up using his arms, wedging the crutches under his armpits with dexterity. It was surprising the strength that he'd built up since that day, dragging himself to the bank, being discovered and brought to Cork, then Dublin and finally Surrey. Those excruciating months in the hospital and now this half-life, lived without the bottom half of his left leg.

People assumed he was just one more of the walking wounded. It was fortuitous timing in that regard at least, and he never lied about his injury, a shot in the leg, but he never disavowed them of their assumption that the bullet was a German one.

He made slow and painful progress across the room. He'd have the porter whistle for a *tana*. Some people felt it was degrading to be pulled along in a rickshaw by another human being, but he had no such scruples.

The staff at the Orchid knew better than to try to help him. He'd barked at enough do-gooders who thought he could use their assistance. He didn't need anyone, and nobody needed him.

The piercing whistle of the porter caused him to wince. Everything about this country, the aspects of India that he used to love – the heat, the noise, the rawness, the sense that one was truly living – had evaporated. All he had left now were a cold gnawing bitterness and a desperate appetite for revenge.

The End.

· · ·

I SINCERELY HOPE you enjoyed this book, and that you'll be happy to know the third book in this series, *The Harp and the Rose*, can be preordered here:

PRE-ORDER THE HARP AND THE ROSE

If you enjoyed it, I would be grateful if you would consider leaving a review.

If you would like to join my readers club please pop over to my website www.jeangrainger.com

There you can download a free novel and sign up to stay in touch and hear from me now and again. It is 100% free and always will be.

ABOUT THE AUTHOR

Jean Grainger is a USA Today bestselling Irish author. She writes historical and contemporary Irish fiction and her work has very flatteringly been compared to the late great Maeve Binchy.

She lives in a stone cottage in Cork with her husband Diarmuid and the youngest two of her four children. The older two show up occasionally with laundry and to raid the fridge. There are a variety of animals there too, all led by two cute but clueless micro-dogs called Scrappy and Scoobi.

The West's Awake is her twenty third novel.

f

ALSO BY JEAN GRAINGER

The Tour Series

The Tour

Safe at the Edge of the World

The Story of Grenville King

The Homecoming of Bubbles O'Leary

Finding Billie Romano

Kayla's Trick

The Carmel Sheehan Story

Letters of Freedom

The Future's Not Ours To See

What Will Be

The Robinswood Story

What Once Was True

Return To Robinswood

Trials and Tribulations

The Star and the Shamrock Series

The Star and the Shamrock

The Emerald Horizon

The Hard Way Home

The World Starts Anew

The Queenstown Series

Last Port of Call

The West's Awake

The Harp and the Rose

Standalone Books

So Much Owed

Shadow of a Century

Under Heaven's Shining Stars

Catriona's War

Sisters of the Southern Cross

Made in the USA
Las Vegas, NV
30 September 2021